GENETIC ROULETTE

"Charlie, there's something wrong with the acid in those Gloryhits. They've been causing miscarriages and deformities in fetuses being carried by women who took them." He hesitated a second. "I want to urge you two to terminate the pregnancy."

"Jesus, Doc, don't scare me like that. Ann didn't take any while she was pregnant; it was a month before."

"That's the problem. All these women took the stuff before they became pregnant. It's not a teratogenic agent; it's some sort of mutagen, and it's causing mutations . . ."

AND IN ANOTHER OFFICE, NOT TOO FAR AWAY . . .

"Thank you, Major, I'm glad you could see me on such short notice." Pearson sat down, opened his briefcase. "I'm afraid that it's become rather important for us to get an idea of the passages to extinction for your various mutator genes. We need to know whether we're talking about tactical weapons . . . or doomsday machines!"

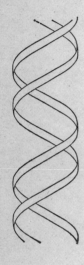

GLORYHITS

Bob Stickgold
and
Mark Noble

A Del Rey Book

BALLANTINE BOOKS • NEW YORK

A Del Rey Book
Published by Ballantine Books

Library of Congress Catalog Card Number: 77-6130

ISBN 0-345-27226-9

Manufactured in the United States of America

First Edition: February 1978

Paperback Format
First Edition: December 1978

Cover art by Richard F. Newton

*This book is dedicated to Jessie
and all the other children of the world,
that they may grow strong and healthy
as nature designed.*

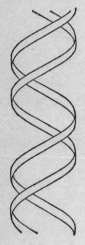

PART
I

Spring

Major Stanley Johnson envied the secretaries and technicians. Their work ended at five o'clock sharp, and by five after they were gone, jobs forgotten until the next day. But Stanley Johnson was no longer a part of the mindless nine-to-five research pool. He stared despondently out the window at the peaceful Maryland countryside, putting off the unpleasant task of calling his wife to tell her he'd be missing another dinner. On the horizon, some sixty miles away, he could just make out the smudge of polluted air that was Washington.

Forty-two, Johnson was losing his hair and gaining bulk around his waist, although in a military uniform he still looked healthy and alert. Returning to his desk, he picked up the dispatch from Intelligence that had been delivered just ten minutes earlier, and read it for the seventh time.

Why can't we ever get a decent jump on those bastards? he thought. Just one year into this research program, and now we find out that they've been at it at least nine months, maybe longer. Can they steal every idea we come up with? Or is it that all our brilliant ideas are so tediously obvious?

"Five top Soviet DNA researchers definitely out of public sight. Karpovich gone at least nine months." That was the extent of the memo. Enough to tell Johnson that the Russians were trying it, too. He poured himself a glass of gin and raised it in a mock toast. "Here's to the great Soviet–American gene-manipulation race," he muttered, and emptied the glass.

3

Saturday, August 1

"My God, you've let it grow!" Ann Merrill stepped aside to let Doc into their house. Tall and slender, he sported a full mustache and a huge head of curly hair. Both were new since she had last seen him, two years ago.

Doc gave her a big hug. "Ann, you look simply radiant. Charlie told me the news, and I'm delighted." At thirty, she could still pass for a college student. Long black hair and bold, attentive eyes distracted most people from the more subtle signs of age that closer scrutiny of her face revealed. "Speaking of whom," he added, "where is he?"

"I'm keeping your dinner from burning. Come on out to the kitchen." Charlie Cotten stuck his head out of the kitchen door and waved at Doc. "Everything's at that watch-it-or-lose-it stage." Turning back into the kitchen, he called, "That hair is great. How do your patients like it?"

Ignoring the question, Doc followed Ann into the kitchen, glancing around the house as he went. "Looks as if you've found a nice place," he commented. They had purchased it just a month ago, and only this week had moved in, following the long drive from California to Boston. Located in Cambridge, the house was an easy ten-minute walk from Harvard Square and the subway.

She shrugged her shoulders. "It still looks pretty sterile. But give us a little while and we'll get it nice and messy."

Charlie laughed. His large, rough hands worked

4

unconsciously on preparing the meal as he looked around the kitchen again. "Ann has a phobia about buying a house like her parents', and absolute cleanliness is the supreme characteristic of their house."

Transferring a large covered pot from the stove to the oven, he wiped his hands on his jeans and turned to the others. "Dinner's in twenty minutes. Let's go sit down and relax."

In the living room, Ann selected an old Charlie Parker record and then joined Doc and Charlie.

Doc smiled at her. "Ann, I can't tell you how delighted I am to hear that you're pregnant. I've been wondering when some of the old crowd would get around to it. What with all the kids I see over at the office, I've started to like them."

"Well, I'm glad to hear your attitude," Ann said, "because a lot of people seem to be down on kids lately."

Charlie interrupted. "Ah, they're just afraid of taking on the responsibility, afraid that they'll get all bogged down like their parents did. If they'd stop and think about it, they'd realize that's not what caused their parents to be the way they were, but they don't."

"Well, I'm just delighted," Doc repeated. Turning to Ann he asked, "How's it been going?"

"The nausea I could do without," she replied, "but I love the idea of being pregnant, with another whole person just growing perfectly inside here." She patted her stomach. "And from what I've gathered, my nausea hasn't been nearly as bad as it might have been. It just sort of makes the mornings not so pleasant."

"It makes me wish I could spend more time at home," Charlie said. "I feel sort of left out, like I'm missing the whole thing. But I've got to get the lab set up before classes start. Once I start teaching, it's going to be hard to get anything more going in the lab."

"How do you feel about being a professor?" Doc asked.

Charlie shrugged. "Ambivalent. I love the idea of having my own lab, and being able to start working on the things I want to, but between this course I have to

GLORYHITS

teach and the damn committee work I'm getting involved with, I'm worried that I won't get to spend as much time in the lab as I want."

"And he doesn't like being called a professor—makes him feel too old," Ann added.

"It's just so strange," he explained. "All my life I've been on the other side of the fence. Now I'm one of 'them.' It's just a strange feeling, because I still feel like old Charlie Cotten, the kid."

Doc laughed. "Well, as I remember, it was your idea that you all should call me 'Doc' instead of Fred, so maybe I should encourage people to call you 'Professor' instead of Charlie. It would be a just desert."

Charlie frowned. "I'll go back to calling you Fred first. I suppose it wasn't so funny for you, was it?"

Doc shrugged and smiled. "You learn to accept what you are, and ignore it when people put tags and trips on you. There's not much else to do."

A timer rang in the kitchen. "That's dinner!" Charlie announced. "You and Ann go on out to the dining room; I'll bring it in."

Over dinner they exchanged gossip and brought each other up to date. Ann and Charlie had spent the last three years in California, in only infrequent touch with Doc and their friends in Boston. It was good to be back.

After a while, Doc asked Charlie where his research was going. In response, Charlie's face lit up like that of a brand-new father getting a chance to show off pictures of his two-week-old daughter. He began to describe his efforts to screen teratogenic agents using tissue culture systems. When Doc interrupted him to ask for a quick explanation of the techniques, Charlie dove in enthusiastically.

"Well, as you must know," he began, "teratogenic agents are chemicals that interfere with the normal developmental process in a fetus. That's what thalidomide does—it interferes with limb growth—and German measles causes retardation by a similar process. And some people claim that LSD also causes birth defects if a woman takes it during the first trimester. But the screening process is really tedious, consisting basically of giving the chemical to pregnant rats, hamsters, guinea pigs, and monkeys, and looking for birth defects. So what I'm trying to do is get a procedure worked out where we grow small pieces of human nervous tissue in the laboratory and then look for changes when we add possible teratogenic agents. It would make the screening much faster, cheaper, and more reliable."

"Which is enough science for one evening," Ann interrupted. "If you two get started, it can go on all night."

Doc laughed. "Some things never change, do they?"

"Hell," Charlie said, "some things better not. Almost everything else has. Why, since Ann became pregnant we don't even get stoned any more."

"I've imposed that on him," Ann explained. "With all this worry about teratogenic agents, I haven't done any drugs since before conception, and I can't stand to watch Charlie get stoned if I can't."

Doc nodded in approval. "I meant to mention that to you. When you're pregnant, the more you can avoid unnatural chemicals, the safer you are. I even recommend to women that they avoid aspirin. It's just too important a process to take any risks with."

"But it's such a drag!" Charlie pouted. "We haven't touched a thing since we took those Gloryhits, way back before Ann got pregnant."

Ah, yes, Gloryhits. In just a few months they had become a legend. LSD appeared in batches and each batch had its own name: Owsley, Sunshine, Microdots, Blotters, Chuckles, and so on. And there'd been Gloryhits. It was the finest acid Charlie and Ann had ever experienced—a small, one-time deal, and Charlie had been fortunate to have been visiting in Boston at the time. They smiled at the memory.

Only Doc seemed unhappy.

"What's the matter?" Ann asked, seeing Doc's frown.

"I'm just not happy with that acid," he said. "I think we'd have been better off without it." He turned to Charlie. "How the hell did you get any? Was it on the West Coast, too?"

"Oh, no," Charlie explained. "Bill Lauter got me ten hits when I was here last year. But why get so uptight? We had it analyzed, and it was clean."

Doc was upset. "Well, why the hell did you two go taking it if Ann might have been pregnant?"

"Come on, Doc," Ann chided him, "we're not neolithic! We were sure I wasn't pregnant when we took them."

"How soon after that did you get pregnant?"

Ann shrugged. "Just a couple of weeks. We sort of look on the acid as good luck. We've still got seven hits stashed away in the freezer."

Doc seemed lost in thought. Turning to Charlie, he asked abruptly, "Do you have access to those Medline searches here?"

Charlie, puzzled by Doc's sudden change of topic, gave a shrug and said, "I'm sure I can. Is there something you want searched?"

"What's this?" Ann interrupted.

While Charlie explained the Medline service—a computerized index and cross-referencing system for scientific journals, which was used to obtain lists of articles on a particular topic rapidly—Doc sat quietly, his attention focused on his own thoughts. When Charlie finished his explanation, he looked at Doc.

"Well," Doc said, still lost in thought, "maybe I'll stop by in a few days and talk to you about it."

They sat and talked for a while, but Doc remained vaguely unsettled and distracted. Finally, he got up to go. At the door he said good-bye to them both. "And welcome back to Boston. I'm delighted to have you two settling so close by. I'm really glad you didn't stay out West."

"We couldn't," Ann joked. "It's so uncivilized out there!"

They walked out to his car. "One last thing," Doc asked. "Would you do me a personal favor, and just keep those Gloryhits on ice until I talk to you again?"

"Doc," Ann insisted, "what is the matter? I've never seen you like this."

"Oh, nothing, I'm sure," he replied. "Just a funny

feeling I have, not something to worry about. We doctors are paid to worry more than we need to." Smiling a last good-bye, he drove off.

Spring

A chance meeting with an old friend from graduate school had given then-Lieutenant Johnson the first glimmer of his idea. Last year's Federation meetings had been embarrassing because when asked for whom he was working, Johnson had lied and made vague allusions to industry instead of answering "the army." He feared that old friends would dump him if they knew he worked in biological warfare research. No, that phrase was wrong—in fact, outlawed by international treaty. He conducted biological research for the army, part of a health research project established to carry out research needed to protect American troops from possible biological hazards in various parts of the world. It managed to legitimize a myriad of classified projects that came as close to biological warfare research as anyone dared tread. But it wasn't biological warfare research. You could lose your job for making that slip at the wrong time.

Fortunately, Johnson's former colleague was so delighted to talk about his own research that Johnson had no problem with the deception. And from his friend's descriptions had come the germ of an idea. But from that point on, the idea was totally his own. He had read the scientific literature in his spare time, figuring out how each step of the project could be tackled. Recent advances in genetic manipulation, the science of transferring genes from one species to another, had made it almost trivial. So his—and only his—name had been on the letter he sent to General

Westland, the head of all army "health and allied fields research." Going over the heads of his superiors had been risky, but channels had a way of turning into mazes that might have separated Johnson from his proposal. While he wandered lost in the maze, some upper-level bureaucrat would have waltzed his idea through to the general. But now, he hoped, would come the payoff justifying that earlier risk.

Sitting tensely in Westland's outer office, an attaché case on his lap, he silently watched the secretary respond to the hum of the intercom and speak softly into it. Turning to the terrified Johnson, she smiled and nodded to the door on her left. In continued silence he rose and walked slowly into the general's office.

For a moment Johnson was disoriented in the huge office. Some forty feet away, Westland rose from behind his ornate hand-carved desk. "Come on in, Johnson," he quipped, "we don't eat anyone above private first class." Startled by the loud but somewhat gentle voice, Johnson closed the door and crossed quickly to the general's desk.

Returning Johnson's stiff salute, he grinned. "At ease, Lieutenant. I've read the proposal you sent to me, and I'll tell you, it rather caught my fancy."

"Thank you, sir."

"Of course, my background is in chemistry, you know, not biology, so I'm personally in no position to judge its scientific value . . ." He seemed lost in thought, then rummaged through a pile of papers on his desk. Finding what he was looking for, he flipped through a file and grunted quietly. "So, with considerable personal inconvenience, I managed to find a half dozen good biologists whose reports, which I have here, confirm the scientific and military merit of the proposal . . ." He stared at the file, then dropped it back on the desk. "Or at least that's what they're saying after you cut through all the bullshit." He looked at Johnson, who was still standing nervously at ease. "You know, Lieutenant, there are channels which you could have sent such a proposal through—it would certainly have been a lot easier for me if you had— and I was wondering, Lieutenant, why you chose to do it this way." Westland pulled a folder from his drawer and looked over the letter Johnson had sent him. "Why did you, Lieutenant?"

Johnson shifted his feet nervously. "Well, sir, I guess I felt it would be read faster, maybe get the project rolling a bit sooner."

"Humph!" Westland seemed irritated. "You know, Lieutenant, I didn't make general by accident, and I didn't make it by taking a back seat to flunkies above me, either. Maybe what you just said is the reason you sent it straight to me. I've guessed wrong about people before, and if that's so, there's no real problem; there are channels that this proposal can be turned over to for development . . ."

"But it's mine!" blurted Johnson. "It's not that I want all the credit, sir, but when you send it through channels, everybody has to change it a little bit and take a little of the credit. Well, that's all well and good, sir, and I wouldn't begrudge them a little credit. But somehow, sir, by the time they all get done with it, there'll be nothing left for me, and they'll have changed the whole thing beyond recognition. I mean, I put a lot of time and thought into this proposal and I think it's damn good—excuse me, sir—just the way I wrote it."

A smile crept across Westland's face, and he pulled a pack of cigars from his pocket. "Well, sit down, Lieutenant, sit down. I think we can start talking seriously now."

They sat there the rest of that afternoon, and all the next day, planning the research facilities, the equipment, the personnel needed, and on and on. Westland, when he decided a project was worth running, had a reputation for not sitting on it. But Johnson was almost in shock as he watched the rapidity with which his paper proposal was becoming a reality.

"Probably the best thing for you to do now," Westland suggested at the end of the second day, "is to go home and tie up any personal affairs that you have back there. We'll have the army move you down here at the start of next week. We can keep all your stuff in storage while you and your wife find a house. It'll

end up being a couple of weeks at the least before
equipment and whatnot really starts getting assembled.
Don't worry about the details of your transfer—we'll
handle them all from this end, and they'll be pushed
through by the end of the week."

And so it went. In a month Lieutenant Johnson was
promoted, and promoted again, to Major Johnson.
Personnel began to arrive to work in his lab, and
Project Vector began to move forward. By the end of
a year, it was clear that the project would work, that
the virus could be constructed, and in a reasonable
length of time. But there was the rub. Now with the
Russians working on some clandestine gene-manipulation project of their own, the definition of a reasonable length of time was becoming considerably shorter.

Westland responded quickly to the change in circumstances, and two weeks after Johnson received the
dispatch concerning Russian work in the field he
found himself speaking to a meeting of an enlarged
research staff.

The talk had, he felt, gone quite well. Looking over
the audience of some hundred and twenty workers, he
concluded his remarks: "I've given you an idea, I
hope, of our position here. Since this speedup was approved, our lab space has doubled, our staff trebled,
and our funding has become almost limitless. Those of
you who have been with me from the start will, unfortunately, find things a bit more formal now. But we've
been quite clearly told that this project has become a
critical one, that its objectives must be met. I can tell
you that what started out as a rather small research
project has grown considerably. We now find ourselves racing with other nations for the development of
these techniques. The project was initiated out of a
concern that other nations might at some date attempt
to set up such techniques and was intended as a means
to explore the health protection procedures appropriate for a response to the intentional or accidental release of new viruses produced by these techniques. But
I'm afraid that these techniques might in the end be
more potent weapons than anything we have seen to

date, including conventional and nuclear weaponry. Potent not in pure destructive power, but potent in their ability to apply force toward a political settlement if future wars should break out. With our increased space, personnel, and funding, we *can* meet our objectives, but only with the help and energy of all of us working together."

By the time Johnson made his way back to his office, his optimism had begun to wane. Westland wasn't going to be impressed by his ability to give pep talks. Westland wanted that damn virus, and nothing else would make him happy. Sure, an enlarged staff would facilitate the work so long as everything progressed smoothly. But unforeseen problems might not yield so easily to the brute force of money alone. Sometimes you just have to sit back and think about your results, allowing the data to sort themselves out in your mind before you go on to the next step. Back in his office, his thoughts were interrupted by the harsh buzz of the intercom announcing the arrival of Major Pearson.

Major Stephen Pearson was from Military Intelligence. He was tall, wiry, and intense. He constantly crossed and uncrossed his legs, folded and unfolded his hands. Clearly an office man, thought Johnson. With all that fidgeting, he'd be useless in the field.

Pearson began: "I appreciate your making this time available to me, Major. In Military Intelligence we've been trying to form some idea as to the sort of experiments the Russians might be trying. I thought I might benefit from discussing the virus project with you. Perhaps I can learn something that will help us to understand what the Russians are up to." Pearson flashed a half smile at Johnson.

Nodding thoughtfully, Johnson asked, "If there's no official transcript being prepared, perhaps I can eliminate all the rhetoric about health maintenance?"

"Feel free, Major," Pearson said. "I'm not making a tape, and if I write down anything that's sensitive, I can make the appropriate additions." Giving a wry smile, he lamented, "It's one of the pains that still hangs around from Watergate. Even stamping a folder 'Top Secret' won't keep Congressional committees out anymore. So anything that gets written down will be appropriately phrased."

"Fine," Johnson replied. "It makes discussion so much easier." He settled into his chair, lit a pipe, and thought for a moment before starting. "It all began with a chance conversation I had with an old colleague who's now a big-time professor on the East Coast. He's working on gene manipulation in plants and was telling me how easy it is now to cut a gene out of almost any type of living organism and add it on to a bacterium or a virus. Then the bacterium or virus will express whatever information is contained in that new gene. For example, they've cut the gene for insulin from human cells, added it to the chromosomes of some bacteria, and the bacteria make human insulin, which is a lot better and cheaper than the stuff the pharmaceutical companies used to sell.

"Well, a couple of days after talking with this guy, the concept of Project Vector popped into my head, almost in final form. Botulism is a serious food poisoning caused by ingesting a toxin made by a strain of bacteria called *Clostridium botulinum*. What, I wondered, would be the feasibility of taking the gene that codes for that toxin and putting it into a normal flu virus? The virus would then also produce the toxin, and we would suddenly have a very deadly flu virus.

"Now, there's a problem in that most people are resistant to the flu, but we can get around that. New epidemics normally arise due to mutations of the virus, which change it just enough so that the body's defense systems can't recognize it. We can speed up that process of mutation in the lab, and we've already produced several flu strains that no one should be resistant to."

Noticing that his pipe had gone out, Johnson paused to relight it. After a satisfactory cloud of smoke had risen from the bowl, he continued. "The only problem left is how to stop the virus once it's released. Vaccinating—and thus immunizing—ourselves and our allies wouldn't work. The flu virus normally mutates at a slow rate, so people immunized against the botulinum flu would eventually be hit with a new strain that they weren't resistant to. That strain could wipe out everyone."

Johnson paused for a moment. It had been months since he had talked in any detail about the project with someone not directly connected with it. He was proud of the project, especially of the solution to the problem of restricting the virus's spread. That had been his act of genius.

He had found the answer in something called mutator genes. They had been discovered back in the early fifties by agricultural geneticists working with corn. The mutator genes, or M-genes, caused genes adjacent to them to mutate with a greatly increased frequency. Johnson had reasoned that by hooking an M-gene to the botulinum gene before transferring it to the flu virus, they could get a strain that would lose its deadly nature. Different M-genes worked with different efficiencies, and so they could make a series of virus strains, some of which would become nonlethal quickly and others that would take a very long time.

He explained all this to Pearson, answering questions as he went along. When he was finished, and Pearson seemed satisfied with the explanation, he was thrown completely off balance by a question.

"How much tissue culture work do you do?" Pearson asked.

Johnson could get no feel for the direction of the question. "Well," he began slowly, "we grow some nerve cells, in order to do tests on the botulinum toxin." He shrugged his shoulders. "It's a standard procedure, nothing very sophisticated."

"Do you have much of a staff working on that?"

"No," Johnson replied. "It's pretty much straightforward, and the pharmaceutical houses automated the process years ago. We've only got four people who do it all." Trying to determine if they had need of any other tissue culturing, Johnson asked, "Are the Russians doing tissue culture stuff? It's hard to believe they're so far behind that they'd need any more than a few technicians."

"That's what we thought," Pearson said. "But we're not even sure that the tissue culture people are concerned with the same project as the DNA people. It's just that they disappeared at about the same time."

For the next two hours Pearson grilled Johnson— on Project Vector, on tissue culture work, and occasionally on subjects the relevance of which was lost on Johnson. Finally Pearson seemed satisfied.

"Well," he concluded, rising from his chair, "I appreciate all the time you've given me, Major. You've been a real help."

"I certainly hope so," Johnson replied, somewhat exhausted.

"I assume you realize that everything we've said here is top secret and should be discussed with no one?"

"Of course," Johnson replied.

Pearson took one last look at his notebook, which he had slowly filled during the preceding two hours. "Oh, one last question. Who was the colleague that gave you the idea?"

"The colleague?" Johnson seemed confused. "Oh, you mean Haenners. Lloyd Haenners—he works in Boston, I think. He didn't really give me the idea, just started me thinking."

"Yes, of course." Pearson smiled, writing down the name.

"Why do you ask?" Johnson inquired.

Pearson shrugged. "Thoroughness, that's all."

Wednesday, August 5

It wasn't until Wednesday that Doc found time to stop by Charlie's lab. Arriving unannounced, he was disappointed to find Charlie absent, and after transferring some boxes from a chair to a counter, he sat down to wait for his friend's return. The stark lighting and the clutter did little to lift him from his depression, and he was almost surprised to see Charlie return in an obviously cheerful mood, accompanied by an attractive woman with shoulder-length brown hair and a pleasing face. In their clean white lab coats, she and Charlie looked the part of dedicated young scientists.

"Why, Doc! What brings you to the ivory towers?" Then, remembering their conversation of Saturday night, he said "Oh, that's right. You said you'd be stopping by." He gestured to his companion. "Like you to meet Beth Cordell. Best postdoc in Lloyd Haenner's lab, across the hall." Beth accepted the compliment with a smile.

"And, Beth," Charlie continued, "this is Fred Blake, an old friend of mine who went straight and became an M.D. As punishment we all call him Doc."

"Nice to meet you," Doc murmured politely. Turning to Charlie, he asked, "Is this a bad time to talk?"

"Not at all," Charlie said. "We were just trading lab stories, and I was telling her horror stories from my graduate school days."

"But small doses are all I can take," Beth insisted. "You two talk—it sounds serious." Turning to Charlie, she added, "We can continue another time." Saying good-bye to Doc, she left the lab.

17

Doc rose and poured a cup of coffee from a pot on the windowsill. He stood there for a minute, staring out the window without speaking. Finally he turned around and came back to his seat, looking suddenly exhausted.

"What's the problem?" Charlie asked apprehensively.

Doc took a deep breath and let it out slowly. "It's the Gloryhits, Charlie—and Ann." He swirled the coffee in his cup and took a sip; then, looking up at Charlie, he said, "I would have talked to you sooner, but I wanted to check my information before I did, just to make sure.

"Charlie, there's something wrong with those Gloryhits. They've been causing miscarriages, and deformities in fetuses being carried by women who took them." He hesitated for a second. "I want to urge you two to terminate the pregnancy."

For a moment Charlie stared back dumbly. But then a wave of relief washed over him. "Oh, Jesus, Doc, don't scare me like that! Ann didn't take any *while* she was pregnant—it was a month *before* she got pregnant. We're sure."

But Doc persisted. "Charlie, that's the problem. All these women took it before they got pregnant. It's not a teratogenic agent; it's some sort of a mutagen—it's causing mutations or something."

Charlie refused to believe it. "Doc, that makes no sense. It's just unheard-of!"

Gently but insistently, Doc replied: "Look, Charlie, I can't pull a 'The Doctor Knows' trip with you. That's not my style, and anyhow, you know far more science than I do. I'm not going to challenge you on that. If you say nothing works like that, I'll say fine, nothing known works like that. If you say it doesn't make sense, fine, it doesn't fit in with anything I've ever heard of, either. That's why I want to do that Medline search, to see if there is any precedent. But with or without scientific doctrine behind me, I've got enough data to say that those Gloryhits are causing miscarriages and grossly deformed fetuses, and I'm convinced that Ann should have an abortion."

The calm, rational, analytic mind that Charlie prized
so highly shut down. It refused to think rationally, to
listen to the argument. Instead, he simply denied it.
"It can't be," he said simply. "I don't care what kind
of data you think you have, it can't be."

A quiet sigh escaped Doc's lips, and he told Charlie
what he had pieced together over the last three months:
that seven women who had taken Gloryhits in the
month prior to conception had miscarried at either
three or five months, that Gloryhits were the only thing
these women had in common, and that he had seen
two of the fetuses. Both had grossly enlarged foreheads, like a horror-movie image of the brilliant mad
scientist.

Charlie laughed bitterly. "So now you want me to
believe that not only is it a mutagen, but that it causes
specific mutations? Doc, I can't buy it. It flies in the
face of everything science knows."

When Doc didn't reply, Charlie continued: "You
said two were deformed. What about the other five.
Were they normal?"

Doc forced calmness into his voice. "I don't know,
Charlie. There's some guy from New York who's doing a study of spontaneously aborted fetuses to see if
they have a high incidence of deformity. He's doing
extensive autopsies and all, so I can't get my hands on
any of them. All of the obstetricians in the area are
cooperating. I never got a chance to see the others before they were collected."

"Come on, Doc," Charlie said, "what does the guy
doing the study say? If he's doing detailed autopsies,
he should have all the data you're claiming to have."

Doc was getting more upset. "Give me a little credit,
will you, Charlie? I've been trying to contact him for
a month, but all I ever get is an answering service that
says he'll call me back, and he doesn't."

"So you can't get the information?"

"Calm down, Charlie. A friend who's an obstetrician
promised to call me when Greene—that's the guy's
name—when he comes around again. He should be by
in a couple of weeks at the latest.

"But, Charlie, don't take chances like this with your

child! I don't care what science says. One of those
fetuses made it to five months, and I've just got a
feeling in my bones that others could make it to term.
You can start again, Charlie. In five months you'll be
back where you are now—and sure that you've got a
healthy baby coming."

Charlie glared angrily at him. "Two months to get
pregnant, Doc, right? Well, try two years, because
that's how long it took us.

"Sure, for two months, but not for two years. If
Ann aborts spontaneously—like all the others you
know about—then she does. Then I don't know what
we'll do. Maybe we'll just call the whole thing bust
and give up. But we're not giving up that baby on purpose, not after all this time."

He crossed to the coffeepot and filled a cup. Looking out the window, he continued. "It wears you out,
Doc, month after month, hoping, but afraid to hope too
much." He turned and faced Doc. "I couldn't take it
again." His gaze dropped to the floor. "Please, let's
drop it for now. I'll help you with that Medline search,
but next week, okay?"

Doc walked over to the window and stared with
Charlie at the shabby tenements across the street.
"Okay, Charlie, I'll drop it for now. But think about
it, and think about the risk. And talk about it with
Ann. You have to do that. It's not just your decision
to make alone." Without answering, Charlie stared out
the window. "Charlie, it's my duty as your doctor, and
as your friend, to give you my opinion, and I have. But
I want you to know that whatever you two decide, I'll
be there with you, to help however I can." He picked
up his coat. "I'll stop by early next week."

Charlie turned from the window and finally met
Doc's gaze. Finding nothing to say, he turned back to
the window again, the need to cry burning in his eyes.
He heard Doc's footsteps head down the hall, and he
was alone with his arguments—and his doubts.

Slowly, mechanically, Charlie sorted out glassware
and chemicals that had come in that morning. There
just isn't enough data to make an intelligent decision,
he told himself. There just isn't enough data.

Tuesday, August 11

It wasn't until the following Tuesday that Doc talked to Charlie again. He arrived to find Charlie and an older man hovering over a huge piece of electronic equipment covered with dials and lights. He sat down quietly behind them, as yet unnoticed, and watched as they fidgeted with the machine. It reminded him of a pinball machine. One of them would adjust a dial, and the other would pound on a meter, trying to get the needle to jump. Finally, after a series of fruitless thumps and punches, they gave up. In frustration, Charlie turned and almost stepped on Doc.

"How the hell you can spend fifteen thousand dollars on a piece of equipment and not have it work is beyond my comprehension!" he exploded. "Now it'll be a week before I can get anything going, unless I want to trek across town with samples and borrow someone else's machine."

He stomped over to the coffeepot and poured himself a cup of coffee. Suddenly realizing that the other two had not met yet, Charlie apologized and introduced them. "Doc, this is Lloyd Haenners. He's in charge of the lab across the hall, and has been helping me in trying to get set up here."

Doc smiled and returned Lloyd's greeting. "Beth Cordell works with you, right?" Doc asked. "I met her last week."

"That's right," he replied. In his early forties, he had the build of an athlete. His hair was modestly long, breaking just over the collar of his corduroy jacket. With just the smallest of beards, he looked the image of the intellectual liberal professor, which he was. "She's a highly prized member of my lab, too," he continued. "Almost invaluable, I'd say." They chatted for a few minutes, and then Lloyd left Doc and Charlie alone.

Charlie pulled over a chair and sat down with Doc. "Haven't seen you in a week. How're things going?"

"Hectic," Doc replied. "That air inversion has been hell. Between the pollution and allergies, it seems like half the city can't breathe. Poor Kip called me up between sets Saturday night begging for some aid, complaining that he'd sneezed his way through most of his first set."

Charlie laughed. "Where's he playing? Ann and I have been meaning to go see him." Kip was one of Charlie's closest friends, a professional guitarist he had known well in college.

"Wouldn't be a bad idea," Doc answered. "He'll be playing at the Hungry Fox again in a couple of weeks. He and Justine have both complained that 'El Profesor' seems too busy to see his old friends anymore."

"Shit!" Charlie muttered. "This lab isn't going to get set up by itself. Ann's been complaining, too. Dammit, I've been working my ass off around here." He gestured at the lab. "But let's see if Warren and Justine are free one night. We can all go and catch a show. Maybe I could invite Beth along."

Doc nodded. "Sure, a fresh face would be nice." He paused for a moment. "How's Ann?"

"Oh, pretty good," Charlie said, avoiding the implied question. "The nausea seems to be over now, and I think she's feeling a lot better. She went down to New York last Friday to spend a week there with some friends she hasn't seen in over a year."

"Did you talk to her?"

Charlie looked uncomfortable. He had avoided telling Ann of the possibilities of losing the baby or of its being deformed. In fact, he still hadn't really admitted the possibilities to himself. He hedged around the real reasons. "I mean, it's no good hitting her with the whole thing just before she goes on a vacation. It would have ruined the week for her, and besides, there's no rush anyway. She's too late for a vacuum abortion, and most OBs would just as soon wait till five months to induce an abortion at this stage."

Doc didn't seem too happy with the answer. "That's all very well and good," he said, "but you can't go and put off the discussion until five months. That's not fair to Ann."

"All right, already, I know that," Charlie replied sharply, "but you don't have to keep harping on it. I'll talk to her about it as soon as she gets back. Look, what about amniocentesis? Couldn't we check it out . . ."

"Charlie, you're not even thinking straight! With amniocentesis you manage to get a few fetal cells out of the amniotic sac, but what would you check for? You have to know what you're looking for with amniocentesis. I'm not trying to harass you, Charlie, it's just that I think you'll feel better, too, once you've both talked it out." He fished around in his pocket and pulled out what looked like a shopping list. "Anyhow," he continued, "that's not why I came here. I thought we'd be able to set up that computer search, if you had the time."

The tension drained from Charlie's face. "Fine," he said, glad to leave the discussion of Ann and abortions. "Let's go into my office—I've got the information on it there." They spent the next hour setting up the Medline search. The cross-referencing service set up by the National Institutes of Health was a well-designed, straightforward system, which meant it got a lot of use. It would take a week to get the information Doc wanted, covering mutagens, teratogens, hallucinogens, and cranial deformations in newborns. Once the search was set up, all they could do was wait.

A week later, Doc returned to find Charlie poring over a thick sheaf of computer printout. Looking up, he waved a hello to Doc. "You don't happen to read Italian, do you?" he asked. "We definitely should have checked 'English Only.' I never know what to do with these foreign-language titles." He held up the printout, which contained easily three hundred references.

"Most of them look irrelevant, but a few seem worth checking out."

Doc pulled a chair up to the desk and sat down. "Anything particularly exciting?"

"Nothing obvious," replied Charlie. "There's no title that says 'Contaminated LSD causes enlarged foreheads in human fetuses,' if that's what you mean. But there are several papers on the teratogenic effects of most of the drugs that we listed, and there are some papers on birth defects that look as if they might be interesting." He handed a file folder to Doc. "I made a Xerox of the listing, so you can go through it at your leisure, and I've marked those that I think are worth looking up. You should check out any others that you think might be interesting."

Doc thumbed through the listing. "From the number of marks, it looks as though we might be busy for a while just looking these up."

Charlie threw an evil glare at the now silent electronic equipment behind him. Then he smiled. "Bertha here is due to be 'realigned' next Monday, so I can spend part of this week reading. I think I can get through most of it in three days of half-assed reading. Oh, and by the way," he added, "I've started a search on LSD or any other drugs causing specific mutations like deformed heads, since that's what you seem to think is going on."

"You don't believe that it's happening?" Doc asked in surprise.

"It? What's it? If you mean do I believe that a lot of people who took Gloryhits had spontaneous abortions—sure, I believe that. If you mean that two of the fetuses had deformed heads—okay, I'll believe that, too. But if you mean that the acid, or something in it, caused specific mutations, I won't buy that. I keep talking to other scientists around here, and they look at me like I'm crazy. Maybe it could be true, but it contradicts everything known about mutations. It'll take a lot of convincing." Charlie folded the printout and put it in the top drawer of the desk. Wanting to change the subject, he asked, "Did you ever get to talk with that guy who's been collecting all those aborted fetuses?"

A look of irritation swept over Doc's face. "That," he said, "depends on your definition of 'talking to.' Dan Studeman called me when Greene got to his office, and I intercepted him before he got out of the building. I've never seen anyone look more unhappy to see me. You wouldn't believe the runaround I got. He told me that he was just overseeing the project, that other people were doing the autopsies, that the autopsies were done by a coded system, and that they couldn't tell until the end which fetuses had come from which doctor, and that he'd see what he could do, but he couldn't promise me anything, and no, I couldn't have his office number, the answering service was the best way to reach him, and he was sorry he hadn't contacted me sooner, and he'd talk to some of the other people in the project, and it wasn't his decision alone, and I'd need release statements from the doctors and the patients, and on and on and on! If I could think of a good reason, I'd say the guy was trying to avoid giving me the information, but that makes no sense at all. I told him I wasn't into research and so he didn't have to worry about competition, and I guess Studeman told him the same thing. Anyhow, the short of it is that I got nowhere. At the end he promised that he'd try to get me the information, and that was it. I was nice and polite and didn't try to push him too hard, but I have a feeling that I won't hear from him until he comes through again next month. It was one hell of a frustrating conversation." He filled a cup of coffee, took a sip, and poured the whole cup down the drain. "I'm so pissed off I don't even know what I'm doing. All I need now is a little caffeine, and I'll shake my way back to the office." He sat down again and tried to relax.

"Isn't it pretty hard to get approval to do work on human fetuses?" Charlie asked. "Maybe you could talk to the commission or whatever that approved it."

"Not for spontaneous abortants," Doc answered. "The only restrictions are for elective abortions, where it's feared researchers could pressure people into abortions."

Charlie shook his head in amazement. "There sure are some crazies running around in academia," he said. "When it's dog-eat-dog, and the results aren't of any immediate importance anyhow, things like that are bound to happen. But you made it clear that this was of immediate medical importance, didn't you?"

"Of course I did!" Doc bristled. "In fact, I went further than that. A patient of mine had an elective abortion, and it turns out that she had taken a Gloryhit a few weeks before the time she thinks she conceived. Anyhow, Studeman did the abortion, and at my request saved the fetus. I'll bring it over for you to see, Charlie. It has the same deformity.

"I told Greene that, leaving out the connection with the Gloryhits. But I impressed on him the fact that my patients were involved and that I needed the information in order to counsel them."

"And that didn't help?"

"Help? That got him upset. He told me that I had to turn the fetus over to him for the study. I pointed out that it was an elective abortion and so of no relevance to his research, since he's looking for spontaneously aborted fetuses. But then he started to make up crazy reasons. At the end he suggested that if I wanted him to be more cooperative, I should consider the same course of action. Once he was convinced that I wouldn't turn it over, he just said he'd do whatever he could, and then left."

"Amazing." Charlie shook his head. "What a bastard. If we knew whether all seven were deformed, or if the others had that same deformity, it'd make decisions a lot easier."

Doc agreed. Then, looking up at Charlie, he asked, "I take that comment to mean that you and Ann haven't decided yet whether to abort?"

Charlie avoided his gaze. "Christ, Doc, there just isn't enough information to make a decision to abort. Maybe, if we find something in these literature searches, or maybe if that ghoul would give us some definitive information, maybe we'd have some grounds to decide on. But at least until I've gone through those articles, I don't see how we can make any decision at all."

"Ann agrees?" Doc asked.

"I'm sure she would," Charlie muttered.

"Would?" Doc was furious. "Cotten, are you telling me that you haven't talked to Ann about this yet?"

Charlie rose from his chair and stomped to the window. "Talk to her about what?" he asked angrily. "That you've gone and gotten some crazy idea in your head that our kid is going to be deformed and she should have an abortion? She doesn't need that kind of worry. She'd just accept my saying that there's no basis for your idea anyhow, so why put her through that?" He turned from the window and met Doc's eyes. "Look, if something comes up, either from that ghoul or from these articles, I promise you I'll talk to her the same day."

Doc cut him off. "What kind of crap is that?" he demanded. "Charlie, you can't treat Ann like that. She has a right to know about this, and if you refuse to tell her, then I'm going to."

"All right, all right," Charlie replied angrily. "Look, she only got back from New York last night. Give her a day to rest, okay? I'll look through these articles and talk to her. Call me on Friday, after I've had a chance to read some of them, okay?"

"Okay," Doc agreed, "but you have to talk to Ann."

"I know, I know," Charlie replied. Doc got up to leave. "Hey, before you go," Charlie called, "I forgot to tell you. Warren and Justine say Saturday is okay with them, and Beth said she'd like to come too, so let's count on it?"

"Fine. I'll talk to you on Friday."

August

"Please be seated, Major Johnson." Pearson politely offered him the most comfortable chair in the room. Johnson smiled and sat down. Major Pearson's constant twitching gave Johnson just the slightest feeling of superiority and took the edge off being on unfamiliar ground. Of the five men present, only Pearson was familiar. The others seemed both calmer and sharper. With Pearson, he never was sure whether he was being understood. "We appreciate your coming up to Washington to talk to us," Pearson continued. "We realize that it's a considerable inconvenience for you, especially at this point in your research, but I'm afraid it would be quite impolitic for all five of us to be seen going somewhere together." He flashed a knowing smile at Johnson, one that the other four chose to ignore. Johnson replied politely, then waited for Pearson to continue. The other four made Johnson just a bit uneasy.

"Well, Major, let's see. I haven't talked to you since last June. Perhaps you could start by bringing me up to date on what you've done since then." Sometimes it's tedious to listen to these answers, Pearson sighed to himself. He had read Johnson's reports in detail, and two hidden microphones were recording every word for later analysis. But he still listened, far more carefully than Johnson realized.

Since June, Project Vector had moved ahead rapidly. By cutting the *Clostridium botulinum* DNA and attaching small pieces to the chromosome of a common laboratory bacterium, *E. coli,* they had succeeded in

28

isolating the gene coding for the deadly botulinum toxin. Westland's seemingly limitless money had allowed them to screen thousands of bacteria in search of the one in a thousand that produced the toxin, and they had found it. The next step would be to attach the mutator genes to the botulinum genes.

After listening to Johnson's recitation, Pearson seemed lost in thought. Finally he asked, "Now that the toxin gene is in *E. coli,* how much more dangerous is it?"

Johnson was shocked. "It's a million times more dangerous! Why, the *Clostridium* bacteria are killed by exposure to air. That's why you only get food poisoning from canned foods, where the air has been sealed out. But *E. coli* is all over the place; you've got billions of them living in your gut, right now, and even a few million of them with the botulinum gene would be enough to kill a man."

Pearson squirmed nervously. "I assume appropriate safeguards . . ."

Johnson laughed, amused at Pearson's discomfort. "The best."

Pearson looked at his small notebook. After what seemed a long time, he raised his eyes to Johnson. "What would you need to put together a highly communicable virus that caused cancer?"

The question caught Johnson completely unprepared. "Well," he stammered, "I don't know that we have the knowledge . . ."

"This isn't an exam, Johnson. You're not being graded." It was one of the silent four, as Johnson had come to think of them.

Pearson agreed. "I realize that you might not have given this any thought before, but perhaps, off the top of your head? . . . I just want some sort of idea of what would be involved." He seemed as nervous as Johnson.

"Well," Johnson replied, "if you just want a wild guess at the problems involved, I suppose first you'd have to isolate a gene that caused cancer, or something like that. Maybe, if you had a virus that caused cancer, you could take the whole viral DNA and hook it to some other, more communicable virus—I'm not sure." He sat thinking about the problem.

"How would you select those viruses which had received the cancer-causing DNA?" Pearson asked.

"How?" Johnson repeated. "I guess you'd have to have some cells, human cells, and try to infect them. I guess you'd want to do it in tissue culture. Grow some human cells in tissue culture and try to infect them."

"Would it be routine tissue culture work?" Pearson asked.

"No," Johnson said slowly. "I don't think it would be all that straightforward. It's tricky telling when a cell has been transformed—that is, turned into a cancerous form. It's rather sophisticated work."

"Could you use a lot of people?"

"Sure," Johnson answered. "I could use two dozen top men in the field."

Pearson seemed satisfied. "Well, Major, you've been most helpful to us." He rose from his chair and escorted Johnson to the door. "Hopefully, if there's any more information I need from you, I can come down to your labs to talk about it."

Johnson was baffled by the brevity of the interview. "That's all?"

"Believe me, Major," Pearson replied, "you've been immensely helpful. My secretary will take care of any details involving your return. Thank you again." Johnson found himself alone with Pearson's secretary.

Back in the office, they were all talking at once. It was the plain-looking man, third from Pearson's left, who finally stopped the chatter. "I want each of your opinions on the probability that the Russians are working on a cancer virus applicable to warfare."

The man on his right, second from Pearson's left, objected. "First I want to know if we've gotten the transcripts from Asilomar yet, and whether they've been digested."

Number four interjected, "If you'll give me about four minutes, I think I can review the entire Asilomar picture." Number three nodded in agreement. "The

1975 Asilomar meeting was held as an outgrowth of a committee of the National Academy of Sciences, to try to set up international guidelines for the safe use of techniques for passing DNA from one organism to another. For reasons that are not clear, but which appear perfectly honorable if naive, a delegation of Russian researchers was invited. This delegation came, obtained as much information as possible, at the least expense of their own information, and photographed all the slides of research presented by American workers.

"Although the meetings were taped, no transcript was ever made, and the tapes have not been opened to the public. We have obtained copies of the tapes, transcribed them, and studied them. The conclusions are simple and terrifying. Anyone having the information presented at those meetings could, without great effort, set up a project similar to the one Johnson has been working on. With good minds, they could attempt the cancer project. In fact, as a result of our analysis of the original tapes, and considering the lack of security surrounding them, we have had them surreptitiously erased. If no one else has gotten them, no one else will.

"It should be presumed, on the other hand, that the Russians hold copies of the tapes. I might add that the four members of the Russian delegation are among those who have disappeared in the last year. That's it." There was no trace of emotion in his voice.

Number two spoke next. "Does anyone think that they're *not* working on a cancer virus?"

"Has it been verified that cancer-virus people have been transferred to Russia's biowarfare labs?" Pearson asked.

"No," answered Two. "All we know is that three of them have disappeared from the public eye. But I don't know where else they might be."

There was silence for several seconds. Finally, Three spoke. "Then it appears that we want to go on the assumption that they are trying it." He looked from man to man, receiving a nod of agreement from each. "Then that leaves us with just one more problem. As you all know, in addition to the invited guests, several uninvited members of the press also attended. We have been carefully going through photos taken at the meeting to verify the identities of these reporters. At this moment, we have two who don't seem to fit. One we can't get any label on—it appears he never registered. The other registered as a reporter for the Boston *Globe*. The name matches a new science writer of theirs, but the face doesn't. We are currently going through all channels to try to track them down. They have been code-named Mohair and Gabardine. You will receive folders on them in the morning, but there's nothing in them that I haven't told you."

"Are there any other points to cover?" Pearson asked.

No one spoke.

"Then we'll meet again next Thursday."

The four filed out silently, leaving Pearson alone in his office.

Tuesday, August 18

Depressed after his talk with Charlie, Doc drove the two congested miles back to his office. He didn't like the idea of having to tell Ann himself, but if Charlie didn't, he'd have no choice. He was confused by Charlie's behavior. Had he changed that much while in California?

He worked through the day, his mind constantly drifting to Charlie and Ann, and the aborted fetus he'd gotten from Studeman. He hated that fetus but at the same time was fascinated by it. Last Friday, in desperation, he had put it on a high shelf behind innumerable other things, to get it out of his sight. But that hadn't gotten it out of his mind.

The day, as usual, ran late, and it wasn't until six-thirty that the last patient left his office. Sharon and Karla, his receptionist and his nurse, were getting ready to leave. One short look, Doc thought, irritated with his continued fascination with the fetus. Pushing a stool over to the shelves, he climbed onto it to get the jar down.

It was gone. He stood there, staring at the empty space on the back of the shelf. Confused, he looked behind other jars and bottles in case it had gotten shoved over. But he knew it was gone. Turning, he called out to Sharon and Karla.

Karla came into his office. "Sharon's gone. Can I help?"

He stood up there on the stool, feeling like a fool. "You haven't done anything with that jar with the fetus since Friday, have you?"

She shook her head. "I thought you had it lower down, over there." She pointed to where it had been before he moved it.

"No, I moved it last Friday. So you haven't touched it?"

"No."

"What about Sharon, did she mention anything to you about having messed with it?"

Karla frowned. "Not a word. I can't imagine why she would. Did she even know where it was?"

Doc climbed down from the stool and sank into his chair. "No, you're right. I moved it at the end of the day Friday, and I guess I didn't mention it to either of you. But for God's sake, where could it be?"

"Do you think someone took it?"

"But no one knew it was there!" Doc exploded in exasperation. "In fact, except for the three of us, Studeman was the only person who even knew I had it. Besides," he added, more calmly, "why would anyone want it?" He looked around his office. "If someone actually broke in here, they passed up a lot of stuff for that fetus."

Karla said nothing.

"Oh, hell, I'll call Sharon later on. Maybe she has

some idea. Someone must have put it somewhere."
He looked back at the shelf. "Actually, it wouldn't be
such a bad loss."

Thursday, August 20

Leaning back in his chair, Lloyd Haenners laughed.
"Shame on you, Charlie. You would have missed
the very first question on our graduate-student qualify-
ing exam last year. It's a contradiction in terms for a
mutagen to have a specific effect. Mutations must, by
definition, be random." He displayed a wry pleasure
in catching a colleague on such a simple point. Now it
was Charlie's move.

Haenners had made a name for himself developing
techniques for raising plant cells in cell culture conditions. It took months for a corn plant to develop,
which meant months for each experiment. By using
tissue culture techniques, it became possible to do large
numbers of experiments quickly and even within the
confines of a small laboratory. With the advent of
genetic manipulation, Haenners had set out to develop
a blight-resistant strain of corn by using gene-transfer
techniques. Beth Cordell was now in the process of
constructing an artificial virus which would carry the
genes into the corn cells.

Charlie shrugged his shoulders at Lloyd's cut. "That's
what I thought, but a strange sort of question came
up, and I wondered if there was something new in
the field. So, for example, thalidomide couldn't be a
mutagen."

"Of course not," Lloyd snorted. "First of all, it only works if taken when a woman is already pregnant, and second, mutagens don't work that way."

Charlie felt relieved, if somewhat irritated by Lloyd's style. He had adopted Lloyd as a role model, impressed by his successful integration of research and politics. Haenners was outspoken about his refusal to take money from the military, although a lot of his support did come from an industrial source, an agricultural research firm called Crop Research Associates.

"Fine," Charlie continued, "but let's suppose, hypothetical situation, a woman ingests an unknown substance and two weeks later conceives a child. There's no way that substance could cause a specific defect?"

"Well, wait a minute," Lloyd insisted. "Now you're not talking about a mutation necessarily. Maybe it's a chemical that screws up, for example, the pituitary gland in the mother, and somehow that causes a teratogenic effect later on. I don't know if anything like that ever happens, but it seems possible."

It might have been possible, but it didn't happen. The computer search had convinced Charlie of that. Teratogenic agents didn't hang around for two weeks in the body, and although interfering with various organs of the mother could cause fetal defects, they were always due to general nutritional failure and were easily identified. There was almost no imaginable way that the sort of event Doc was suggesting could happen. Almost.

It was one of those references that the computer would sometimes provide for no apparent reason. It was an old paper, from the early seventies. A research lab in England had been doing some work with a virus thought to cause certain types of cancer. Called an adenovirus, it always attached to a certain spot on one of the human chromosomes. Why it attached only to that one spot, and how it caused cancer, if indeed it did, wasn't at all clear. But there were cancers of the nervous system, and conceivably a specific virus could attach to some point on a human chromosome in a sperm, or an egg, and cause a tumor of the brain. It was a good idea, but there were no such viruses.

"What about a virus?" Charlie asked.

"Unfair." Lloyd smiled. "You said a chemical, not a biological agent."

Charlie was exasperated by Lloyd's debating tactics, and was tired of the game. "Okay," he said. "You're right. But let's consider viral agents now."

Lloyd thought for a moment. "Well, I've got to admit it's theoretically possible. You know, German measles can cause specific neurological defects in fetuses, but the mother has to catch it while she's pregnant. It has to be active while the nervous system is developing."

"On the other hand," Charlie countered, "a woman can get syphilis and pass it on to a fetus ten years later. So she wouldn't have to first get the infection when she was pregnant."

"Syphilis is a bacterial infection, Charlie. You asked about viral infections."

Charlie couldn't take it any longer. He was talking about his unborn child, and Lloyd was playing with words. "Lloyd," he demanded, "not academically, but really, do you think something like this could happen?"

Haenners was surprised by the tone. "No," he replied. "Maybe in theory, but not in practice."

Charlie sighed in relief. "Thanks," he muttered and rose to leave.

"If you're interested in viruses that affect the genetics of the hosts they infect, you might sit in on our lab seminars now and then," Lloyd suggested. "That's one of the approaches we're considering for the blight problem. I think Bill's talking today, but you should check with Beth—she's in charge."

Back in his own lab, Charlie sank into a chair. There were no grounds for thinking that Doc's hunch was right, but he didn't feel as confident as he had an hour ago. He was exhausted by the doubts and confusion of the last two weeks. Up and down, up and down, positive of the child's safety, fearful for its life. He felt like a straw in a hurricane, waiting to be finally dropped in some unknown place. Depressed and still unsure of his decision, he looked through the results of the computer search, but he could find nothing there he hadn't seen before. Finally he returned to setting up his lab.

He worked steadily through the early afternoon, forgetting completely about Lloyd's suggestion that he attend the lab seminars until Beth stomped into his lab and threw herself into a chair.

"That idiot is going to drive me stark raving mad!" she exclaimed, her face flushed with irritation.

Charlie turned to her with interest. "And who is this lucky person that has gained your undying gratitude?"

Her eyes flashed with anger. "That fool, Bill Hebb!"

"Lloyd's research associate?"

"His so-called associate," she replied angrily. "How he ever got a Ph.D. is beyond my comprehension. That idiot has the organization of a laundry hamper! I don't believe that he just spent an hour and fifteen minutes telling us that nothing seems to have worked in the last month. And then I discover he took *my* bottle of phosphate solution and put a different kind of phosphate in it without changing the label or telling me, so now my experiments for the last week are ruined. I'll kill that guy yet, I swear I will!" She stood up and began roaming around the lab, trying to calm down.

"It's time to get you away from the lab for a bit," Charlie suggested. "What say we wander down to the cafeteria? I could use a break myself."

"Fine," she growled, "but I might make mean company."

Back in his office, Charlie collapsed heavily in his chair, his emotions frazzled. Beth had kept her promise and been mean company. With Charlie offering a sympathetic ear, she had attacked not only Bill but also Haenners for the anarchistic way he ran the lab, and in the end she had placed responsibility for Bill's destructive influence on Lloyd, who refused to recognize its existence. To make matters worse, when Charlie had come to Lloyd's defense, she had turned and attacked him.

Normally he wasn't bothered by criticism of his

scientific life. But Beth's opinions seemed more important, especially in light of the antagonism he had felt toward Lloyd during their discussion. Besides, he was attracted to Beth, he realized, and was hurt by her attack.

Ann too, he realized, had disliked Lloyd from the first time she had met him; a second meeting had only strengthened the feeling. Charlie had put it down to jealousy over a new friend whom Ann couldn't comfortably share, but if Beth's opinion corroborated Ann's, he didn't know what to think.

Charlie picked up the printout of the literature search he and Doc had run. It hadn't turned up any articles of interest, and that, at least, was a relief.

He was leafing through the pages for one last check when the phone rang. "Hi, Charlie, it's Doc. I'm running behind here at the office, so decided that I'd replace a social visit with a call. What'd you turn up?"

Charlie set the printout down on the desk. "Nothing, Doc—not a thing. There are no mutagens, no teratogens, no nothing that causes that kind of deformity. There exists a rare genetic disease that seems to be something like what we're talking about, but the fetuses are always born alive. I think that what we've seen is the result of a very unlikely coincidence, and that's about all. So it looks as if Ann and I are going to have a baby, nice and normal."

Doc sounded unhappy. "I take it, then, that you've talked it over and have both agreed that that's what you want to do?"

Charlie hesitated for a second. "Well," he started, "as a matter of fact, no, we haven't talked about it. But, Doc, you've got to realize that there just isn't anything to talk about." He kept going, not giving Doc a chance to object. "Look, you had an idea, and we thought it might be right. That's why we did the literature search. But the answer is that your idea is wrong. It can't be what you thought it was, so there's nothing to worry about. What is worth worrying about is the effect of stress on the development of a fetus. That *is* well documented, and there's no reason to expose Ann to any unnecessary pressure—especially when it took so long for her to get pregnant. That kid means a lot to us, and I don't want to stir up a mess. I don't know if there's any common cause behind the miscarriages you've found or not, but even if there is, which I doubt, it's really unlikely that Ann and I are connected with it. Besides, even if we are, and we do lose the fetus, we'll feel a lot better about trying again that way than if we abort what turns out to be a perfectly normal fetus."

There was silence for a moment, and then Doc asked, "Are you finished?"

The question caught him off guard. "I don't see that there's much more to say," he replied.

"Charlie," Doc said, "I can't believe that you're being such an ass! Big Charlie Cotten, protecting his frail mate from the terrors of the outside world. Charlie, I'm sorry, but apparently I didn't make myself clear last time I talked to you. Ann is going to be told. I'm her doctor as well as yours, and it's my responsibility to see that she knows. Charlie, I can't believe that you think you have the right to make this kind of decision for her!"

Charlie was furious. And scared. He wanted nothing to do with telling Ann, but he couldn't let Doc do it. He tried to sound calm, reasonable. "Doc, I'm not trying to play God! It's just that there's nothing to gain by talking it over with her. You know as well as I do that in the end she'll defer to my judgment, because she doesn't know anything about the subject. I've gone through the literature, and you've seen the results yourself. We searched for mutagenic and teratogenic effects of LSD, for mutations affecting neural development, and even for mutagens that specifically affect anything! There's just nothing like this, that's all there is to it. I even talked with one of the big shots here who's working with genetic-manipulation techniques, and it just doesn't make it."

Doc spoke in a quiet, strong voice. "There was another one yesterday, Charlie. Another miscarriage, another deformed fetus. You can come with me and see it for yourself if you want. It's sitting in Dave

Butler's office. Another coincidence, Charlie? You're the scientist—what are the odds?"

Charlie found nothing to say.

"Charlie, it's Thursday now. Monday I'm calling Ann. If you haven't talked to her by then, I will."

Charlie stared silently at the phone, then hung it up without replying. He turned to the computer print-out with all the evidence that Doc's fear wasn't real. Finally, shoving back his chair, he left the lab.

Emerging from the subway in Harvard Square, Charlie was assaulted by the manic congestion of what had become Cambridge's major shopping dis-trict in addition to the home of five thousand college students. Avoiding the direct route home, he walked up Brattle Street, turning down the cobblestoned alley behind the Coop. He stopped at the top of a flight of stairs leading down to the Hungry Fox, suddenly realizing that his subconscious had been leading there. Inside, he found Kip reading a paper in the now empty coffeehouse.

Long blond hair down to the middle of his back and an embroidered cotton shirt gave Kip the look of the archetypal hippie. As undergraduates, he and Charlie had been involved for two years in political organizing, and despite three years of little contact, they still felt close.

"What brings the professor to this dank hollow be-tween nine and five?" he asked cheerfully.

"Hi, Kip. Lemme sit down a minute first, okay?"

"Sure." Kip could see the tension and exhaustion in Charlie's face. They had spent many a long night together, planning and organizing, and each could read all the signs in the face of the other. "Looks like you've been having a hard time."

Charlie sat quietly, refusing the potato chips Kip had shoved toward him. "Kip, has Doc been acting more grouchy, more authoritarian, since I've been gone? I mean, in his professional, medical sense. Is he pushing things on you more, or something like that?"

Kip smiled. "You haven't changed, Charlie, but neither have I. No cryptic questions. What's up?"

Charlie smiled gratefully, understanding better why he had sought out Kip to talk to. He was the one person with whom Charlie could talk honestly and openly, without fear of attack or deprecation. Even with Ann, he realized, there was too much at stake to let everything go unchallenged. With Kip, the relationship was just loose enough that they could avoid getting defensive and attacking the things the other one said.

"You can't believe how pissed I am at Doc. I feel that he's ruined our friendship in one fell swoop by trying to play God."

"What happened?" Kip asked gently.

"Oh, Christ, Kip, it's all so confusing. Did you ever hear of some acid called Gloryhits?"

"Sure I did. It was beautiful stuff." Kip looked confused. "Is there something about it I don't know?"

"Yeah. Maybe a nightmare. Hell, I don't know, either." Slowly Charlie got the story out. Talking about it with someone other than Doc for the first time, Charlie realized how upset he really was. By the end, he was shaking. "I don't know. I was convinced that Doc was on a wild-goose chase, but now I'm not so sure."

"You seem awfully upset for someone who doesn't think there's a problem," Kip agreed.

"Well, dammit, what if he's right?"

"Charlie, I don't grasp the problem. You don't want to lose the baby, and I can understand that. But if Ann miscarries, is that so different from losing it by an intentional abortion?"

Charlie shook his head. "That's fine, except for Doc. He thinks it could go to term, even with the deformity—and that's just plain bullshit. I mean, he has no data to support it, no reason at all, and he admits it. I think he just said it to scare me into an elective abortion, and that's why I'm so pissed off at him. If they all abort by five months, and they all have, then his argument really doesn't hold water. So I feel as if he tossed in that ringer to get around it. That's why I asked you about his getting more authoritarian. It didn't sound like the old Doc to make something up just for the sake of convincing a patient."

"No, it doesn't sound like him at all," Kip agreed. "And he hasn't changed that much since you left, not so I've been able to tell."

"But then, how could he say that?" Charlie insisted. "There's absolutely no reason for him to think it. He says it's just a feeling he has, and that doesn't sound very scientific to me."

"You don't have to agree with him, Charlie, but don't sell him short. I don't think he's lying to you. It isn't his style."

"But what am I supposed to say to Ann?" he demanded. "Even though Doc's argument has more holes in it than a sieve, I still have to present it!"

Kip nodded in sympathy. "Do it like you did with me. That wasn't too unreasonable, and I don't think Doc could ask you to do more." Kip stirred the rapidly melting ice in his drink. "It's gonna be hard, Charlie, damn hard. I don't envy you at all. But don't blame it on Doc. He didn't make it hard, it just is."

Charlie wasn't satisfied. "I don't know, I'm still pissed off at him. He seemed so goddamn callous about it, and showed about as much sympathy as a slaughterhouse worker does for a steer. I think I can do without him for a while."

"What about Saturday?" Kip asked.

"Oh, shit!" Charlie lamented. "I forgot all about that. Look, Kip, be a good guy and beg off for us. If I talk to Ann, neither of us is going to want to come, and I don't want to see Doc if we haven't talked yet."

Kip nodded understandingly but said, "You're wrong cutting Doc off like this, but it's your decision. I'll tell them that you didn't feel well and weren't sure that you'd make it. What about that woman you work with?"

"Beth?" Charlie asked. "I think she's catching a ride with Doc, so I suppose she'll come anyhow. Be friendly to her—Doc's the only one of us she's even met before."

"Will do, Charlie."

Charlie looked at his watch and sighed. Ann would be expecting him home for dinner soon. He wasn't looking forward to the evening.

Sensing the situation, Kip rose from his chair. "You'll have to let me go now, Charlie. I've got to run through a few numbers before the show starts, and I like to do it before dinner." He reached for his guitar case.

Charlie got up from his chair. "Okay, Kip, I guess I've got to go, too." He started toward the door.

"I'll dedicate one to your kid tonight," Kip called out. "For good luck."

Sunday, August 23

Charlie had gone home that evening dreading the unavoidable confrontation. But somehow he had gotten through the evening and Saturday and most of Sunday without bringing up the subject. Finally, after dinner on Sunday, there was no more delaying possible. Tomorrow Doc would be calling Ann.

"You seem to have gotten into a funk awful fast," she complained. The dinner had been good, and they had talked extensively about plans for the house and yard. Now, in the living room, Charlie sat silently, unable to begin the conversation. When he didn't respond, Ann became more serious. "What is it, Charlie? You've been drifting off into that vaguely unhappy look of yours all weekend. Can you tell me?"

Charlie nodded, but then just sat there, silent, without turning to Ann.

Ann came over to his side. Putting an arm around him, she gently turned his face to hers. "Come on, Charlie, what is it?"

He started in a monotone. "Doc has some crazy idea, and he's insisted that I talk to you about it. I guess I'm convinced that his whole idea is wrong, and that even if he's right, there's nothing to be done about it. But still, we really need to talk it over, because it affects us both."

"Charlie, what are you talking about?" There was a trace of apprehension in Ann's voice.

"Doc thinks that our kid is deformed because of the Gloryhits we took, and that it'll abort spontaneously at five months." He blurted it out, anger in his voice. "In which case we have two ugly months to wait for it to happen or, more likely, to not happen." He sat silently for a moment and then finally turned to her. She was shocked, and tears were just beginning to appear. "Ann, I'm sorry to throw it at you that way. I've been trying to find some way to bring it up for the past two weeks, and I just haven't been able to. He's wrong, I'm sure of it, and I just haven't wanted to worry you about it, I guess. But Doc convinced me that you should know and share in making the decision."

"Not the baby, Charlie—oh, Jesus, not that!" Tears flowed down her cheeks. "Not something wrong with it. I think I can bear anything, but not that!"

Charlie put his arms around Ann, rocking her gently. "That's what I'm trying to tell you. It isn't real, what Doc's worrying about. It's just a crazy idea he's gotten somehow, and gotten all blown out about. So we have to deal with it, and worry about it, but no, I promise you, there's nothing wrong with our kid."

She sobbed into his shoulder. "Charlie, I couldn't handle a deformed child—you know that, don't you? I don't want to bring one into this world. I couldn't handle it, Charlie, I just couldn't."

"But I'm telling you, Ann, even if it is deformed, like Doc thinks it might be, it'll abort by itself at five months. The deformity is lethal; the fetus can only make it halfway through development. So at the worst, we'd lose it then. But there won't be any deformed child." In that instant Charlie realized that he would never tell Ann that Doc thought it could survive.

Staring forward, she forced a hard smile and said, "So after two and a half years we can just start all over again. Just like that?"

"Ann, nothing's going to happen! You've got to believe me. No deformed baby, no aborted fetus. Just a normal, healthy baby." He almost screamed it at her.

She turned to him, a stony, blank look on her face. "Okay," she said, "now tell me what it is. Tell me why Doc thinks we're going to lose our child."

So for the second time in three days Charlie told the whole story. But this time he did not mention the possibility of a live deformed child. It was absurd, he told himself, and it wasn't even clear that Doc was really willing to stick by it. He had only mentioned it once or twice.

He told Ann about the deformity and its correlation with the people who had taken Gloryhits, about the literature search and how it had revealed nothing, and about his talk with Lloyd.

"You told Haenners?" Ann asked in dismay.

"No, not really," Charlie explained. "I just sort of talked to him about the theoretical possibility of something like that happening."

She wasn't convinced. "It sounds to me like you really did tell him. You don't think he might have guessed that it wasn't just a random conversation?" Now she was angry.

"For chrissake, Ann, I told you he didn't. In fact, he took it almost as a sophomoric debate. Why do you always get so riled up over him, anyhow? Would it be so terrible if someone else knew?"

"I don't like him, okay?" she shouted. "Do I have to like all of your damn scientist friends, regardless of how creepy they are? I just don't want him coming up to me at some damn party, tossing me a wink, and saying, 'Hi, I hear you're going to have a de-

formed baby.' " She turned away from Charlie, on
the verge of hysteria.

He pulled her back to him and gently settled her
head against his shoulder. They sat there silently,
both trying to calm down. He wished that he could be
the one crying, and Ann comforting him.

"Charlie, please don't tell anyone else about it?"
Her voice was soft, pleading. "I guess I can live with
it, wait the two months, but I don't want to have to
talk to anyone else about it. I don't want to cry in
front of anyone, and I don't want to have to be strong,
either. I just don't want to talk about it at all. Promise
me?"

"Sure, I promise." He did not mention his talk with
Kip. It would only upset her more. Silently he drilled
it into his memory to tell Kip not to say anything.

Gently rubbing the back of Ann's neck, he mur-
mured, "So now we wait. Wait for the fetus to move.
None of the others ever quickened, ever moved at all.
Once it moves, we're safe."

"But two months, Charlie, two months that were
going to be so beautiful—they're going to be terrible
now."

"I know," he whispered, and finally, he cried for
his child.

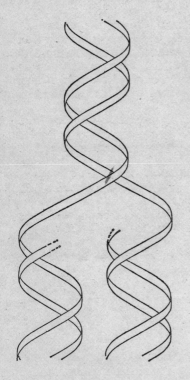

PART
II

September

Stanley Johnson looked out at the mid-September sunset. A hint of the impending fall could be found in the trees and in the crispness of the air. But hermetically sealed windows, air conditioning, and bright office lights prevented the climate from penetrating into his office. To Johnson, the sunset merely pointed out that another evening at home would be lost. In the outer office he could hear Carol, his secretary, typing. At least she gets overtime pay, he thought.

The parking lot had been full the last few weeks. Overtime was becoming the rule rather than the exception as the big push slowly built up steam. And with the steam came the inevitable pressure, emanating from Pearson's office in Military Intelligence. Pearson was impossible to talk to. Or, rather, to talk with. He was easy to talk to, but nothing ever came back from him except vague intimations that in some way things were more serious than Johnson thought, that Project Vector was more important than he realized. And that he didn't like. Somehow, when he had first thought of the project, it was just that, a project. But now it seemed to be more of a weapon, a weapon that at least Pearson seemed to think was needed, and needed fast. Even tomorrow's visit was unsettling, in that Pearson had called just that morning to set it up instead of waiting for their monthly meeting. And he had told Johnson specifically what the meeting was to cover. It put that much more pressure on him, and he would be up late, working with one of his top men, deciding just what the best tack for to-morrow's meeting would be.

Behind him, Peter Stanker continued the discussion. "Why the hell can't you just say, 'Look, we don't have enough information to give you the precise estimates you want, but these are our best guesses'? They can't expect us to do the impossible!" He was the only person in the project who could talk to Johnson that bluntly. A decade older than Johnson, Stanker appeared to have neither hope nor interest in rising any higher than he had, and considering his age and unspectacular, if impressive, record, Johnson felt no threat.

"Pete, I'd love to. But those bastards just aren't scientists, and they don't understand science. They're cloak-and-dagger boys, and when they say they want to know the number of passes to extinction, they think it's like saying 'Find out if Joe Shmoe is passing secrets to the Russians.' They think that you can just whip out an experiment and have 'ten' or 'twenty' printed out by the computer, all nice and neat."

Stanker nodded in sympathy. It wasn't a pleasant situation to be in, which was part of the reason he was happy with a lower-level position. "But what if you just stated that determination of the number requires actual human studies with the botulinum virus, which we haven't even isolated yet?" he asked without pushing too hard. "Wouldn't that be a rea-sonable answer?"

Johnson turned back from the window and sat down at his desk. The myriad stacks of papers on his desk seemed to reinforce his feelings of helplessness. "Who ever said they were reasonable people? I'm afraid that if I said that they'd go find someone else to ask, someone who would just make up a number to get points for coming up with an answer, and if that's what they're going to do, I'd just as soon give them an educated guess. We're certainly in the best position to do that."

Stanker reluctantly agreed. "I can't even imagine where they'd go to get another guess, but I suppose they'd find someone. You're right, Stan, if that's the choice, I'm sure we can give them the best guess. Just so they realize that we're not one-hundred-percent certain of the numbers."

Johnson sighed. "I just hope they'll listen when I tell them."

Together they pored over the meager data at their disposal, noting frequently where they had to make estimates or, on occasion, guesses, and it was one-thirty in the morning before Carol had finished typing their conclusions. Johnson finally was out of the building at two, looking forward to a half-hour drive home, which he hoped would loosen some of the knots in his stomach. Pearson had insisted on an eight-thirty meeting, so Johnson was going to be woefully short on sleep.

The knots finally loosened at three-thirty as he fell into a troubled slumber.

"Major Pearson, sir." Johnson looked at the clock. It was eight-thirty-one.

"Please show him in, Carol." He spoke into the intercom, wondering if Carol was as exhausted as he was. With only three and a half hours of sleep, he had come in with no breakfast and had grabbed a doughnut and a cup of coffee in the cafeteria not ten minutes earlier. His head throbbed; he was angered at the lack of sleep, and his stomach wasn't any happier with the doughnut.

Pearson looked as cheerful as ever. If *cheerful* was the word. The man always had a half grin on his face, one that never quite broadened into a full smile. In fact, thought Johnson, the man looks exactly the same every time I see him. Johnson rose from behind his desk and shook Pearson's hand. "Good morning, Major, good to see you again." He smiled, curious to see if Pearson would smile back.

For an instant the half grin broadened into something just short of a full smile. "Thank you, Major, I'm glad you could see me on such short notice." With no more ado, he sat down and opened his brief-case. "I'm afraid that it's become rather important for us to get an idea of the passages to extinction for your various mutator genes. We need to know whether we're talking about tactical weapons or doomsday machines." He smiled at his little joke and began the constant crossing and uncrossing of his legs.

Johnson smiled back, a bit nervously. For the first time, Pearson had referred to the viruses as weapons. "Well, for a start, let's say it can't be a doomsday virus. Even if we hook it up so that the virus never mutates into a harmless form, there are some people who will be resistant to the flu just by chance, and even some who are resistant to the botulinum toxin. Besides, don't forget, a true doomsday machine kills all human life, while we can easily vaccinate at least some people against the toxin."

"And their children, and their children's children?" Pearson asked.

Johnson was startled. Maybe only because he was so tired, but the question seemed more astute than Pearson's usual inquiries. "Well," he responded slowly, "I guess I never thought about it that way, but sure, why not?"

"Perhaps," Pearson suggested, "because it would take a lot of survivors to maintain a technology capable of producing antitoxins. Don't you think?"

"I suppose," Johnson agreed slowly. He was clearly on the defensive. "But there are clearly a lot of unknowns involved in answering questions like that. It seems pretty clear, for example, that the viruses with the botulinum gene would be selected against by normal viruses."

"Oh?" Pearson seemed surprised. "That's a new thought to me. Why don't we start with that." He sat back with his notebook in hand.

Johnson breathed a sigh of relief. He wasn't going to be too fast on his feet today and was much happier sticking to materials that he had prepared and was comfortable with.

"Because it kills the person it infects," Johnson explained. "You see, one of the big problems that came up, an ironic one, is that the virus is way too deadly. Although we obviously haven't tried it out with the influenza virus in humans, extrapolations from experiments on animals suggest that the infected person would die after only a very small number of his body's cells had become infected, because the toxin is so potent. The typical victim would, in fact, die before he had begun to spread the infection, so there wouldn't even be an epidemic effect. Ideally, there would be a day or two between the start of the infection and the death. Otherwise the people who were first infected would die, and no others would become infected. So we've isolated a mutant that has a less active botulinum toxin—several thousandfold less active, in fact—and that should just fit our requirements."

"Is the normal botulinum antitoxin effective against the mutated toxin?" Pearson asked.

"I'm not sure," Johnson stammered. "We've only recently isolated the mutant, and haven't had time to check out that kind of thing." In fact, he hadn't considered the possibility.

"Have you prepared an antitoxin to the mutant, then?"

"No, but we're in the process. It takes a while."

"Then right now you're not sure that you have any antitoxin that would be effective against the virus if, say, it got loose?"

"Oh, well, it's not into the influenza yet; it's still only in the bacterial carrier." Johnson suddenly felt relieved that it wasn't. Not having prepared the antitoxin was a bad oversight, a consequence of the speed with which they were moving.

"Of course," Pearson replied. "I had forgotten." He made a note in his book. "Well, I'm sure you're working on it as fast as you can." The grin widened for another instant.

"Yes, we are," Johnson lied. Pearson's behavior was entirely different than it had been in the past. He's sharper than I thought, Johnson told himself. "Anyhow," he continued, "the ideal influenza virus, from the point of view of the survival of the virus, is one that doesn't even affect the host, so that it can be spread as widely as possible. The botulinum influenza, regardless of how much we restrict its lethality, will be less effective at being spread. So, over time, it will be outgrown by other influenzas already in the environment. It's a standard evolutionary pattern," he concluded.

Pearson seemed convinced. "Okay, so we at least won't have an ultimate doomsday machine. Do we have something pretty close?"

"Close," Johnson agreed. "Well, reasonably close, I'm sure. The question is, what fraction of the population would be hit by the virus? I think we can say that we'll have much better than a ninety-nine-percent kill in those that are infected, but would everybody become infected? Normally when a flu epidemic comes around, anywhere from ten to sixty or seventy percent of the population actually catches it. Presumably the low values are for flus that aren't very different from other flus that have been around in the past, and most people are resistant from the last batch that came around. Well, we can mutate the influenza enough so that nobody's immune system will recognize it. In fact, we've already done that. We tried it on a couple of hundred army volunteers, and they all got the flu, so it's okay from that point of view."

"Well"—Pearson smiled—"at least they would survive the doomsday bug, now that they're resistant, right?"

"Yes," Johnson agreed. "I guess in effect they're the first people to be immunized against it. Which is why we took precautions to see that they didn't spread it to anyone else. In theory, they could have started an epidemic, and then everyone would have become resistant. So they were kept in isolation for a period of fourteen days, much longer than would be necessary."

"Then why wouldn't it have a ninety-nine-percent kill rate?" Pearson asked.

"Well, that brings in the whole concept of epidemiology. Once a government realizes that it has a plague on its hands, it's going to start restricting travel and quarantining people and areas that are infected. Just how effective such procedures would be really isn't known. Plus, once you start talking about

a thirty- or sixty-percent kill, you have sanitation
problems that start getting out of hand. No one wants
to handle dead bodies that may still be infectious.
Then, with big cities, how do you get food in past a
quarantine? And who's going to keep the power and
water and gas running? It's a problem that can't be
answered yet. All we can really talk about is the fraction of a city's population that would be killed by the
virus itself, if people weren't expecting it. For that I
think we can say that with just the stripped-down
botulinum virus we can get ninety- to ninety-five-
percent kill." There were a lot of *if*'s that Johnson
left out, but with Pearson so aggressive a more complete discussion would have been too much to deal
with.

"And it would spread from city to city as fast as
a normal flu epidemic?" Pearson asked.

"Yes," Johnson agreed, "except insofar as travel
is restricted and quarantine procedures introduced."

Pearson scribbled furiously in his notebook, nodding
either to himself or to Johnson—it wasn't clear.
"Then," he said slowly, finishing writing his notes,
"then the stripped-down virus would have an almost
infinite number of passages to extinction, except for
natural selection?"

"If that's how you define 'passages to extinction,'
yes. The term can be defined in a number of ways,
I suppose."

"How do you mean?" Pearson looked up from his
notes, clearly confused.

"Well," Johnson replied, "the term 'passages to
extinction' is tied in with the mutator genes. You
remember that when I first talked to you about this
project, I said that the one major problem remaining
was that the flu normally mutates every few years, and
so even people immunized against the botulinum influenza would be susceptible after a few years, when
the virus had mutated a bit. We needed to make sure
that the virus would die out, somehow, before that
could happen. The solution we settled on was the
attachment of mutator genes to the front of the
botulinum toxin gene. M-genes were first discovered

back in the fifties in corn. More recently a huge number have been found throughout the plant and animal
communities and, finally, in bacteria. The bacterial
mutator genes apparently work by causing a short
segment of DNA next to the mutator gene to be cut
out of the chromosome. So whatever is located after
the mutator gene will be lost. Hooking up a mutator
gene in front of the botulinum toxin gene would cause
the eventual removal of the toxin gene. We've obtained
mutator genes that cut out the attached DNA with
frequencies ranging from once every ten cell divisions
to once every hundred thousand. In the first case,
every time the virus replicated, there would be a ten-
percent chance of the toxin genes being lost. So after
ten replications only one-third of the viruses would
still be infectious."

"That still doesn't sound like it would die out too
fast," Pearson objected.

"You're forgetting how many times the virus rep-
licates in one person," Johnson explained. "If the
virus goes through thirty replications before the victim
starts to infect other people, then only four percent
of the viruses will still have the botulinum toxin genes,
and only four percent of the people the victim infects
will be killed."

Pearson still seemed confused. "Then how does it
die out?"

Johnson went to the blackboard. "Let's say we start
out with a hundred people, all infected with the botulinum influenza. So that hundred will all die. But now
let's say they each infect five people. So five hundred
get infected. But remember, only four percent are
infected with the botulinum influenza. The mutator
gene has inactivated the rest. So only twenty get
botulinum influenza. Next round, the five hundred infect twenty-five hundred, of which the twenty with
botulinum influenza infect one hundred. But again,
only four percent get unmutated influenza, so this
time only four out of twenty-five hundred get the
botulinum influenza. Next time, the twenty-five hundred infect about twelve thousand people. But the
four with botulinum influenza only infect twenty, and

only four percent of these will get botulinum influenza, or less than one person. 'Passages to extinction' is simply the number of times the virus is passed from one person to another before there is less than one person receiving the botulinum virus per hundred people originally infected. In our example, one hundred people passed it to twenty, the twenty passed it to four, and the four to four-fifths, or less than one person, so there were only three passages to extinction. Altogether there would be only a hundred and twenty-five people killed for every hundred people initially infected, and the virus dies out very rapidly."

"I see," Pearson said slowly, going over the figures that Johnson had written on the blackboard.

"The stripped-down virus, with no mutator gene, would have a number of passages to extinction equal to infinity, since it almost never mutates," Johnson continued. "When we define it this way, we don't take into account things like evolutionary selection of other strains of influenza. That's why I said it depends on your definition. I think ours is the more stringent definition, and I guess I'd rather err on the side of safety."

Pearson nodded in agreement. "That makes good sense. But back to the frequencies. As the frequency of mutation decreases, the number of passages to extinction slowly increases?"

"Not so slowly," Johnson answered. He returned to the blackboard. "If you look at the number of people who got infected with the botulinum influenza each time, it went from one hundred to twenty to four to less than one. To achieve extinction, the number of people getting the botulinum virus has to keep getting smaller. Now if twenty percent of the initially infected people transmit the botulinum genes, and each passes the virus to five or more people, then the first hundred would infect five hundred others. Of these, twenty percent, or one hundred people, would get the botulinum genes. So there would be no decrease in the number with the botulinum genes, and there would never be extinction, at least in the sense that we've defined it. But even so, with each passage of the influenza virus a smaller and smaller percentage will receive the deadly botulinum genes."

Pearson nodded in understanding, writing down all the numbers.

Johnson transferred figures from a notebook to the blackboard. "If you assume thirty replications in a person before infectivity, and five persons infected per person, then the numbers look like this:"

Frequency of transfer (%)	Passages to extinction	Number killed in city of one million
1	2	105
2	3	111
3	3	118
5	4	133
10	7	197
20	—	639
30	—	2522
50	—	25,731
70	—	145,186
90	—	561,082
95	—	754,226
99	—	946,133

"So, as you can see, we pretty well have the possible range covered. We have frequencies of transfer from four percent to ninety-nine percent. Ninety-nine percent would give a ninety-percent kill throughout the world starting from a hundred infected people."

Pearson seemed pleased. "How accurate are these figures?" he asked.

Johnson phrased his answer as carefully as possible. "They're as close as we can possibly get without doing some sort of field testing. But it would have to involve the botulinum influenza with human subjects. And it would have to be in the field, not in the lab, so I'm not sure that any improvements at all are possible on these estimates. You know, it's not like the A-bomb, where you can go test it on a desert atoll or something."

"So with the strongest mutator, essentially only those

people infected by the initial spray, or whatever, would be killed by it?"

"Essentially," Johnson agreed. "There'd be about twenty-five people killed by infectivity for every hundred initially infected."

Pearson thought for a moment. "If you got accurate figures on that one, could you extrapolate?"

"Why, uh, yes," Johnson replied. He didn't like the implication of the question. "But it would take several hundred deaths to get accurate measures."

Pearson, realizing Johnson's thought, laughed. "Don't worry, Major, we're not about to do field tests."

Johnson smiled uneasily. It was the first time he had ever seen Pearson laugh. "Besides," Johnson pointed out, "we've got the mutator hooked to the botulinum genes, but we still have to get them from the bacterial host into the influenza, and that'll take a while."

Pearson nodded. "We have faith in you, Major. We're sure you'll have it soon enough."

Saturday, October 3

"Help like that I can do without," Charlie said. He picked up a pillow from the floor and threw it at the couch.

"Well, I don't see how you're in any position to complain," retorted Ann. "You get all in a huff at Doc for doing what you know damn well he had to, and should have done, and then do one of your stupid trips and refuse to see him. Well, it's been six weeks now, and I'm tired of it. If you want to sneak out the back door before he gets here, that's just fine with me." She lit a cigarette and began to smoke, something she only did under stress. "Do you want to tell me exactly why you don't want to see him? Is it anger or embarrassment? If I were you, I'd be embarrassed."

"Maybe I just don't like everybody else planning my life for me!" he shouted. "Like telling me ten minutes beforehand that you've invited them all along with us. I do like to think of myself as being able to decide for myself who I'd like to go out with."

"Except I'm tired of living in social isolation. We haven't gone out with anyone in six weeks, Charlie, and I'm fed up with it. They're my friends, too, and I invited them." She was four and a half months pregnant and was beginning to tire more easily. "Come on, Charlie, don't do it for me—do it for Disney." It was the name they had given the fetus. They would change it when he or she was born.

Charlie sank down onto the couch, still upset. "Okay," he agreed. "For Disney."

"Thanks," she said, giving him a gentle kiss. They sat there, in each other's arms, until the bell rang.

"Hi, Doc, come on in." She ushered him into the living room, where Charlie had started a tape of Miles Davis. He turned to greet Doc.

"Good to see you again," he said, forcing a smile.

Doc returned the smile. "And it's good to see you two again." He looked around the living room. "You two have done wonders with this place since I was here last." It was a gentle way of acknowledging the separation.

"Not so much *we*," admitted Charlie. "Ann has done almost all the work herself lately. I've been buried under the pressures of getting this damn course ready to run. College teaching is supposed to be a breeze, but the first time you teach a course it's incredible how much you have to do. The lab's been at a virtual standstill these last six weeks."

"It's true," Ann said. "I've hardly seen him. He rushes off in the morning, rushes home for dinner, and then afterward rushes up to the study. We even agreed that I'd pick up more than my share of the work around here for a while, until the course is running smoothly." She smiled at Charlie. "But he'll pay for it later. The truth is that he really loves it. It was all I could do to get him to take this evening off to go hear Kip."

"Oh, to be a student again," moaned Charlie, "free to live the easy life. I'm turning gray from the work."

"Poor boy," sympathized Doc. "But at least those students don't get you out of bed at three in the morning." He accepted a slice of cheese and a cracker from Ann. "But you've already started teaching, haven't you?"

"Just a week ago. Classes start at the end of September so that the term can end before Christmas. Then there's a recess until almost the middle of January."

"Doesn't starting relieve most of the pressure?"

"Well, it eased the fear," Charlie admitted. "But I'd wanted to be a full month ahead in preparation before the course began, and I'm not. So I'm trying to gain just one more week on my lectures. Then I'll slow down. I live in terror of preparing a lecture the day before I have to give it."

"It's his favorite nightmare nowadays," said Ann.

"And how are you doing, Ann?" Doc inquired. "If you've been doing all this work in the house, I take it you're feeling pretty good!"

"It's true! The nausea ended just before we saw you last time, and since then it's been just fine. It's so exciting, watching myself get big."

"It should be quickening soon," Doc commented.

"I know," said Ann. "We've been waiting nervously for that. None of the others ever quickened, did they?"

"No," said Doc. "I guess now I'm willing to agree with Charlie that if the fetus quickens, you're out of risk."

Ann was confused by the qualification Doc put on the statement. But Charlie spoke before she could say anything. "Not 'the fetus.' *Disney*. That's its name until it's born."

"Disney?" Doc asked.

Ann explained: "It's better than 'the fetus,' and it isn't male or female. Plus you'd never want to keep a name like that. So it's just a fetal name. I hate calling it 'it,' so I call it Disney."

"Okay," Doc said. "Disney it shall be."

The front door swung open to admit Warren and Justine. "Come on," called Justine. "We're not going to wait all day for you people. And if we don't get moving, we're going to miss the start of Kip. Don't want him to get mad." The pair looked like brother and sister, both short, with round, cherubic faces and wide smiles.

"Well, come on in a minute," Charlie said, ushering them inside. "Just because you two are late is no reason to rush us."

Warren held up a pair of ink-stained hands. "We didn't even get to wash up before coming over. It's that press that made us late. It's going to just quit altogether one of these days."

"Amazing Grace?" Justine asked. "She's good for another twenty years of printing. Those presses don't know how to die."

Doc rose from his chair. "I know. The print just fades away." He herded them all toward the door. "Come on. If Beth's meeting us there, we shouldn't make her wait by herself."

"You're just worried that she might *not* wait by herself," teased Justine.

Doc grunted an unintelligible answer, while Charlie looked at Justine with a question on his face.

"You shouldn't have finked out on us last time, Charlie. Poor Beth showed up, and Doc was the only person she knew. We tried to sit her far away from him, but he weaseled right in there next to her."

Doc pulled on his coat and pushed Justine back out the door. "I will not stand for gossip about me in my presence," he gruffed.

"Don't worry," Warren whispered to Charlie in a stage whisper. "He can never compete with a real professor."

It was a pleasant ten-minute walk down Cambridge Street and through Harvard Square to the Hungry Fox. Outside, a few hardy souls sat by the basement windows of the Fox, choosing uncomfortable but free seats for the show. Inside, they found Beth at a table way up front. The coffeehouse was dimly lit even before the show, and a dozen tables were squeezed two deep right up to the front of the slightly raised stage. Latecomers had to settle for hard chairs arranged in ten rows behind the tables. The place was packed, mostly with college students, back from their summer vacations.

Ann noticed how casually Doc took a chair next to Beth. "You must have gotten here pretty early," Ann commented, "to get a table up here."

"Nope." Beth smiled. "It was packed when I got here, so I asked if you all were here yet, and the guy said no, but that Kip had saved us a table. I just got here a couple of minutes ago. If it weren't for Kip, we'd be stuffed in a corner by the bar."

"Where you can't hear a thing," commented Doc.

By the time they had ordered drinks and gotten settled, Kip had begun. The audience was good, and Kip responded. Slowly Charlie unwound. To himself he thanked Ann for arranging the evening. His had been a guilt-induced anger, and he was relieved to have it over with. Besides, he was curious about Doc and Beth. She had mentioned casually that she had enjoyed Doc's company after that evening some six weeks ago, but had not mentioned him since then. It was obvious that they had seen each other in between. There was a touch of jealousy in Charlie's mind, but mostly, he was just curious.

Between sets, Kip came over to join them. He gave Ann a peck on the cheek. "Long time no see, you two," he chastised. "Ann, stand up and let me look."

Ann blushed. "Later, Kip—you're just embarrassing me. But look." Still sitting, she pulled the fabric of her dress around the shallow bump that was Disney. "I can't fit in my damn jeans anymore, so I'm stuck with dresses until I get elastic panels to put in the jeans."

"Aha," he replied. "I thought maybe the dress was for a faculty wife. I hear Charlie's even teaching now."

"Grumble," Charlie muttered. "So far, being a professor reminds me more of being a dishwasher than of being a student. You may not realize it, Kip, but I actually have to *work* now. Ah, for the good old days."

"See, Kip," Justine chimed in, "he's just like before, always complaining and whatnot. Why, he hasn't even objected to our calling him by his first name." They all laughed.

"It's not funny," Charlie protested. "All those kids call me Dr. Cotten, and it makes me feel like telling them to take two aspirins and go to bed. Even when I tell them, 'Please, call me Charlie,' they're nervous about it. They want me to be an insulated authority figure."

Doc smiled. "Tell me about it, Charlie. If you think you have problems, try being a medical doctor. I've actually lost patients because I asked them to call me Fred. And all of you call me Doc."

"Well," replied Warren, "at least Charlie and Ann seem to have survived the rise in status without totally deserting their old friends." Winking at Ann, he added, "Why, stirred on by their fine example, Justine and I have actually started to consider having a kid ourselves."

Charlie laughed sarcastically. "I'd talk to Doc first, if I were you."

Warren looked at Doc curiously. "Are you antichild now?" he asked.

Doc forced a smile. "Don't you know you're supposed to check with your doctor before you ever do anything?" But his tone of voice betrayed the lack of humor in the statement.

"Actually," said Ann sharply, "maybe they should talk to you, if they're serious about this." She glared angrily at Charlie.

Warren and Justine both looked confused. "Wait a minute!" demanded Justine. "What's going on?"

Charlie gave in. Avoiding Ann's angry, pained glare, he muttered, "I brought it up, so I guess I should have to explain." He thought for a minute. "But look, this has got to be kept just between us. No one else, no matter who they are." Charlie looked around for signs of agreement, avoiding Ann.

"Charlie, what are you talking about?"

So once again Charlie told the story. But this time,

he noticed, he was able to tell it calmly. The fetus Ann carried was due to quicken in the next few weeks, and he had become certain that there would be no problems.

"Wow," said Warren. "I can see why you don't want people finding out about it." He turned to Justine. "But didn't we hear from someone else that they'd seen some of the stuff?" He turned back to Charlie. "Not around here . . . Some other friends down the coast mentioned Gloryhits. But who the hell was it?"

Doc shot up like an arrow. "Of course! Why didn't we think of that? Of course we're not the only people to have gotten it." He turned to Charlie. "And that would be our control for things other than the acid. Warren," he said, turning back, "you've got to remember where you heard of it."

"Was it Eric," asked Justine, "down in New Haven?"

"No, I'm sure it wasn't," Warren answered. "He hasn't been into that sort of thing for a couple of years."

"Look," said Charlie. "Just think about it, okay? It'll come to you in the next few days, for sure. Don't push too hard—that can really make you lose it."

Kip thought for a moment. "Let me check around, too. There're a lot of people who pass through here who might have seen some of it. But I can't remember anyone's mentioning it." He sat there, thinking about it.

The silence bore in on Charlie, unsettling him. He turned to Doc and asked, "What ever happened to that guy who was checking out the abortants? Did you find out what you wanted to know?"

Doc took a deep breath. "Later. It's a lousy story."

Beth turned to Doc. "Fred, is that the creepy guy you were telling me about?"

"What?" he asked. "Oh, yeah. That's the one. I get mad even now, just remembering the bastard."

"Come on, Doc, you can't leave us all hanging like this," Kip insisted. The rest agreed.

"All right, already," Doc complained. "It's just an irritating story. But I guess I'd be interested in hearing your opinions of what he meant. Oh, hell, I'm getting

like Charlie—never saying what I'm talking about."
He paused for a moment, then began to explain.

"I had talked with this guy once before, and it was
pure runaround. So this time I decided to confront him
a little more strongly. I'd seen a few more abortions
take place with women who had had the acid, and I
felt I was in a better position to pressure him into
releasing information. That is, if he wasn't going to
be cooperative. In a word, he wasn't. I spent the day—
it was last Tuesday—waiting at a friend's office, where
he was supposed to stop by. He finally showed around
two in the afternoon. He seemed not to remember me
when I introduced myself to him, so I explained to
him again how I was a local physician, interested in
the survey he was working on.

"Well, he seemed out-and-out friendly. Started chat-
ting about the research and what they hoped to learn
from it. He's working with some research group in
New York City. He gave me a card with an address
and phone number. I think it was a post office box.
Anyhow, he explained how it was known that over
half of all spontaneous abortants had chromosomal
abnormalities or obvious deformities, compared with
almost none in normal-term babies. But they want to
do careful autopsies on the fetuses, to see what physical abnormalities might show up."

"Aren't there hospitals doing that already?" asked
Charlie.

"Oh, definitely, but Greene—his name is Alex
Greene—insists that his project's autopsies are much
more thorough, with histological stains and everything. Apparently they're also collecting from several
different communities to see how much difference there
is from one town to the next. By having a single group
of researchers do all the autopsies and tests, you can
avoid having to equate the results of several different
laboratories. The work is clearly valuable and worth
doing. But that's not the issue. Last time I'd talked to
him, he'd said that he'd try to get the information
about those fetuses for me, and now it was as if he had
never seen me before. Finally, after a lot of prodding,
he seemed to remember—or, more likely, decided to

remember. And then he mumbled something about the director not wanting the data 'tampered with.' "

"Wait a minute," Charlie interrupted. "I thought he was the principal investigator. What's this 'director' crap?"

"I don't know," Doc answered. "He sure tried to give the impression of being in charge last time."

"Sounds pretty typical," said Kip. "Lots of people try to act like head honchos if they think they can get away with it."

"Except that he wouldn't give me the director's name or phone number. He said I could just write to 'Director,' care of the address on the card he gave me, which I'll do. I called the number, but it was just an answering service. I left a message to have the director call me back, but that was Wednesday morning, and I haven't heard a word. Anyhow, that's getting ahead of the story. When I asked him what he meant by 'tampering' with the data, he went into this song and dance about how all the results are being stored in a computer, and the researchers aren't supposed to know what the results are for any of the other fetuses being autopsied since that might make them more prone to look for those same defects."

"That's a common enough practice," Beth interrupted. "We do the same sort of thing in a lot of our experiments. It's an important technique."

"But I'm not arguing with that!" Doc insisted. "I said I would dig up the funds to pay some disinterested person to pull out the necessary data. It was that important to me. And then he started to mutter about how he'd love to be cooperative, but it wasn't really his decision to make, and it would really be a hassle to have strange people piling through the data banks, and on and on. When I pushed him a bit further, he suddenly said that it was a stipulation in their grant that no results be made public before a complete report was filed with the funding agency, so it would definitely not be possible, but if I would give him my name, he would send me a copy as soon as it came out."

"You don't believe his comment about the funding agency?" Justine asked.

"Christ, no!" Doc insisted. "You could see him just making it up on the spot. But it was also clear that he was ready to stick by the story."

"Well, there's no doubt about it," said Warren. "The guy is definitely an asshole."

"You know," said Beth, "you hear all this propaganda about how science is an open, cooperative venture. But when you get down to it, it's not so different from everything else. Status, jobs, funding—it's competitive as hell. Some so-called scientists will even lie to throw people off the right track." She looked to Charlie, who nodded in silent confirmation.

"I don't know," Doc argued. "I can spot those highstrung superaggressive researchers, and he didn't seem like one at all. Anyhow, that's not the whole story.

"When it was clear that he was just going to politely refuse any vague requests I made, I decided to play a few cards I had stored up. I pulled out a list I had made of the women who had taken the Gloryhits and then aborted and of the obstetricians who had in each case passed the abortants on to him. I also pulled out a batch of release forms, signed by the women, asking Greene to release the information on the abortants to me. I told him that all of these women were my patients, aside from seeing the various obstetricians, and I thought it might be very important to know if the fetuses had any common malformation, such as might indicate the widespread use of a teratogenic agent in their environment."

"And he still refused?" Kip asked.

"He told me I had been reading too many sciencefiction stories. He informed me that spontaneous abortions happened everywhere and were not indicative of anything more than a natural process at work. He said that this community was no different from any other in the country, and I was chasing after straws thinking that my patients had something special wrong with them.

"And, there's more. Because, remember, I'd seen two of the abortants with the deformed heads, and I told him that, and that it was so unlikely a phenomenon that I felt the deformities had to have a common cause. I even hinted very vaguely that I might have a lead on what that common cause was.

"All of a sudden Greene is interested. 'Oh,' he says, 'playing a little Sherlock Holmes?' I assumed he wanted to know what I thought it was, but he soon made it clear that he didn't care. 'The last thing I want,' he says, 'is the fantasies of untrained people playing scientist. If I were you,' he says, 'I'd concentrate on medicine and stop trying to play private eye.'

"Then I got pissed, and I guess I raised my voice. I asked him who the granting agency was that was sponsoring the work, threatened to contact the AMA or the registration and discipline board. I shook those consent forms in his face and told him that he had no option but to release the information. I was furious!"

"And still nothing?" asked Justine.

"Well, not exactly. But not what I expected, either. All of a sudden he backed off, and switched from being arrogant and aggressive to being sneaky and defensive. It actually looked like he got shorter, and he physically backed off. 'Okay, Blake,' he sneered, 'looks like you're going to get mean about this, aren't you?' It sent shivers down my back, the way he said it. 'Well,' he said, 'I guess I'll have to check with my superiors about it. You'll hear from us within a week. Will that make you happy?' I mean, he was really creepy about it."

"Well, what did you say?" asked Warren.

"I didn't back down, which I feel good about in retrospect. I said I was happy that he was going to talk to his boss, but that I wouldn't be happy if the boss gave the same answers he did. And then, in this super-sinister way, he said, 'Don't worry, he won't!' and left." Doc shook his head, depressed and confused again, thinking about Greene.

Suddenly Kip let out an awkward laugh. "Doc," he said, "that's one of the finest presentations I've heard in an age." The conversation had not helped him to relax between sets. "Look, I've got to head backstage now, but if you ever get tired of medicine, we can use you on the stage." Rising from his chair, he waved good-bye to the group. "He must be great around campfires," he added and headed off toward the stage door.

Doc looked around the table, somewhat bewildered. "Am I really building it up that much?"

Ann spoke for the first time since the conversation had started. She was hurt and angry, and felt betrayed by having her secret discussed so openly and so casually. Her tone harsh, she replied bitterly to Doc's question. "How the hell can we tell? Maybe Greene's just a pig." She tried to make it sound as though her anger were directed against Doc's antagonist.

"Come on, Ann, give Fred some credit," Beth objected. "He could tell if someone was just acting differently—I mean, like different from us." She turned to Charlie. "Doesn't Greene seem a bit heavier than usual? It almost sounded like a threat at the end."

Charlie laughed, but uncomfortably. Was he the only one who understood why Ann had responded so hostilely? "That's the advantage of getting to tell the story yourself. After all, it was Doc who threatened Greene with the AMA and state discipline board. Personally, I'd say that Greene's response was rather restrained." Then, turning to Beth, he added, "Come on, Beth, you don't have to defend everything Doc says."

She looked irritated with the comment, and didn't respond.

Embarrassed, Charlie turned back to Doc. "Did he bring up that abortant again?"

"What?" Doc had drifted out of the conversation.

"That elective abortion that your friend did, remember? You said that you got a deformed fetus from him, and that Greene had demanded that you give it to him."

Beth interrupted. "Fred, you mean Greene knew about it before it disappeared?"

Surprised by the realization, Doc nodded in agreement.

Warren was about to ask about it when the lights dimmed and Kip came out on stage. Doc sat morosely through the first song, staring at the table. When it ended, he turned to the others. "Look, I think I'm going to catch a bus home. This whole thing with

Greene has me too upset—I can't get into any music now. Explain to Kip, will you?" He rose to go.

Beth got up, too. "I'll give you a ride, Fred. I've got a lot to do tomorrow, and if I stay for the second set, I'll sleep till noon."

Doc accepted her offer. Beth turned to the others. "Tell Kip I really liked him tonight," she said. "I've enjoyed the evening."

Everyone said good night, and the two left.

"Just what is going on with those two?" Charlie asked.

Justine smiled. "Where've you been lately, Charlie?"

Beth and Doc drove silently down Storrow Drive toward the Back Bay. He still felt confused and uneasy about his encounter with "the ghoul," and the week was almost up, without any word from Greene or his alleged superior. Somehow, Greene's tone had convinced him that something would really come of it.

"How come you never told me the whole story about Greene before?" Beth asked.

Doc turned and smiled thinly at her. "Now, please, don't you start getting paranoid, too. *That* I couldn't take tonight. It's just that there wasn't any way I could without telling you about Ann and Charlie, and they're my patients. Doctor–patient confidentiality is a serious thing with me." He paused for a second. "I was going to say, 'especially since you know them,' but that's not true. Lots of doctors entertain their friends with stories about unidentified patients, and I can't stand that."

"No, I can understand that," Beth agreed. "It's just that I had been wondering why you were so grouchy this week." She reached across and rested her hand on the back of his. "Christ, it must be terrible for them, not knowing whether they're going to lose that kid or not. I feel as though I should have been gentler with Charlie this last month."

Doc said nothing, just squeezed her hand gently. After several moments of silence, Beth asked, "When the fetus quickens, then the problem is over?"

Doc shrugged. "I tell you, Charlie and I are really

close friends, but that's the sort of thing I can learn to hate about him." Beth looked confused. "Look," Doc continued angrily, "I know of seven spontaneous abortions among people who had taken those Gloryhits. Five came after three months, and the other two came at just about five months. None of them had quickened. What does that tell you?"

"Well," said Beth, "that probably if it quickens, it's safe."

"Probably," Doc repeated. "But only probably. I don't know. I told Charlie, and I take it he didn't tell Ann, but I've just got a feeling in my bones that that damn deformity could go to term."

"And survive?" Beth asked.

Doc threw one hand into the air. "How the hell can I know? Maybe he's right, five months is the cutoff. Maybe it can survive, and be a genius. How should I know! It's just a feeling."

Beth pressed the back of his hand. "You think Ann should have had an abortion?"

Doc nodded silently.

"How long have you known them?" she asked curiously.

"Years," he answered. "Charlie and I roomed together for a couple of years when we were both undergraduates, what, eight, nine years ago, and we both stayed in the Boston area for graduate school. Except for the last three years, when Charlie was out West, we've been pretty close."

"How long have they been together?"

"Since Charlie's first year in graduate school. They met at a workshop on radical medical care and hit it off right away."

"Ann's into politics, too?" Beth asked.

Doc shrugged. "I honestly don't know." He paused, then with a strong trace of regret in his voice, continued. "Ann seems to just follow along behind Charlie. When he was doing political work, she did the same thing. Now Charlie's drifted out of politics, and Ann doesn't seem to be going near it on her own."

They turned up Clarendon and drove the few remaining blocks to Doc's apartment in silence. Beth pulled up in front and turned off the engine. "Coming in?" Doc asked.

"Sure," she smiled.

He lived in a beautiful renovated apartment with twelve-foot ceilings and parqueted floors. A stained-glass window in the living room cast an eerie light into the dark apartment. Heading straight for the kitchen, they ransacked the refrigerator, and Doc put water on for tea. Sitting around the kitchen table, eating bits of cheese and leftover salad, they waited for the water.

"And what about you?" Doc asked. "I've never asked you what you're planning for the rest of your life."

Beth smiled. "No, we haven't talked about that before." She nibbled on a piece of lettuce. "I've ruled out being an industrial researcher, so I imagine I'll end up on some biology department's list of faculty. But I haven't done much about it yet, aside from thinking about it.

"I find myself watching Charlie, wondering how he'll turn out. I guess I'm playing role models. I know I'd rather teach high school biology than turn out to be like Lloyd Haenners."

"Ah, yes." Doc nodded. "Your boss." He took her hand and teased, "I wouldn't be too worried. You're much too nice a person." Leaning over, he kissed her gently on the lips.

"Mmmm," said Beth, "I doubt that Lloyd would even approve of my having a relationship with an M.D. instead of a Ph.D." She kissed him back.

"I'm not so sure Charlie would, either."

"What's that supposed to mean?"

"Oh, just that he seemed to be watching us as much as he was Kip. I think the man has it in him to be just a bit jealous."

"But we never even touched each other," she protested.

Doc shrugged. "No," he answered, "just left together."

Beth made a long face. "Well, he can just live with it. That kind of college professor I can live without."

"Oh, I'm sure Charlie can adjust to it without too

much difficulty. I'm painting too dark a picture of him.
Besides, what with 'Disney,' I think his time and energy
are pretty well tied up." He rose and lit a couple of
candles. "How would you like to roll a joint?" he
asked, slipping off his shoes.

"Sounds nice," she agreed. Removing her own shoes,
she crossed to the chest of drawers in his living room
and tugged on the bottom drawer. "Oomph! It's
jammed," she announced.

"Let me check it."

"Sit down," Beth told him. "I may be just a woman,
but I can unjam a drawer with the best of them." She
removed the middle drawer and started looking for
the obstruction below.

"No," Doc explained, "that's a screwy drawer. It has
a lock, and unless you close it right, it locks by itself."
He looked at the lock. "Yeah, that's what happened.
I've got the key in the top drawer." He started rum-
maging through the top drawer. "I hope it's not going
to start locking all the time. I'm sure I closed it carefully before I left for Charlie's this evening."

Beth peered over his shoulder. "Mmmm, let's see
what the doctor keeps in his top drawer." She stuck a
finger into the drawer and started poking around.

"Here's the key!" Doc announced. Ducking out from
under Beth, he stooped to unlock the bottom drawer.
Above, Beth continued her poking.

"Oooh!" she cooed. "A plain brown paper bag. I
wonder what's in it." She pulled it from the drawer
and peeked inside. "A plastic bag!" she exclaimed in
mock surprise. She removed the bag and held it up. It
contained an ounce or more of a clean white powder.
"What is it?" she asked curiously.

Doc looked up from the bottom drawer. "I don't
know," he said. "Where'd you get it?"

"In the top drawer." She handed it to him.

He turned the bag over in his hands. "Strange," he
muttered. "I'm sure I've never seen it before." He
opened the bag and smelled it.

"And you don't know what it is?"

"No, but I've got a strange hunch." He took the bag

into his study, turned on the light, and closed the curtains.

"What are you doing?" she asked.

He pulled some bottles and glassware from his desk drawer. "I'm going to check for morphine content. On occasion, I've assayed heroin for patients who were withdrawing and needed accurate dosages. Lots of times they want to use street junk, just because they're more used to it."

"You think it's heroin?" Ann asked.

"That's what it looks like." He added a tiny scoopful of the powder to a tube and watched it turn a deep purple. "Jesus Christ!" he muttered.

"Is it heroin?"

"Not only is it heroin, but it's the strongest stuff I've ever seen."

"Isn't that a lot of it?" Beth asked, shocked.

"A lot?" Doc murmured. "That bag's probably worth fifty to a hundred thousand dollars. I guess that's a lot."

"But where'd it come from?"

"I don't know, and I'm sure not too happy about it." He thought for a minute. "I'm tempted to think that someone hid it here for safekeeping, but I don't even know anyone who would have anything at all to do with that much smack."

"Couldn't they have sneaked in when you were out?" Beth asked.

"Not likely," Doc answered. "I keep some prescription narcotics in the house, so it's kept locked about as tightly as possible. It would take a top-notch professional to get in without breaking anything."

"What about a plant?" Beth asked. "Is there anyone who would like to see you busted?"

Doc thought for a minute. "I'd love to think the AMA was after me, or even the local police. But my politics just aren't that threatening. Besides, you don't realize how much is in that baggie. Nobody would waste that much on a plant unless they had tons of it, which rules out just about everybody except maybe the mob."

"The police could, couldn't they?"

"I doubt the local police have this much to play games with, but I guess it's possible. But if it were a plant, you wouldn't expect them to leave it here long enough for me to find it."

They sat there, the tea kettle screaming from the kitchen.

"Fred!" Beth jumped up. "What are we doing? If that's a plant, then you've got to get rid of it. If you're sure the drawer wasn't locked, then it must have happened while we were at the show tonight."

Doc rose quickly and headed for the front door. "Goddamn, you're right. The bust could come any time!"

"Where are you going?" called Beth, heading out of the study after him.

"To lock this door up," he explained, locking the door, the deadbolt, and the chain lock. "Check the back door, will you?"

Running through the kitchen, she checked the door. "Tight as can be!" she called.

She almost crashed into Doc coming back. "Get the bag of grass and dump it in the john," he called out. "I'll get the smack from the study." Quickly they gathered up the drugs and flushed them down the toilet. "Flush it a couple more times when it fills," he called to Beth. "I'm going to make sure there aren't any roaches or anything lying around."

When Beth rejoined him, he was going through drawers in the study. "One of the side effects of being a doctor is that you don't have very much time, so I have a woman who comes in one day a week and cleans. Luckily, she was here yesterday, so I went over the place carefully the day before. But there might be stuff in a drawer somewhere."

"I'll check the living room," Beth said and headed out of the study.

Forty-five minutes later two exhausted people dropped onto the living room couch. They sat there for a few minutes, recovering from the frantic search that had turned up three roaches and an ounce of grass that Doc had lost six months ago. "Fred," Beth finally asked, "who could have done it?"

He shook his head uncertainly. "I don't know. I can't figure who would be out to get me."

"What about your work with heroin addicts and your refusal to testify against them? Are there narcotics officers angry at you over that?"

"Oh, they're angry at me, all right," Doc admitted. "But it's hard to believe that they'd be that mad." He sat and thought for a minute. "Although, actually, I guess some of them are. I know Diederson got up before the state legislature and called one of my proposals 'a program designed by pushers and addicts for their mutual benefit.' I've also been fighting against a bill before the state legislature that would force doctors to report addicts among their patients to the police."

Beth seized on the idea. "But then, don't you see? If one of the proposal's main opponents turned out to be a pusher, that would prove his point. Do you think your arrest could increase its chances of passing?"

Doc thought about it, and then nodded. "It would. I've talked personally to a lot of the legislators who were swing votes. If I got busted with that much heroin . . ." His voice trailed off. "Christ, it gives me the creeps just to think of someone's trying that." He laughed. "You know, it's funny. I know that the police do this sort of thing, and I've even gone out on a limb for a friend who was busted by a plant, but I never thought it could happen to me! Charlie was right," he concluded. "Years ago he said that the government will always turn out to be meaner and sneakier than you can imagine, and time and again he's been proven right."

Slowly Beth traced the outline of Doc's fingers with hers. "Well," she said, "now we know that no matter what else happens, all in all this relationship's been worthwhile. It's probably put thirty years back into your life."

Doc smiled. "That's right. And I never even thanked you for the ride home."

Beth rose and took his hands, pulling him to his feet. "I know how you could thank me," she suggested.

"Oh, no!" Doc laughed, pulling Beth back onto the

couch. "This happens to be the state of Massachusetts, my dear, which, in its own endearing way, still lives back in the days of the Puritans. I'm damned if I'll give them the satisfaction of busting me for 'unlawful carnal knowledge.'"

Beth pouted. "You doctors are all the same—stuffy."

"Oh," asked Doc, "have you tried many?"

She gave him a quick kiss and jumped to her feet. "I'll never tell—the room might be bugged!"

Doc rose to his feet and gave her a big hug. "Look," he said, "I'd love you to stay and stay, but I'm getting uptight about this damn bust and I don't want you here when it happens."

"Why?" she asked. "You could probably use some support when they come."

"Not if it happens to be at four-thirty in the morning. That's just asking for trouble." He gave her another kiss. "Look, you take off for home. I promise I'll call you right after it happens—or in the morning in any case—okay?"

Beth agreed. "But be sure to call right away. I'll be going out of my mind worrying."

Doc smiled. "That's nice of you to say."

A long, slow kiss later, Beth left, and Doc fell exhausted onto his couch, trying to sort out the events of the evening.

Sunday, October 4

"All right, already, I'm coming!" Doc woke from a fitful sleep and turned on the light. "You don't have to knock the door down!" The clock showed four-thirty. "Right on time," he muttered to himself.

The pounding began again. "I said I'm coming!" he bellowed, wrapping a bathrobe around himself. "No use waking up the rest of the building!" Padding barefoot across the living room, he slowly unlocked the door and opened it a crack. Impressive, he thought. Three in uniform, two plainclothes. All for little old me. "What the hell do you want?" he asked in an irritated voice. "It's the middle of the night."

"You *Doctor* Fred Blake?" a uniformed policeman asked, the title "Doctor" pronounced with great sarcasm.

"Yeah, that's me." Doc recognized him. It was Diederson.

"Open up. We've got a search warrant." Diederson stuck the paper through the partially opened door, casually placing his foot in the doorway.

Doc took it, looking at Diederson again. The guy was bigger than he'd remembered. I wonder, he thought, if it's because he's closer, or because I'm seeing him from the other end of a warrant. He read through it carefully, checking the signatures. The judge who'd signed it wasn't a hysterical antidrug person. They must have had an alleged eyewitness to get it. It was in perfect order.

"This is the craziest thing I've ever seen," he muttered out loud, "but it looks legitimate. You'll have to let me close the door, to get this chain off," he told Diederson.

Diederson smiled and shoved a tin plate in by the doorjamb. It would prevent the door from being locked once Doc closed it. "Be my guest."

The second the chain was off, the door was shoved violently open, smashing Doc's bare toes. Four men pushed in past him and fanned out through the apartment, the fifth staying in the hall. "Sid down, and keep your hands in your pockets," Diederson ordered after frisking him.

"No one else here," the other uniformed officer said, sitting down in a chair opposite Doc.

"Well"—Diederson smiled—"this shouldn't take too long." The two plainclothesmen and Diederson began to search the apartment. Diederson turned to one of them. "Take your time, Patterson, and be thorough."

The plainclothesman responded with a grunt. "Just worry about your own men, Diederson." There was a trace of mutual dislike in the exchange.

Doc watched with curiosity. Patterson apparently was an outsider of some sort. Wonder what brought him in, Doc thought. Somehow he didn't look like a cop. His hair was a bit too long, his clothes a bit too expensive. And there was something about his manner —Doc wasn't sure what—that just didn't fit.

After searching casually behind the drapes and under the couch Doc was sitting on, Patterson crossed straight to the chest of drawers. Starting with the bottom drawer, he searched through it in a very casual manner. He went on to the middle, and finally to the top drawer. In the top, he started in the corner opposite from where the heroin had been planted. When he got through the drawer he seemed confused. Then, slowly, he started through the drawer again, taking items out one at a time, going through pockets, shaking out sleeves and pant legs. Finding nothing, he hurried back to the middle drawer, clearly anxious, clearly upset, but still precise and careful in his search. The man knows his trade, Doc thought. Finishing the third drawer once again, he examined the interior of the chest with its drawers removed, looking for a secret cache. He found nothing.

Patterson turned and glared at Doc, who tried his best to maintain a look of concern and confusion. He hoped frantically that no trace of a smile was breaking through.

Obviously frustrated, Patterson turned to the rest of the room, sometimes searching in precise detail, sometimes with utter sloppiness.

After about fifteen minutes, Diederson came back to the living room and looked at Patterson. "Well?" he asked.

Patterson crossed to Diederson and, turning his back to Doc, started to whisper to Diederson.

"What?" exclaimed Diederson. Then they whispered rapidly back and forth, each obviously angry at the other. Suddenly Diederson's voice rose to an audible level. "Bullshit! My men didn't even know where they were going when we got in the car. You better check over at your office, Patterson. That's the only place it could have leaked."

Doc smiled to himself. Always good to see inter-departmental squabbles, he decided. Maybe they'd take it out on each other. The two officers separated and continued searching the house.

Finally, at six-thirty, Diederson called his men back into the living room. He turned to Doc. "Blake," he said, "don't think for a minute that you've gotten off. I'm nowhere near done with you. I can smell how badly you and your cronies want that bill passed. It'll do wonders for business, won't it?"

Doc only stared at him, blankly.

"A doctor, no less! You're about the most disgusting example of a man I've ever seen, Blake. You don't even need the money. Do you do it just because you like to see those kids destroyed?"

Doc started to pale. Diederson clearly thought it was a legitimate bust. He was too angry to be faking it. Doc looked at Patterson. Patterson never said a word, simply stared at Doc with what looked like part hatred and part irritation. He seemed to be thinking, as if deciding what to do next. Finally Patterson stood up. "Come on Diederson. We're done here." Diederson and the other two rose and filed out of the room. Patterson turned to Doc before leaving. "Have a good day, Doctor."

October

Stanley Johnson picked up the handwritten report and handed it to Carol. "This should get out to Westland as soon as possible, and I suppose you should send a copy to Pearson, too. He's been making a lot of noise about my getting this part done, so you might as well let him know officially that it's finished now."

Carol took the papers and leafed through them. "It doesn't seem like General Westland's been in contact much. Has he?"

"No," Johnson agreed. "I've been sending him weekly progress reports, which I'm convinced he's reading because he occasionally drops a note asking for a clarification. But I think basically he's leaving me pretty much on my own. I like to think that means he's happy with my work so far. Which is more than I can say about Pearson."

Carol looked at him quizzically. "What's Pearson's part in all this? Isn't he from Military Intelligence?"

"Yep," Johnson replied. "But his role isn't at all clear to me. At first I thought he wanted my advice on possible Russian activity in the area of genetic engineering, but recently he's taken an almost hysterical interest in the work we've been doing here. And he's pushier than hell."

"Does he have that power?" she asked. "It isn't obvious to me that he's any higher than you are in the structure."

"Officially, he's not," Johnson agreed. "But Westland sent me a note about a month ago, stating that Pearson's work was of absolute importance and that I should consider him to be speaking with the approval of Westland himself. I've never heard of anything like that, but it carries all the weight it needs. In fact, sometimes I think that the reason Westland doesn't talk with me more is that he's working through Pearson."

"But I thought the work was going well," Carol asked. "How come Pearson's being pushy?"

"Actually, he was probably right," Johnson admitted. "The problem was that we were going so fast that I wasn't keeping tabs on everything that needed to be done. But that should make him happy," he said, pointing to the papers in Carol's hands. "We've gotten a good antiserum prepared against the mutated botulinum toxin now, so we don't have to worry about that."

Carol smiled. "It's nice being a secretary to someone whose experiments are always successful. You're not as grouchy as some others I've worked for."

"We're both lucky," Johnson laughed. "I've never heard of a project moving along so much like clockwork. We've gotten every break possible. In fact, we're so far ahead of schedule, we'll be doing immunizations next week."

"Immunizations?" she asked. "Against what?"

"The influenza we made and the botulinum toxin we're planning to put into it. Remember, they've been mutated so that people won't have any natural resistance to them, and we don't want any of the workers here to have any problems."

"But it's no more dangerous than any other flu, is it?" she asked.

"Not yet. But as soon as the immunization is completed, we'll be ready to start putting the toxin genes into the virus. And then it'll be about the most dangerous thing around."

Carol feigned a nervous shudder. "Well, make sure I get an immunization shot, too."

"Don't worry," he assured her with a smile. "We won't miss a soul."

"Well," Carol said, rising from her chair, "if you want these out today, I suppose I'd better get going." Smiling a good-bye, she left Johnson's office.

Sitting there alone, Johnson sighed with relief. He
was glad to be done with the report. Pearson had called
twice since their meeting a month ago when Johnson
had admitted to not having an antiserum against the
new, mutated botulinum toxin. Pearson was a lot
sharper lately, Johnson had noticed.

He looked at his calendar. Everything was running
smoothly. In the next month, with luck, they'd have
the genes transferred out of the bacteria and into the
influenza viruses. Then they'd be ready for assaying in
tissue cultures. He frowned, remembering Pearson's
comments about field tests. No further mention had
been made of it by either of them. He leafed through
the calendar for the next month and was reminded of
the DNA meetings in Squaw Valley scheduled for the
first week of November. It would be a week of reports
from the top labs in the country concerning their work
on genetic engineering, and the meeting could be of
considerable value to the work that Johnson was doing.

But it was Peter Stanker, not Johnson, who would
be going. Johnson was unhappy about the decision, but
with things moving so quickly around the lab, he clearly
couldn't just up and leave for a week. So Stanker, his
right-hand man, would go instead. Still, Johnson would
never switch positions with the man. Stanker was a
follower, doing basically what he was told. Johnson
was a leader, now. With a hundred and fifty people
working under him, he probably was directing one of
the largest research labs in the country. It was like an
answer to a dream.

And maybe it was better that he didn't go to the
meetings. He'd go crazy, keeping inside him all the
work he had done and the progress he had made. He
had probably done more real research, made more significant progress in genetic engineering during the
last year than any of those academic greats. In the past he
had always been jealous of the scientists who had made
it in the academic world. They were the creative ones,
they were the ones doing exciting research, pushing
back the frontiers of knowledge, and all that, while he
just turned things around, doing old things in slightly
different ways.

But that was before. Before Project Vector. He could just imagine himself, giving a talk to all those hot shots at Squaw Valley. He'd flabbergast them!

Laughing to himself, he thought, One day I'll go to one of those meetings and just not say a word. Listen to all those guys who think they're doing such great research. His thoughts turned to Pearson and his vaguely disapproving attitude. Pearson, too, he thought. I'll bet his pretty ass that the Russians aren't moving along as quickly as we are.

Thursday, October 15

The morning sun shone in through the bedroom window as Charlie lay in bed, his hand on Ann's ever-growing stomach. Five and a half months pregnant, it was more beautiful than ever. A ventral stripe was slowly appearing, passing above and below her navel. But still they had felt no movement.

It was mid-October, and autumn was in the air. It was a time for consolidation, for strengthening in preparation for the winter. But still their entire existence was up in the air. They dared not plan, assume, even hope too hard. It was past five months, past the time of the latest abortion Doc had found; it should be safe. But it was also past the time that those first gentle movements of the fetus are usually felt. "There's a lot of variation," Doc had said, trying to calm their fears. "Some women feel their children move at three months, others not until after six. It doesn't mean a thing." Not a thing, Charlie thought, except that we can't be sure it's to be our child.

They spent a little while like this every morning, now fourteen days, since Ann had reached five months. They talked little about it, about being past five months, about the fetus not having quickened. And they didn't talk about names, or whether it would be a boy or a girl. It wasn't theirs yet, to plan for.

Though this Thursday morning was bright and crisp, Charlie felt drained. A day that would charge most people full of energy, to Charlie it underscored the depths of his depression. He was barely a week ahead of his class in preparation, and his lab-work was at a complete standstill. Every time he tried to relax his mind, to let it deal with his research or his teaching, he would see the deformed fetus Doc had described to him floating in its bottle of formaldehyde. And his mind would clamp shut.

A couple of days he had stayed home, wanting to be with Ann, afraid that the child would be lost, but Ann had finally asked him to leave. His depression made her own unbearable. And so he had returned to the campus, not taking any more days off.

But the lab was even worse. Every time the phone rang, his hopes would die because he expected to hear either Ann or Doc telling him that it was all over. But the calls were always just the normal calls that came every day, and the fetus grew and grew, to every outward sign healthy and normal.

And in return, he had this time in the morning, when the child was his, warm in Ann's abdomen, under his hand. He lay there quietly, trying to feel only with his fingers, not with his heart or his mind. The skin, stretched taut, felt like that of a baby. He loved its feel. Ann would lie there, ever so quiet, breathing as shallowly as she could, and they would both try to sense motion.

It felt like a twitch, a tremor in a muscle, but not like that, too localized. Charlie felt it, and didn't say a thing. Ann felt it and froze motionless. They lay there, one minute, two minutes, three. And it came again. It wasn't a twitch, or a tremor in a muscle. It was a kick. One minute more, and it came a third time.

Quietly, Ann began to cry. Charlie rolled onto his side and took her in his arms. Tears stung his eyes.

"It's alive," she sobbed, "it's moving in there." Now the tears came fast, and her whole body rocked with the tremors of all the fear of the last two months.

"It's over," Charlie whispered, "the waiting's over." He pushed away from Ann, so that he could see her face. "We're going to have a baby."

The day was the most beautiful either of them could remember. They had cleaned the house, talked about a nursery, guessed at the baby's sex, toyed with its name. And they had called those who had known of the threat and invited them all over for the evening.

It reminded Ann of Christmas, her friends seeming like family and an air of joyous celebration all around. Finally they all quieted down a bit, and the conversation turned to topics other than Disney.

Chiding Charlie for his recent lack of energy, Beth teased, "You know, Charlie, you've been acting like Bill lately—forgetful, blank stare in your eyes, always picking things up and then looking at them as if you didn't know what they were. I think you might have some of the people around the lab wondering about you." At Charlie's frown, Beth quickly reassured him. "Oh, I wouldn't worry. They'll have forgotten by the middle of next week. You seem to be back to normal."

"I can believe it," Charlie replied, shaking his head. "I was so tired and depressed, I could have functioned just as well sitting in the john, and then I wouldn't have had to walk there and back. Christ," he wondered, "is that the way Bill feels all the time? Maybe I should be a bit more sympathetic."

Kip interrupted Charlie's thoughts. "Who the hell is this Bill? Sounds like some musicians I know."

"He's a research associate working in Lloyd's lab, allegedly a human—which is questionable. Nobody even *pretends* he's a responsible worker."

Doc winced, tired of the story, but Beth continued.

"His mind has the organization of a two-year-old's room. There's apparently some inner order to it, but

I'll never understand what it is. For example, I needed to use a procedure that he was using. When I finally got him to write it down for me—and that took two weeks—he put the first step last, then the second step fourth. He left the third step out altogether!" She flushed with the irritation of other memories. "The guy isn't even aware of how much he annoys other people. One afternoon at lunch he laughingly related how when he was a graduate student, his advisor made him double-check all the equipment before he left at night, to make sure he hadn't left anything running. And then the same night, after telling us all about this big joke, he went home and left five hundred dollars worth of plastic equipment melting in an oven."

They all laughed. "But really," Justine asked, "doesn't everybody do something like that sooner or later?"

"They do," Charlie agreed. "You should talk to people who work with radioactive chemicals. They all eat food in the areas in which they work, even though it violates federal regulations, not to mention the occasional radioactive spills that do happen to everyone."

"But it goes on and on!" Beth insisted. "Like the time he decided to go on a short vacation and left a dead rat on top of his bench for three days. He can break things by just looking at them! No one in the department will lend him anything anymore. His lab is such a shambles, the cleaning staff refuses to touch it, and I would too."

Warren seemed surprised. "What does your boss say about all this?"

"Oh, I don't know," Beth said, "he just kind of ignores it. At one point he suggested that I try to collaborate with Bill on some experiments, but it was literally impossible, something Lloyd found very hard to believe. But that's because of how he runs the lab. He doesn't interact much, except at our weekly meetings. He's interested in our work, all right, but he wants the results, not the dirty details of how hard it was to get them. I'm sure Lloyd just hopes the problem with Bill will 'resolve itself,' as he would say."

"Enough," Doc pleaded. "It drives me crazy every time I hear about this!"

"Amen," Charlie agreed. "We've been through this before."

"And I'm not sure I've convinced you yet," Beth taunted.

"No arguments, no arguments!" Kip begged. He turned to Doc. "A word from the well-known smack dealer!"

"Hey, yeah," Ann chimed in. "I still haven't got that story straight."

Doc looked from side to side. "Well, I thought I'd kept it well hidden," he whispered. "I mean, I made certain only to sell it to the children of policemen and politicians. I guess it was the classified ad that blew it."

"Ad?" asked Kip.

"Absolutely," Doc continued. "I took out an ad that said, 'Feeling down and out? We've got the answer. New wonder drug, originally developed as a cure for morphine addiction, will give you a new outlook on life.' I suppose the police got a bit suspicious."

Ann threw a pillow in his face. "For chrissake, Doc, you should be more serious than that about it."

"Well, it's at least partly serious," Doc replied. "They used opium to cure alcoholism, cocaine to cure opium addiction, morphine to cure cocaine addiction, and heroin to cure morphine addiction. Now they've got methadone to cure heroin addiction. In a few years they'll be implanting electrodes in your brain to cure you of methadone addiction. Then we'll have electricity addicts, and the Mafia will deal in black-market batteries."

They all laughed at the idea. "Well, Doc," Charlie asked with a chuckle, "who do you think is behind it?"

Doc frowned. "I just don't know. The AMA may dislike me, but I doubt that they have a dirty tricks division. The bust had to be at least supported by the police. Hell, who could come up with that amount of stuff to throw around? I can't fathom that at all."

"What about this guy Diederson?" Ann asked. "I

take it he's aware that you've worked with and helped junkies and have refused to testify against them."

Doc nodded. "Oh, he hates me, all right. He made that pretty clear. But it seems more like a personal hatred. And anyway I doubt that he has enough power to have swung this setup by himself."

"What about Patterson?" Beth asked. "Did you ever find out anything about him?"

"Who?" Warren asked.

"Patterson," Doc replied. "He came along on the bust. In fact, maybe he's the key. I don't know where he's from, but apparently it's a completely different department than Diederson. They were quarreling about it when they couldn't find anything."

"But Patterson's the one who seemed to know where it was, wasn't he?" Beth continued.

"Yeah, you're right," Doc agreed. "Patterson seemed to go straight to the dresser where the stuff had been planted," he explained to the rest, "and was confused as hell when the smack wasn't there. It was clear that he at least knew where it was supposed to be."

"Did you get any feel for whether he thought it was a plant or not?" Kip asked.

"No," Doc answered. "I got almost no feeling from the guy except professional detachment. Diederson, on the other hand, clearly thought it was legit. He was spewing hate. I've never seen anyone quite so hateful toward me."

"So if anyone there knew it was a plant, it was Patterson," Charlie said.

"Right," Doc agreed. "And it seemed that although Diederson was officially in charge, Patterson was running the show."

"What department is he from?" Ann asked.

"I don't know," Doc said. "I tried to find out who the Patterson working with the police department was, and there wasn't any. He could have been in surveillance, or undercover, and the information wouldn't be available, but then you wouldn't expect him to go along on a bust. If he had found the stuff where he thought it was, then he would have had to testify in court, which would have blown his cover. So that seems unlikely. But I can't figure out how else it could be."

"Did you try questioning the police directly about the people who participated in the bust?" Ann persisted.

"I tried, but all they'd give me was the names on the warrant, and those were Diederson's and the judge's. An unidentified 'informer' was also referred to, but that's information I couldn't get unless an arrest had been made. So it looks like a dead end."

"Well," Ann said, "at least they blew it. I'm glad to hear that we can still have you around."

"You can thank Beth." Doc smiled. "If it wasn't for her, I'd be on my way up the river now."

Beth laughed. "He's kept me around like a good-luck charm ever since I found the stuff."

"You even bring yourself good luck," Doc added. "Have you told them yet?"

"No, I haven't," Beth replied. Then, turning to the group, she announced with a flourish, "Today I received my first job offer, along with an embarrassing salary offer."

As everyone else cheered, Kip let out a low moan. "And you seemed so nice, too. But now you'll be turning out just like Charlie, all stodgy and professorial."

"Oh, worse than that," Doc answered. "There's more to the story."

Beth raised her hands for silence. "Ladies and gentlemen," she announced with great solemnity, "I have been offered a job working not for the academic world, but for the wondrous world of industrial research!"

The statement was met with more cheers and hoots. "Wait a minute," interrupted Charlie. "I knew you were looking for a position at some university, but I didn't know you were considering industry jobs."

"I'm not, and it's not a job that I applied for. Tom Darnell, who works in the lab, got the offer made at his request. Tom's just working in our lab for a couple of years," Beth explained. "He works for a group called Crop Research Associates, which is a subsidiary of some agribusiness outfit. He's sort of on sabbatical, learning some of our techniques. I guess he decided that I'd make a good addition to their group, so he swung me an offer."

"If he's anything like this Bill person, I can imagine why you wouldn't want to work with him," Warren commented.

"Oh, no," Beth said. "He's almost Bill's opposite. He screws up every once in a while, just like everyone else, but he faces up to it at least. He might not be as bright as Lloyd or Charlie, but he's absolutely dependable. If he borrows something for an hour, it's back in an hour. If he says he'll be in at two, he's in by five of. Anything he uses comes back clean and functional. It's a delight working with him."

"That should help balance off Bill a little bit," Justine suggested.

"Well, it does help," Beth replied. "He's neat and careful, and really knows the literature, and I daresay he takes more interest in my work than Lloyd does. But he's so quiet. He never sits around and bulls like this. He probably has a better grasp of what's going on than anyone else, Lloyd included, but he only talks when he's actually addressed by someone or when he's getting information related to lab stuff. I'm not even sure if he's married or what. He never comes to any social functions or stuff like that. So you really can't just sit and talk with him. I've tried a few times, but I end up doing all the talking myself."

"Well," Warren said, "he doesn't sound like such a bad sort."

"He's really not. In fact, he's the only plus in connection with this job offer."

"Are you seriously considering it, then?" Kip asked.

"No, not really," Beth replied. "Although I must admit that the salary was high enough to tempt me for just a minute."

"Can I ask?" Ann inquired.

"Thirty thousand," Beth answered. "I doubt I'll see anywhere near that big an offer for quite a while."

"You'd better believe it," said Charlie. "I'd have to be a full professor to get that much. That's a lot of money, you know."

"I do," Beth affirmed, "and in some ways it wouldn't be so bad. They'd set me up in my own lab, and at first I could just continue the work I've been doing with Lloyd. They offered me thirty thousand dollars in equipment money as well as two full-time technicians."

"Well, if you can do what you want, what's wrong with it?" Justine asked.

"Those offers to do what you want never get put into the contract," Charlie explained. "Industrial outfits have one main purpose, and that's to turn the largest profit they can. They'll let you go as long as they think it's profitable. But when you're working in pure research you find yourself going off on tangents a lot. Some of the biggest discoveries in science have come from people making chance discoveries and following them up. In most industrial labs you would never get to follow a lead like that, unless it looked as if it was likely to make a buck. There's a few exceptions, places that let you do whatever you want, but they're awfully rare."

Beth agreed. "That's how the universities can get away with paying half the salary industry does; they know that the work is so much more satisfying."

"Well, at least, it must be nice to know that someone thinks you're worth that much," Ann said.

"That's true," Beth replied. "I have to admit that at lunch I sat and smiled at myself, saying, 'You're worth thirty thousand dollars a year.' All of a sudden I believed the fact that I wouldn't spend the rest of my life in Lloyd's lab."

"I take it finding another job shouldn't be too hard?" Kip asked.

"Not with Lloyd's support," Charlie answered. "He's got a lot of pull around the academic world, and I know he'll back Beth to the hilt, which is all it should take. I daresay you needn't put an 'unless' on your rejection letter. I've no doubt you'll be able to land a job in academia."

Beth blushed. "Well, it's certainly good to hear you say that, Charlie, but until I see the offer in writing, I think I'll still be a little nervous."

"I'm sure you will," Ann told her. "Everyone told Charlie not to worry, and he still used to lie awake at night wondering what he would do if he didn't get a single offer, or worse, if the only offer came from Alabama or Iowa."

After a moment's silence Charlie added, "Maybe now that things are back to normal I'll get to do all those glorious, exciting things we in the academic world have the opportunity to do. For the last two months I might as well have been working for industry myself, for all the 'pure knowledge' I've been chasing after."

"But maybe you could settle for being a week ahead in your class, instead of a month?" Ann asked. "Otherwise you'll be the next six weeks trying to get that far ahead." He was three weeks into the semester, and not feeling quite so intimidated by the concept of teaching.

"Maybe I'll try that," he agreed. "Then at least I'd have a chance to get something done in the lab." He turned to Beth. "Lloyd seems to manage pretty well, teaching and running the lab, both. What's his secret?"

"It's easy," Beth replied. "Give the same lectures year after year with only a meager amount of updating, and run your lab from your office instead of working in it. The job's a lot easier that way."

"Hooray," cried Ann. "I knew I wasn't alone in my views of old Lloyd."

"I see," Charlie bristled. "Now you're going to gang up on me. Personally, I don't think either of you is in any position to talk. You've no idea how much time goes into writing those damn grant applications, attending departmental and committee meetings, not to mention holding office hours for your students. I mean, there are only so many hours in a day."

"But it's a matter of priorities," Beth insisted. "You plan to work in the lab doing experiments, don't you?"

"Sure," Charlie insisted. "I'm just saying that it's not at all as easy as it appears at first glance."

"Well," Kip suggested facetiously, "maybe you'd better blow off academia and take that job with industry. I bet you don't have to write any grant proposals." The idea was met with a chorus of boos.

"Actually, Kip," Beth explained, "the truth is that Charlie's got a crush on this guy, and you know how it is—anyone looks great when you're infatuated." She turned to Charlie. "I haven't kept my promise yet. Remember I said I'd introduce you to some scientists who were worth looking up to? I'll do that next week. Lloyd isn't worthy of being a role model."

"Hey, Warren," Doc asked, switching the subject, "have you remembered where you heard about the Gloryhits?"

"Oh, shit," Warren replied. "I'd forgotten all about it. Let me think a minute." He put his hands over his ears and bent his head down toward his lap.

"Because it's still important," Doc continued. "I'm relieved that Ann seems to be past danger, but there are eight others who lost their pregnancies because of something that I still think was associated with those Gloryhits. If it's in another community, they should be warned at least."

"Is eight a large enough number to be sure?" Justine asked.

"Hell," Doc answered, "if this had been seen in a research hospital, there would have been a huge research project launched around it. Eight cases are definitely more than enough. But what with that damn ghoul Greene, no one except the computers would notice anything."

Warren rejoined the conversation. "Shit," he complained, "I can almost picture the guy, but it just won't solidify. I promise," he told Doc, "I'll really put some effort into it. I'm sure I can remember."

"No one I've talked to has heard of them," Kip informed the group, "except for some who knew that the acid had been around here. But they'll be on the lookout, and maybe one of them will hear of somewhere else that the acid's been sold."

"Well, I suppose all we can do is wait," Doc concluded.

"Warren will remember," Justine said encouragingly. "Give him a few days."

"Really, I will," Warren promised. "It's just a matter of time. But what was that crack about computers?"

"Oh," explained Doc, "it's something the federal government set up some years ago. It's called the Epidemiological Survey Network. In the midseventies some studies were done to determine the frequency of occurrence of various types of cancer as a function of geographical location, and what were called 'local hot spots' were found. Then, over the next few years, it was possible to determine environmental or occupational factors that led to the higher rates in those areas.

"Well, the technique worked so well that the federal government set up a massive network to monitor rates of illnesses, causes of death, and, among other things, frequencies and causes of spontaneous abortions as well as types of fetal and newborn deformities. That way, if something like thalidomide came along, they'd be able to spot it quickly." Doc stopped in the middle of his explanation and looked at Charlie. "Is there any way to hook into that system?" he asked. "We could search for higher rates of spontaneous abortion. Or for that deformity of the head. It might not tell us where the Gloryhits went, but if they're having the same effect we think they're having here, then maybe we could spot it."

Charlie wasn't sure. "Maybe we could. People in the med school probably use that system all the time."

"But do you think we could pull the data out?" Beth asked. "We're not talking about that many abortions, out of the total population."

"I bet it's okay," Doc said. "First of all, the head deformity should stick out like a sore thumb. I've never seen anything like it before, so even one or two in the last six months would be very unusual. I'm sure we can find it that way. And spontaneous abortions between three and five months aren't all that common. Most of them occur either in the first trimester or near term. So seven in, say, two or three months, should stick out. I think they've got the data broken down into pretty small segments geographically so that even neighborhoods can be distinguished from one another. They really went all out when they set up this thing."

Charlie was thinking about the details. "I'm not sure exactly how you go about setting up your search,

but I can guess, and it shouldn't be too hard at all."
He turned to Doc. "Look, if you'll stop by the lab
tomorrow, late afternoon, I'll try to talk to the people
at the med center before you come."

Doc checked his pocket calendar. "No go," he
answered. "Make it Monday. I couldn't get out long
enough to drive to your office and back."

"Good enough," said Charlie. "That'll give me a better chance to find out all I need to know about the
system."

Kip let out a loud sigh. "I don't know," he said.
"Somehow you people always manage to get around to
science."

"Not science," Ann said. "Human lives."

Monday, October 19

Monday morning brought the promise of winter.
Charlie hurried down Cambridge Street toward Harvard Square and the subway, reminding himself to pull
his down parka out of whatever closet it had been
stored in. It was an exhilarating feeling. The initial
release had come Thursday, with the quickening of
Disney, but it took the entire weekend for all the tension to work itself out of their systems. To use a cliché,
he felt like a new man. The crisp, cold air seemed to
clear his thoughts and his mind. Half an hour later he
emerged from the trolley and walked the last block
to the lab.

Once there, he remembered the life he loved so well,
tapping at the thick, obstinate shell that surrounded

every kernel of truth in the universe. The drudgery of the last two months had evaporated.

Beth stopped by late in the morning to find Charlie on the phone. He pointed out a chair to her and mouthed that he would only be another minute. He was scribbling frantically on a scratch pad, occasionally asking whoever was on the other end to repeat a phrase. After a couple of minutes he thanked the person and hung up.

"We're in," he said, with an air of satisfaction. "That was Barbara Waterper, over at the medical center. She does a lot of work with the Epidemiological Survey Network—or ESN, as she calls it—and she said there would be no trouble sticking in our search with her next batch. Otherwise, there's a shitload of paperwork required to gain access. Anyhow, she's sending a request in on Wednesday, and she said if we can get our description over to her tomorrow, she'll have a chance to check it for proper form before she turns it in."

Beth was delighted. "How long do we have to wait for the results?"

"Almost two weeks," Charlie replied, obviously unhappy with the answer. "Apparently there are just too many people using the network, and there's always a backlog to get on. But," he sighed, "I suppose we can wait."

"Especially since we've got no alternative," Beth agreed.

Charlie smiled. "So how go things with you?" he asked.

"Oh, pretty good," she answered. "Getting that job offer from Crop Research has given me the kick I needed to sit down and write a dozen applications for faculty positions. Lloyd's promised to get off letters of recommendation within the next day or two, which means within the week, hopefully."

Charlie laughed. "That's about par for the course. Whereabouts are you applying?"

A faint blush colored Beth's cheeks.

"Well, they seem to be more heavily weighted toward the Boston area than I would have expected a few months ago. Except for that, I guess it's just whatever places have openings. I want to stay in genetic manipulation, and there are only so many openings in the country. Lloyd insists that I only apply to top-notch departments—says it shouldn't be any problem getting into at least one of them."

"The Boston area is because of Doc?" Charlie asked.

"Yeah," Beth answered, slightly embarrassed, "but don't tell Lloyd about it, or he'll have my head. Science *über alles,* you know."

"For sure." Charlie smiled. "Have you written to Crop Research yet?" he asked.

"No, I haven't. I was about to, but Tom made me promise to hold off for a couple of weeks, until I got some feedback from other places. He said he'd relay the fact back to CRA that I wasn't likely to accept the offer."

"You told him, then, that you didn't want it?" Charlie asked.

"Well," Beth admitted, "I didn't want to make things difficult between us, so I sort of hedged on my reasons—said I wanted to stay in academia if possible, that I liked teaching and basic research. I guess I should have been more straightforward, because he argued pretty convincingly against my reasons."

"Oh?"

"He claimed that if my main interest was research, I ought to love industry. I wouldn't have to worry about political hassles for space and wouldn't have to spend a lot of time writing grant proposals. The offer from CRA did say that I could continue my present research for the three years of the contract. After those three years, he said, I could return to a school affiliation."

"Mmmm, I don't know," Charlie replied. "I think he's being a little naive about the barriers one faces trying to return from industry to academia."

"But that's not even the point," Beth continued. "I mean, the real reason I don't want the job is because I think the atmosphere would be stifling with everybody singlemindedly into their own research, and their own progress, and their own Christmas bonus and raise. The thought of showing up every day at nine and leaving at five is terrible."

"So?" Charlie asked.

"So he made me promise not to reject it officially until I had gotten at least a semioffer from some other place that I would prefer. Hell, it makes no difference to me *when* I reject it."

Doc entered with a *humph*. "These kids, always rejecting one thing or another. Don't know what this younger generation is coming to." He gave Beth a quick kiss and smiled at Charlie. "How goes everything?"

Charlie suppressed a twinge of jealousy. "Just great," he answered. "Looks like all we needed was a good kick."

Doc smiled. "Have you checked out the Epidemiological Survey Network?"

"The ESN," Beth corrected him, her nose turned up in the air. "Everyone calls it the ESN."

"We've got it made," Charlie answered, ignoring Beth's tease. "I talked to a woman named Waterper at the med center, and she uses it all the time. If we can get her a search outline by tomorrow, it'll go in with hers on Wednesday. Should get it back two weeks from today."

Doc grimaced. "No way to get it faster?"

"Don't complain," Charlie chided. "If she weren't willing to put it in with hers it would take six weeks to get through an application for access before we could even send a search in."

"Okay," Doc answered. "I won't complain. It's just that, well, you know, I feel as though there are people out there whose futures depend on whether we get to them in time."

"Oh, you're always so dramatic," Charlie said. "You make it sound like a matter of life or death."

"Charlie!" Beth said incredulously. "Have you forgotten so quickly? What are you saying?"

Charlie looked embarrassed. "Oh, I'm just making an ass of myself as usual," he admitted. "I guess I just get caught up in this search more from an academic point of view than as a real medical concern."

"You can't separate them like that, Charlie," Doc said. "You know that as well as I do. That's what scientists have been pretending for ages. And you've spent as much time as I have fighting that attitude."

Charlie turned red. "I can't defend myself. It's true; both of you are right. Christ, I feel as if I'm slipping into the role of a professor. It's scary."

"Comes from using Lloyd as a model," Beth warned. "Tomorrow, lunch, let me introduce you to a friend."

"Okay," Charlie agreed. "It's a deal."

"Well," said Doc, "now that we've got that settled, maybe we should plan out this search. How do we go about it?"

"Oh, it's pretty simple," Charlie began. "I've got it all written down here." He found the pad of paper among the myriad objects on his desk. "In the end, everything is entered as a numbered code, but Waterper said she'd do that part for us." He looked at the pad. "Okay. First we want the 'universe,' which is the part of the country covered by the search."

"Do we want the whole country?" asked Beth.

"I was thinking not," Charlie said. "New England should be sufficient. That'd make it easier to follow up if we found anything."

"Right," said Doc, "and we can continue with the rest of the country if the original search looks worthwhile."

"Agreed," said Beth. "What's next?"

"Wait a minute," Charlie muttered, writing on a clean sheet of paper. "I have to put it down by states." He finished writing and went back to the other sheet. "Okay. Next is 'field size,' which means, how large an area should be averaged over—like, do we want to compare states? Or counties?"

"I thought we wanted the smallest possible area," Beth replied.

Doc and Charlie agreed. "I guess that's hospitals, which isn't the best, but close enough," Charlie said.

"Well, wait," Beth argued, "maybe we want something larger."

"Okay," Charlie agreed, "but I'll have to check with Waterper; I'm not sure how this goes."

And so it went for the next hour. The final result was two searches: for deformities, involving the shape of the head, observed in both living and dead babies whose ages ranged from three months gestation to birth; the other for deaths, from all causes, between three and five months gestational age.

"Then I can walk this over to her this afternoon," Charlie concluded. "I'm sure she'll appreciate the extra time to work on it."

Doc looked at his watch. "If we hurry, I can grab lunch with you two—if you're willing to subject yourselves to cafeteria food. How about it?"

"Great," said Beth. "Can you join us, Charlie?"

"Me?" he asked. "I'm a professor. I never have anything that I have to do."

Laughing, the three of them headed down toward the cafeteria.

"Hey, Doc," Charlie asked as they reached the cafeteria, "did anyone ever contact you about those collected fetuses?"

"No," Doc said, "they didn't. What with the bust, I'd kind of forgotten about the promise to reply within the week. They never called or anything."

Charlie collected his Coke, fries, and cheeseburger and got in the checkout lane. "It's about time for Greene to be coming around again, isn't it?"

Doc frowned. "You're right. I think he's due on the twenty-sixth"—he checked his watch-calendar—"which is a week from today."

The three of them searched for a few minutes until they found a table. "Are you going to try to do anything more about Greene's project withholding information?" Beth asked. "You haven't mentioned it since the bust."

Doc frowned and shrugged his shoulders. "I don't know," he admitted. "In my less rational moments I think I'll either threaten to cave his goddamn head in if he doesn't get me the data or I'll at least try to get the obstetricians here in town to boycott the collection."

"Personally," Charlie suggested, "I think the second idea is better, if less gratifying."

"Would the OBs go along?" Beth asked. "It'd seem to me that once they've agreed to something like that, it'd be hard to get them to boycott it."

Doc disagreed. "The OBs I've talked to aren't all that enthralled with him. He doesn't seem to have given anyone a very good feeling. In fact, we're not the only ones who refer to him as 'the ghoul.' "

Charlie was surprised. "Really? That's surprising. What don't they like about him?"

"It doesn't seem to be something they can put their finger on. I guess they've been offended by his secrecy, but not just about his secrecy toward the data. No one seems to be able to find out too much about who he is or who he's working for or who's backing the project. He just has some weird mannerisms, I guess, that a few of the OBs find offensive. Studeman, that OB friend of mine, thinks that Greene's just a lackey, sort of a low man on the totem pole, who's trying to make himself seem big. Which sort of correlates with what we were talking about last month, but it's really hard to pin down.

"Anyhow," he continued, "I don't think out-and-out confronting him again is going to be of much use, although I thought maybe you could come along next time, Charlie. Maybe another researcher could exert some sort of moral pressure on him."

"I don't know." Charlie frowned. "He doesn't sound very willing to cooperate with anyone." The whole thing was so frustrating. If only they could find out who was behind the survey, then they could get the information they wanted. He wished they had anything at all more definite to go on. "And the fetus you misplaced never showed up again? Damn! If we had that, or some other fetus, we could have shown it to some of the people at the hospital and probably aroused some interest."

Doc threw his hands up in the air and let out an exasperated cry. "Cotten, you're going to drive me up the wall! Over a month ago I told you there was another one you could see."

Charlie looked confused. "When did you tell me that? I don't remember your saying anything like that at all."

Doc looked irritated. "That's probably because you were in such a snit over being forced to tell Ann." Realizing that Beth was unaware of Charlie's having been coerced into telling Ann, Doc quickly went on. "Remember when we talked things over on the phone? It was after the literature search failed to turn up anything. I told you there was a miscarried fetus I could show you. But you never said anything, so it got collected with the rest."

Charlie remembered. He had forced the entire phone call out of his mind. It had been when Doc had given him three days to tell Ann, and he had censored even the memory of the phone call itself. But now it was coming back. Swept by feelings of guilt, Charlie could only say, "God, I really fucked up that one."

Doc swallowed his anger at Charlie and tried to say that it didn't matter. Maybe another one would come up.

Either way, no matter. There was nothing they could do about it now.

Tuesday, October 20

Ila smiled. "Beth said you wanted to hear about the work I'm doing with Science for the People." Ila was an assistant professor of pathology at the medical school; Beth had arranged for Charlie to meet her at lunch.

Charlie nodded. "I did a bit of work with them on

the West Coast and thought I might get back into it again."

"Charlie has just become a professor," Beth teased, "so he probably wants something a bit more genteel."

Charlie made a face at her.

"Actually," said Ila, "Beth can joke, but I went through the same sort of confusion when I became one of the glorious faculty. In fact, I've just organized a faculty rap group for the purpose of talking about being a faculty member and how that relates to one's politics . . ."

Charlie smiled. "Well, I hope I'm not quite so reactionary as to need that. I think I've got a pretty good grasp of what should be done and what sort of forces stand in the way."

"Perhaps," Ila answered in a neutral tone, "but I know I found that there were a lot of subtle pressures, aside from the obvious ones, which were subverting me. It certainly was worthwhile for me, and the administration sees me as a flaming radical."

"Well," Charlie said, "I'd be interested to come once or twice, if for nothing else than to meet some people and see what they have to say. But I guess I was more interested in what sorts of active projects were going on."

"Oh," said Ila. "Well, we certainly have enough of those." She pulled out a file from her attaché case. "These are some old newsletters and bulletins you can keep. They outline most of the projects that are under way in the Boston area. The one I'm most excited about is the professional responsibility program. What we're doing is going around and talking to individual faculty members about specific research they're doing and how it relates to the community, the country, and the world. For instance, a lot of the research at the medical center, valuable research which has as its goal an increase in our knowledge of how human beings function, is borderline in terms of its justification for using human subjects. We've gotten a member of our group on the Human Experimentation Review Board, so we get to give input on that level.

"We've also been talking to people about whether it's

more valuable to do research on heart transplants, which at best will only serve the needs of a small number of relatively rich people, or to put more time and energy into investigating the relationship between diet and heart disease. There are whole industries based on selling products that are thought to be extremely dangerous for people with heart conditions, and they keep pushing their products as hard as they can. We've suggested that certain foods be labeled 'The surgeon general has found that this food might be dangerous to people with heart conditions.' You should have witnessed the uproar the dairy and poultry industries raised. But still, that sort of issue has to be brought up, or people never think of it.

"Or, on another level, some of our members talked to Lloyd Haenners, Beth's mentor, just last week, about his work. In doing some research on the subject, we found that Haenners is trying to transfer blight resistance to a type of corn that seems to be harder than most to work with. From the point of view of world food supplies, there are several strains of corn that would be much, much more valuable."

Charlie turned to Beth in surprise. "Did you know about this?"

"I only found out last Friday," she replied. "And not from Lloyd, either. It's definitely true that it's a lousy line of corn to be using, not only in terms of world food supply, but also from the standpoint of the ease of transferring new genes to the corn."

"Does he acknowledge this?" Charlie asked, somewhat suspiciously.

"Oh, in a sort of ass-backward way," Beth replied. "He went through this big brouhaha about wasting a lot of time worrying about subtle differences, and how it's better to work out a technique in a hard system because then you can be sure it'll work in the easier ones, and shit like that."

"Better in a harder system? I've never heard that argument before."

"Well," Ila interrupted, "the real reason, of course, is that if you read his grant contract, which is on file in the administration building, Crop Research Associates, who've given him the majority of his money, wrote into the contract that they would supply the corn line that he would use. It's obvious that they want it put into their own line of corn, which makes perfect sense in a good capitalist country."

"The majority of his money?" Charlie asked. "I thought it was around one-third."

"Check the office," Ila suggested. "It comes out to seventy-three percent, once you add in this guy Darnell's salary and the fifteen thousand a year they give Haenners for Darnell's expenses, plus travel money and other little things, that all add up."

Charlie whistled. "That's a lot of support."

Despite Beth's efforts, the conversation slowly became more and more technical. Finally, as the lunch hour approached its end, Beth dragged the conversation back. "Before we go, Ila, maybe you should tell Charlie when that faculty rap group is meeting next."

Ila checked in her notebook. "I don't seem to have it written down," she apologized.

"Oh, don't worry," Charlie replied. "I'll give you a call in a couple of days, and you can dig it out for me then." He rose to go. "It's been nice meeting you, and I hope to see you around."

Ila rose and shook his hand. "I always enjoy meeting new faculty who might be interested in doing some politics. There's so much to be done."

"For sure," Charlie agreed.

As they headed back upstairs, Charlie was unusually quiet. "You're surprised about Lloyd's work?" Beth asked.

"I'm not even sure that I believe it. It's so unlike him."

Beth glowered. "Well, if you don't believe it, maybe you should do some checking yourself, rather than assume that Lloyd's doing the best thing possible."

"Hey," Charlie responded, "don't get upset. I'll think about it—I promise."

"And maybe, if it's all true, you'll have to think again about Lloyd?" she asked, pursuing the point.

"I guess I'd have to," he said, not at all happy with the prospect.

Monday, October 26

The following Monday was ghoul day. Doc's friend Dan Studeman had agreed to put Greene off when he came to collect the fetuses and to get him to come back later in the day. That would give Doc, and a rather reluctant Charlie, a chance to get over to Studeman's office. But by four o'clock there had been no sign of him, so Doc and Charlie decided to wait at Studeman's office. The obstetrician was a few years older than Charlie and Doc, and his hair was beginning to thin and show traces of gray. Heavy-rimmed glasses made him look the image of the old-fashioned country doctor.

Studeman greeted Doc and Charlie at the door. "Fred, you look absolutely terrible!" he exclaimed. Embarrassed at his explosion, the obstetrician ushered the two of them into his office. "The afternoon should be clear from here on out. Cancellations can sometimes be a blessing." He turned to Charlie. "You must be Dr. Cotten. I'm Dan Studeman."

The two shook hands. "Charlie," he insisted. "Only the mail gets to call me Dr. Cotten."

"Any word from Greene?" Doc asked.

"Nothing," Studeman replied. "But it's not unusual for him to come right around five. I wouldn't worry." He looked intently at Doc. "Fred, are you feeling okay? I've never seen you look so exhausted."

"Physically, I'm fine, except insofar as worrying can run this poor body into the ground. It's been a hard month." He proceeded to give Studeman the barest summary of the Gloryhits problem and the bust.

108

"Well, I'm not surprised that you're so frazzled," Studeman said in wonder. "But maybe we can make a little progress at this end. I think we can threaten Greene with a boycott next month if he's not willing to give you the information. I'm sure that'll get it out of him."

"I sure hope so," Doc muttered.

They sat around talking until almost four-thirty, when a young man in his early twenties, with limp blond hair that hung over his collar, came into the office. "Dr. Studeman?" he asked uncertainly, looking at the threesome.

Studeman rose and smiled. "I'm Dr. Studeman. Can I help you?"

"Uh, I'm here for Dr. Greene. I'm supposed to pick up some jars with fetuses in them?"

There was a moment's silence. Then Doc exploded. "I don't believe it!" he shouted, leaping from his chair. Startled, the youth took a step back. "Where the hell is he?" Doc bellowed. "He's supposed to pick up these fetuses himself!"

The youth looked at Charlie and Studeman for help. "I—I don't know," he stuttered.

Charlie stood up and put a hand on Doc's shoulder. "Easy, Doc," he said. "We'll find out what we can." He turned to the youth, who looked about ready to turn and flee. "You said you work for Dr. Greene?" Charlie asked calmly.

"Well, not really," the youth began.

Doc turned and began to pace the room. "Oh, this is just too much. Now he doesn't even know if he works for Greene or not!"

Charlie ignored Doc's outburst. "Go on."

"I'm a student at Boston University, and I needed some cash, so I went over to the student employment office to see if they had any jobs where I could pick up some quick cash. Well, there was this card that said, 'Pick up medical samples,' and paid twenty-five dollars for a half day's work, so I grabbed it. It said you needed a car, and not so many kids here have one."

Charlie looked discouraged.

"Well, what are you supposed to do with them after

you've collected them?" Studeman asked. "And how do you get paid?"

"The guy left a padded crate that I'm supposed to pack them in. It's got postage on it and everything. I just have to take it down to the post office and send it registered mail. When I bring back the receipt and this list of doctors with their signatures, they'll give me a cashier's check for the money," the youth explained, showing a typed list of local obstetricians.

"Who's 'they'?" Charlie asked. "Who gives you the check?"

"The student employment office," he explained. "The guy left a check before, I guess."

Doc slumped back into a chair. "You don't happen to remember the address, I suppose."

"No, but it's on the crate, down in my car," the youth suggested. "It's a post office box number in New York City."

Charlie shook his head. "Probably the same one he gave us last time." He turned to the other two. "How about if we put a note in the crate, saying that unless we hear from them and get the information you asked for last time, they can expect a boycott? That should at least get us a phone call."

Doc felt defeated. "I don't think anything's going to have any effect," he complained. "This clearly is not my month."

But Studeman was irritated. "No, I think we should do what Charlie suggests. Personally, I don't think any of the local OBs would want to give Greene any more fetuses if they knew how he was responding to you." He sat down at his typewriter. "I'll get you the samples after I've typed this note," he told the youth. "Be absolutely sure that the note sits on top of the samples. I'll tape it on."

"Sure," the youth responded, "whatever you want. It doesn't matter to me." He was clearly shaken by the intensity of their emotions. Studeman finished the note, taped it securely to the top of a jar, and handed the box of jars to the youth.

"One more thing," Charlie said, turning to the messenger. "If this guy Greene should get in touch with you personally, for any reason, it's worth fifteen bucks to me to get a complete report on what he says, and twenty-five if you can get a phone number or address that isn't an answering service or post office box."

The youth seemed interested. "How do I get in touch with you?"

"Just bring the information here," Studeman said. "I'll see that you get paid, and that they get the story."

Charlie agreed. "I'm sorry if we shook you up," he apologized to the youth. "It's just that we really wanted to talk to him."

"Yeah, sure," he responded, and taking the box, he left the office. Christ, he said to himself, I see why the guy didn't want to come himself.

Sunday, November 1

The next week saw no developments. Charlie, finally getting into the swing of teaching, had begun to set up some experiments in his lab, and the research fever began to return. Disney kicked harder and harder as Ann grew larger. She felt great. All their worries seemed to have evaporated, and Charlie predicted a "golden age."

For Doc, things were not so easy. Still upset about the episode with Greene's stand-in, he awaited what he was sure would at least be a nasty phone call, but nothing came. Beth was preparing for the DNA meetings in Squaw Valley, where she would be presenting some of her results, and hence she had little time for Doc. The final blow came on Friday, when Diederson of the narcotics squad stopped by Doc's office. "Thought I'd start stopping by now and then"—he smiled—"just in case someone I'm looking for might be here." It was harassment, pure and simple, but there didn't seem to be anything Doc could do about it. By Saturday he was feeling irrationally nervous and depressed.

Against this background, Beth flew out of Boston late Sunday afternoon. She had spent the night with Doc, and he had seen her to the airport. It had been a depressing good-bye, made worse by Tom Darnell's presence, which made real communication impossible.

Crop Research Associates had apparently decided it was worth their money to send Darnell to the meetings, and they were paying all his expenses. His usual cheerful but quiet self, he took the seat next to Beth for the four-hour flight to Squaw Valley. He tried to make conversation with her, but when he discovered her unusual sulkiness, he retired into a novel.

They reached Squaw Valley late at night. The moon shone brightly on the towering mountains, already deep in snow. The sudden transition from Boston's still-rainy fall to this beautiful winter scene was like a dream. It only worsened Beth's depression. Picking up her key at the desk, she bade Tom a quiet good night and dragged herself off to bed.

She awoke the next morning to brilliantly clear skies. On her way to breakfast she ran into a group of friends from the Boston area, also up early due to the jet lag, and together they ate a leisurely breakfast. Slowly her depression began to evaporate. She had picked up the abstracts of talks to be given, and the meetings would be even more exciting than she had hoped. It looked as though the whole field of genetic engineering was finally breaking open. By the end of breakfast, her worries about Doc had been pushed, if not out of her mind, at least into a distant corner.

Together the small group went over to the auditorium to listen to the morning sessions. After the first speaker, Beth leaned over and whispered to her companion, "Don't complain—he finished on time." The speaker was a Nobel Prize winner who had done much of the pioneering research on recombining different types of DNA. But as is so often the case, he had done little since then. The talk, which lasted forty-five minutes, contained no information of interest that had not been published at least two years earlier.

But the next two talks were brilliant, and the hall buzzed with excited conversation after the session ended. "Mallory's work is simply elegant!" Beth exclaimed. "I wouldn't have believed that anyone could get that to work."

"It's incredible," her friend agreed. Karen Mae had entered graduate school a year ahead of Beth and was now working at the University of Chicago. They had not seen each other since Karen had left last June. "And not only that, it'll throw these meetings onto the front page of all the newspapers. If it wasn't so beautiful, and really valuable, I'd say it was a grandstand experiment."

Nearby, Mallory was being besieged by reporters. "In a way," Beth commented, "it's dangerous and scary work. Putting bacterial genes into human cells is like opening Pandora's box."

Around them, others seemed to be saying the same thing. In his talk, Mallory had reported successful transfer of a bacterial gene into some human cells growing in tissue culture. The gene, used by bacteria in digesting complex sugars, allowed the human cells to break down cellulose and to use the sugar contained within them for energy. In its own way, it was the first successful step in changing human beings genetically.

At the end of his talk, he had tried to emphasize how far researchers still were from actually changing the genetics of a human being in a specific way, but somehow even he seemed unconvinced by the statement. Ten years ago the concept was pure science fiction. Five years ago it was a long way in the future. Today, Mallory had said, "It will probably be several years. But," he had added, "it is in the nature of science that when practical applications run right on the tail of basic discoveries, time estimates can be off by factors of ten or even a hundred. With luck, people

could start doing it in a year." And that was the message the reporters had heard. Pushing their way
through the excited crowd, Beth and Karen headed for
the lunch hall.

That afternoon they took off on cross-country skis.
The meetings were arranged to leave the afternoons
open for enjoying the Squaw Valley area. An hour
and a half from civilization, the two women stopped
to rest and eat the food they had carried along. The
air was still, and no sign of human existence intruded
on their senses. They sat for a while and soaked in the
tranquillity of their surroundings.

"Sometimes," Beth said softly, almost whispering,
"when I find a place like this, it's hard for me to believe that I live in that supermechanized world back
East and that I like it. I get so depressed sometimes,
realizing how badly we've scarred so much of the
world."

"I know," Karen agreed sadly. "So many of the
really terrible things we've done—pollution, radioactive fallout, almost destroying the ozone layer a few
years back—in retrospect seem so obviously bad."
They both sat for a while in the quiet, watching a
rabbit forage in the snow-covered underbrush.

After a while Beth said, "It's as if we know what
we're doing, but just refuse to take responsibility for
our actions."

"And now that we've screwed up the physical
world," Karen replied, "we're going to start in on the
biological world. God," she said, "if we do as badly
this time as we did with the environment, we just
might not survive."

Back at the lodge, they threw off the afternoon's
melancholy and returned to their meetings. On Tuesday, Tom joined Beth for dinner. He was interested in
the workshop sessions she had attended, since several
had run simultaneously and he had not been able to
go to all those he had wanted to. Beth was happy to
exchange information. Tom paid his usual close attention to details, particularly when they seemed applicable to cell culture and the incorporation of new DNA

into cultured cells. They talked energetically until the end of the meal.

After dinner Tom brought up the issue of Beth's future plans. "Nothing's changed, Tom. I'm still holding out for an academic job."

"How's the job hunt going?" he inquired.

Beth frowned. "Well, a couple of requests I sent off came back with regrets, but they said the space was filled. The University of Southern California is interested, but I don't want to move to L.A."

"Well, at least it's something," Tom answered. Then he added, "Well, much as I'd love to get you to come work for CRA, I'm sure something you want will come through."

Beth smiled in response to his support. After her talk with Karen the day before, she felt more opposed than ever to working for industry. But at the meetings that evening she felt a twinge of uncertainty. Some of the talks that evening, all from academia, seemed at least as scary as anything that industry could dream up.

Tuesday, November 3

Charlie anxiously awaited Doc's arrival for dinner. He had added an extra plate to the four for himself, Ann, Warren, and Justine after Barbara Waterper had brought him the results of their epidemiological survey. They had turned up more than he could have hoped for. While waiting for Doc, he explained the background of the search to the others. "So what we had hoped to get out of it was, first, whether the search was accurate enough to spot increases like ours in the rate of stillbirths, and if so, where else there were similarly high rates. Second, we wanted to find out where else these cranial deformities showed up."

"From your enthusiasm I'd say something interesting has come up," remarked Justine.

" 'Interesting' isn't the word," Charlie replied. "Boggling. Simply boggling." He could hardly contain himself. "But no more until Doc shows up. He deserves to be here."

Ann looked unhappy, but said nothing until Doc arrived. "Come on in, Doc, and have yourself a seat." She smiled warmly at him.

He still looked worn-out, but some of the depression seemed to have lifted. "I told myself that Charlie sounded too happy for the results to have been totally negative and that my theory that everything possible was going to go totally wrong must not be valid any more."

Warren sympathized. "You should see Kip on a night when his guitar won't stay in tune. I've seen it happen a couple of times. He looks like he just wants to return everybody's money and go drown himself. Everybody seems to have runs of luck like that."

"And it probably doesn't help to have Beth gone, either," Ann suggested.

"Dammit," Doc complained, "you're right. That woman is starting to get to me. I'm just not as cold and predatory as I used to be."

Ann smiled. Doc was one of the least aggressive men she had ever met, a drastic contrast to Charlie when she had first met him.

"Well, she's due back pretty soon, now," Charlie consoled him. "It shouldn't be too hard lasting out till Friday."

"Friday evening," Doc corrected him. Suddenly throwing off the frown, he turned to Charlie. "But tell me about these results."

Charlie grabbed an envelope off the table. His eyes shone with excitement as he started leafing through the pages of computer output. "First of all, the unit areas being compared are what they call 'contiguous hospitals.' The computer produces a number for every hospital in New England, and that number reflects the statistics for not only that hospital, but also for all the hospitals surrounding it. That way it averages out a larger area.

"So the first question became 'What ten contiguous hospital areas showed the highest incidences of spontaneous abortions at three to five months pregnancy, for the quarter running from July first through September thirtieth, and what was the breakdown on types of deformities and abnormalities reported?' "

Charlie held up a sheet of paper. "This is the list of contiguous hospitals. They run from New York City up to Boston, and all are pretty much on the coast. Massachusetts General Hospital is number six." It was the one with which most of the obstetricians who had reported to Doc on Gloryhits-related abortions were affiliated.

"I don't see what you're so gleeful about," Ann commented, clearly irritated.

"You don't?" Charlie was surprised. "Why, it means that the survey network is good enough to pick up increases like we've had here."

"And it also means that we've got the sixth highest incidence of spontaneous abortions in all of New England," she snapped. "You forget pretty fast how close we came to being part of that delightful statistic."

"Who says I'm happy with the result?" Charlie countered. "All I'm saying is that since it is true, at least we can find out where else there've been similar occurrences. That's all."

Doc tried to stave off the conflict. "What did they have to say as to defects and abnormalities?"

"Just a small listing of relatively common ones," Charlie answered. "But, and this is what's so exciting, there's also an asterisk under the heading of deformities and abnormalities."

"Come on, Charlie," Justine complained. "Don't play showman, okay? What does the asterisk mean?"

Charlie looked a bit deflated. "It means that, quote, A large number of the abortants were unavailable for report, due to collection for research study, unquote." He still had a smile on his face.

"Whoopee," Warren replied calmly. "So what's new?"

"Just," Charlie announced triumphantly, "the fact that a total of seven of the top ten towns have the same asterisk!"

"What?" exclaimed Doc. "You mean Greene's been collecting from seven of the ten towns with the highest rates?"

"Precisely!" Charlie replied.

"Well, that seems pretty reasonable to me," Ann said. "Why wouldn't he pick towns with high rates?"

"Because his study is supposed to be of normal abortants. Picking high-frequency towns begs the question, since it's reasonable to assume that there's a special reason why they're higher than most."

Charlie looked pleased with himself. "Which means that something even stranger than we thought is going on."

"Is it obvious that the ghoul would have thought up that objection?" Warren asked. "I mean, I would have automatically picked the places with the highest rates, just so I could get as many as possible."

"And, Charlie, before you jump in and say 'Of course he would,' I'm not so sure." It was Doc who objected. "You're the one who's always complaining about how most researchers have vital flaws in their work. Greene didn't seem to be the most brilliant researcher around."

Charlie looked crestfallen. "I guess that's possible. I hadn't considered that."

"It's not the Gloryhits." Ann said it as a statement, and everyone looked shocked.

"What's not?" Charlie demanded.

"The cause of these abortions. They weren't caused by the Gloryhits!"

Everyone shouted at once. "Because," Ann shouted out above their voices, "because the ghoul started collecting fetuses before any of the miscarriages associated with the Gloryhits occurred." They still looked confused. "And if he picked those towns because their abortion rates were high, then the rates must have been high before the Gloryhits!" She looked at Charlie triumphantly. He stared at her silently as he realized what she was saying.

Doc swore softly. "So now we can just start over again, right? Now we're saying that there's no connection between the Gloryhits and these towns?"

Warren was looking at the list. "Except," he said slowly, "for Middletown, Connecticut."

They all looked at him, not comprehending.

"Middletown is number three, and it has an asterisk, too," he continued slowly.

"So?" Ann challenged.

"Tony Belvedere lives in Middletown," Warren said, "and he's the guy who said he'd had some Gloryhits!"

Wednesday, November 4

Wednesday brought a blizzard to Squaw Valley, unlike anything Beth had ever seen. But the resort area took it in stride, and except for the loss of revenues from the skiers who would normally have filled the now closed ski lifts, everything ran smoothly. Beth spent the afternoon with Karen, sitting around the fireplace in the new lodge. They were both surprised and delighted at how little the months of separation had affected their friendship, and they spent the afternoon talking, ignoring the friendly smiles and introductions of a not small number of fellow scientists—all men.

"It was really hard," Karen said, "getting a postdoctoral position, and feeling that I got it not because I was a woman and not because someone owed the guy I was working for a favor." She looked around at the crowd of mostly middle-aged men. "I mean, all the

people you're applying to are here this week, and all
you'd have to do would be return their smiles and sit
and listen to them talk about their research with an
impressed expression on your face. That plus Lloyd's
letter would probably land you the job."

Beth frowned. "And if you tell them to get lost
in any way that isn't supernice, they decide you're a
castrating bitch, and you'll never get the job, no matter who you are." They had seen it happen over and
over again. Science wasn't that different from the rest
of the world.

As the lodge got more crowded, it became impossible to carry on any sort of conversation for more
than two minutes without being interrupted by a
friendly scientist. This place really seems to get their
blood flowing, Beth thought. Looking over the crowd,
she spotted Tom Darnell talking to another man.
"Salvation!" she called to Karen.

Squeezing through the crowd, they finally reached
Tom and his friend.

Tom smiled a hello. "Please," Beth begged jokingly,
"you have to give us sanctuary from this ass-crazed
crowd!" She laughed, out of breath from the rush of
the crowd. "I'm afraid that if one more nice young
man swirls his cocktail around the sides of his glass,
smiles, and says, 'Mmm, hi' to me, they're going to be
picking pieces of glass out of his face till tomorrow."

Tom smiled. "They do look a bit predatory this
afternoon. Without the skiing, they don't seem to know
what to do with their energy."

Karen laughed. "Since Beth is too impolite to introduce me, I'm Karen," she said, poking at the name
tag pinned to her blouse. "And you're nameless," she
said, noting Tom's lack of a tag.

"Oh," Tom explained, "it's here in my pocket." He
pulled the corner out to show them. The tags were
required for admission to the sessions. "I'm not wearing it because they managed to goof it up entirely."
He showed them a tag reading *John Darnle, M.I.T.*
"How they managed that is beyond my comprehension, but I'm afraid that if I try to get it corrected,
they'll tell me that there isn't any Tom Darnell regis-

tered and throw me out." They all laughed at the idea. "By the way, I'm Tom," he said to Karen, "and being more polite than my colleague, I'll introduce an old friend of mine, Jim Karls. We went to Brown together, longer ago than I'd care to admit."

Beth smiled in sudden recognition. "That's right," she said. "You were at the DNA meetings with Tom in Atlantic City last year."

Karls smiled broadly. "I'm flattered that you remember." Turning to Tom, he added, "Although I'm not sure I like being considered no longer a threat to women."

"What brings you here, Jim?" Beth asked.

"Nothing very exciting," he answered. "I'm a science writer for a Great Metropolitan Newspaper, and I'm trying to keep up with this genetic-engineering stuff. It appears to me that this is where the action's going to be for the next decade."

Karen smiled. "A nonacademician. How nice. I'd forgotten that people outside of the groves came to these meetings."

"Oh, sure." Jim nodded. "Reporters, and a lot of people from the pharmaceutical firms are here. And people like Tom, from other industries."

Karen looked at Tom, confused as to his affiliation.

"That's right," Beth said. "I'd forgotten that Tom's with industry. He fits into the academic world so well."

Tom smiled. "Why, Beth, that's very kind of you."

She curtsied politely. Turning back to Jim, she asked, "What paper are you with?"

Karls looked slightly embarrassed. "None at the moment, actually. I'm doing free-lance stuff right now and selling it wherever I can." Changing the subject, he said, "Look, since I'm officially here on business, can I pick your brains on some of this stuff? I'm trying to find out what people's reactions were to Mallory's talk. I've only been getting the opinions of older, established workers. Can I ask you two what you thought?"

For the next hour they discussed Mallory's work, the aspects of it that they liked and those that they didn't.

But somehow, neither Beth nor Karen brought up the reservations that they had expressed to each other on Monday, skiing in a different world.

Beth didn't see Tom or Jim again until Friday morning at the final session. The closing talks were on the social aspects of genetic engineering, and Beth went more out of a sense of duty than from any great interest. Somehow such talks always alluded to the "great future humanity could expect under the aegis of controlled evolution." And, somehow, scientists who had reservations about the field didn't get invited to speak on the panels. She hoped some good questions would come up.

The talks went more or less as expected. The first speaker lectured on the tremendous potential for improving the world with the technique of genetic engineering. A cheap source of vital drugs, the development of new plants, possibly even the curing of genetic diseases. The next two speakers said the same thing in slightly different terms. Only the last speaker was truly interesting.

Marilyn McCulloch, an associate professor at Berkeley, wondered aloud about some of the more surreal aspects of genetic engineering. For instance, what was to prevent the development of completely new species of animal life to fill existing ecological niches, such as a bird that would prey on the much hated snails of California—and maybe slugs, too, while they were at it? That seemed a logical extension of all this work.

"Or," she suggested, "go beyond that. People in chemistry are working on organic polymer materials which will have useful properties as semiconductors, for example. Once a protein is developed which is useful, then it would not be unreasonable to construct a segment of DNA that would code for that protein, and insert it into bacteria, thereby getting the bacteria to synthesize a totally artificial protein. Or at least," she suggested, "we should be able to take genes from fireflies and put them into some bacteria, so that we can feed old grass clippings to bottles of bacteria in order to get light. Even now," she challenged, "we're close enough to being able to get bacteria to make oil and natural gas for us to make the proposition worth investigating." It was far and away the best talk of the session.

After her talk the floor was opened for questions. "Wouldn't it be possible," a man in the back asked, "to select genes for increased human intelligence, and breed a race of supergeniuses?" Turning to see who had asked the question, Beth discovered that it was Jim Karls. He was sitting way in the back, next to Tom. The question met with a certain amount of jeering from the audience.

"I would have to say," McCulloch began, "that as far as we know, it is at least theoretically possible. But first it would take a lot of work, for a start, to define intelligence. It's clear now that whatever it is, it isn't measured by IQ tests, so we're sort of left without any way to get at it. Besides, I'm not sure that there's been any good research that indicates a genetic basis for intelligence as opposed to its being based on one's environment and upbringing."

Karls interrupted her. "But what if you went about it another way? What if you could just do something like increase cranial capacity, so you could get a larger brain? Wouldn't that be useful in increasing intelligence?"

There were more laughs from the audience, while McCulloch merely shrugged her shoulders. "I doubt that it's as simple as that, but I'm afraid the question is well outside my area." Looking out over the audience, she asked, "Would anyone here like to respond to the question?"

Amid further hoots and jeers, the question found no takers, and several picayune questions later the meeting ended.

After promising to write soon and saying good-bye to Karen, Beth headed back to her room. She was anxious to return to Boston and Doc. I hope he hasn't had another bad week, she thought. I'm not sure he could take it.

Monday, November 9

Doc was in high spirits when he met the plane. Except for the survey, nothing extraordinary had happened, but the day-to-day routine of the office had been particularly pleasant that week. And Beth's absence had brought home to Doc the realization that her presence meant a lot to him.

After telling Beth the survey results, Doc swore her to silence on anything relating to Gloryhits and swept her off to the cottage of a friend in Vermont for a weekend of rest and relaxation.

On Monday morning Beth wandered over to Charlie's office to see the computer printout. "So now you know as much as the rest of us," Charlie said, rocking on the rear legs of his chair. "The only thing we can conclude is that the high rate of spontaneous abortions was present before Greene picked his towns, unless he's working a hell of a lot of towns. Even if he were, the odds against picking seven of the top ten towns at random must be better than a million to one."

Beth frowned. "There're too many inconsistencies. Greene started collecting before Gloryhits came to our area. If he did pick the towns because of their high rates, then that means the Gloryhits are not connected to the high abortion rate. But Warren's friend in Middletown is also in a high-abortion-rate town, which is unlikely unless Gloryhits were all over the place."

Charlie shrugged his shoulders. "Don't argue with me about it. Kip tried to find the person who sold him the Gloryhits—someone by the name of Larry Seigal.

124

Unfortunately, the guy disappeared shortly after dealing out the acid, and Kip's had no luck in tracking him down."

"What about going through Warren's friend?" asked Beth.

Charlie shook his head. "Warren's been calling twice a day, but no luck. I guess he's out of town or something. No one's answering his phone, so we can't get any lead on him at all. But Warren should be getting in touch with the guy soon, I guess. Until then, we just wait."

Beth pursed her lips and made a clicking noise with her tongue. "Well, at least that's more than we had two weeks ago. It seems like the first break we've had with this thing, and it's certainly lifted Fred's spirits a lot. I think he had come to the conclusion that the whole world was plotting against him. Did you hear that Diederson stopped by again on Friday?"

"At Doc's office?" Charlie asked.

"Yep. I gather he's into a weekly harassment trip. Fred's convinced that Diederson thinks he's pushing smack out of his office and that his visits will scare off Fred's clientele. Anyhow, Sharon offered him coffee and doughnuts, which apparently freaked him out. To hear Fred talk about it, he almost looks forward to the visits for comic relief."

"The weekend must have helped, too," Charlie said with a slight edge to his voice.

Ignoring his tone, Beth merely smiled and nodded affirmatively. Then she said, "But he's still uneasy about what this survey might be turning up. No matter how you explain it, it doesn't come out very likely."

"Uneasy?" Charlie asked. "I can see being excited, but why uneasy?"

"Just because we still don't know for sure if the acid is causing the deformity, and we don't know why the abortion rates are so much higher at Mass. General."

Charlie grumped. "Him and Ann," he complained, annoyance in his voice. "I can't understand why they get so upset about these numbers. We knew that there were going to be ten top areas; there have to be. Why is it so much scarier if we're one of them? I mean, sure it's scary, but they almost seem to be unhappy that we found out. Isn't it better to know than to be ignorant?" he insisted. "This way, maybe we can do something about it. I mean, if it's a contaminant in the acid, maybe we can alert people to it or something."

"If it really is something in the acid," replied Beth. "The only way it seems that could be possible would be for Greene to have known about the Gloryhits ahead of time. I'm not quite paranoid enough yet to believe that."

Charlie looked frustrated. "I know, I know. It doesn't make any sense. But that's not so unusual in scientific work. You know as well as I do that when we've got enough information to piece it all together, it'll seem perfectly reasonable. But that doesn't explain why they have to get so riled up over it. That isn't any way to carry on research. And Doc should know that, too."

She answered slowly. "I think Fred realizes that as well as you and I do. Maybe even more so, because he's the one who was so insistent that something was going on in the first place. But his patients are involved, and that's hitting him hard. He's reacting to both of those feelings, not necessarily mixing them up. I think I feel more the way Doc does. How can you not be scared about something like this? I'm sure that the people who first suspected that thalidomide and those defoliants we used in Vietnam were teratogenic had feelings like ours. Don't you think so?"

Charlie was silent, and Beth decided to press the point. "We're human beings, Charlie, not just disinterested scientists. You can't treat your research as only a scientific matter, denying its effect on you and on others as well. Charlie," she challenged, "if you're going to slip into being just another normal, uninvolved scientist, it's going to be through things like this. It's perfectly reasonable to become emotionally involved in your experiments and their implications without allowing that involvement to distort the results. Not to realize that is a lethal mistake."

Charlie shuffled some papers on his desk. Her com-

ments had stung deeply. Trying to joke about it, he
finally said, "It sounds as if you've got me pinned out
pretty accurately. Lemme think it over."

Beth didn't respond. She made a mental note to have
Ila call him when the next faculty rap session came
up. Maybe Charlie would see the value of it now.

"How was Squaw Valley? Anything interesting?" He
was clearly finished with the other subject, at least for
the time being.

"Really exciting," she replied. And for the next
half hour she related the high points of the talks. She
glossed over most of the technical reports. Outside
Charlie's field, they would be essentially meaningless
to him. But he was interested in Mallory's results in
putting bacterial genes into human cells and found
the description of Marilyn McCulloch's talk fascinating.
"Then this friend of Tom's, a newswriter, asked a question about transferring intelligence genes into people,
and the audience cracked up."

Charlie smiled. Newspeople had a way of pushing
scientists just past the edge of all reasonability. "How
was it spending a week with Tom?" he asked.

She made a face. "I guess at the time it was sort of
nice. But it left a sour taste afterward. I realized how
strongly he's pushing me to take that job. He's very
subtle, and I didn't realize it then, but I feel as if my
parents have just made it clear that they think I should
take the job."

He laughed. "Uncle Benny!"

"What?"

"My uncle Benny. My mother's brother. He's an industrial maggot. Every time I see him we talk about my
work for a while, and then he says, 'Charlie, my boy,
I know people in the chemical industry who'd pay
you five times what you're making now if you'd come
and do the same thing for them. Don't be so proud!
It's industry you want to get your message to anyhow,
isn't it?' And then I give him the same argument that
always seems so lame when I'm around him." He
laughed at the memory.

But Beth had found Tom's attitude more disturbing
than humorous. To her, the world of industry was still

a foul-smelling swamp, a breeding place of noxious chemicals and equally noxious attitudes. "It upsets me," she explained, "to see a guy who seems to be so intelligent and so considerate of others, but who comes to such a completely different conclusion after being presented with the same basic information that I've gotten. It just seems that with all that was exposed about Watergate, the Vietnam War, the CIA, ITT, and on and on, that he'd be more sensitive to the negative aspects of industry."

"Aha! Now you're asking people to look at data from an entirely neutral position, to not let their feelings and emotions interfere with logic. That's the opposite of what you just said. Everybody looks at the same data, but they weigh different factors differently, they interpret the data differently, and sometimes they even seem to get different raw data. For example, you seem to start out from the assumption that the good of the people is paramount. But that's just a postulate. Maybe if you assume that the good of the nation is paramount, you'd end up somewhere else."

Beth said nothing. She considered Charlie's reasoning merely an excuse for Tom that he didn't deserve. She picked up the computer printout and looked at it again. They couldn't even figure out what that meant. Suddenly she turned to Charlie. "How long have we been in the top ten?"

"You mean Mass. General?" he asked.

"Yeah."

Charlie grinned proudly. "Ask me in a week or so. This is just the results when July through September are averaged. After we got these back, I called Waterper to initiate a search that would give the past two years' monthly rates, compared with the norm, for all the towns in the top ten."

Beth was still annoyed by Charlie's debating tactics, and the childish grin now plastered on his face was more than she could tolerate. Gracefully complimenting Charlie on his good thinking, she went back to her lab.

November

Mid-November is an ugly time in Washington. Even in a nonelection year, all the politicians trying to decide the significance of a million minor elections for garbage collector and dog pound administrator in their individual districts. The cool air seemed to trap the ever increasing pollution over the dirty city. Pearson could remember when at least the government district maintained a semblance of cleanliness, but even that had finally been beaten back by increased pollution. If he squinted hard, he could pretend that the smog was just a gentle haze surrounding the Pentagon, cutting it off from the rest of the world.

He was upset by his conversation with General Westland. Johnson had complained about the pressure that Pearson was applying, and Westland had sided with Johnson. Worst of all, they were right. He had been unconsciously transferring to Johnson all the blame for Intelligence's slow start on Russia's genetics research.

In fact, Johnson's work was moving faster than anyone had any right to expect. He looked at the latest report. The bastard had actually gotten the botulinum genes into the influenza virus! Whether the genes would be expressed. and the toxin produced, hadn't been checked yet, nor did they know if the mutator genes had also gone in. But they were testing that in tissue culture, and it was reasonable to expect the results within a month. The guy was either phenomenally lucky or a true genius. Pearson suspected the former.

129

Depressed by the way things were going at his end, he decided to replay the tapes of the last executive committee discussion. He felt something had occurred that he hadn't fully grasped yet. Setting up the recorder, he cued up the tape and leaned back, his eyes closed as the tape began.

"The purpose of this meeting is to review our information on enemy work in genetic engineering. We have three reports: one on the Russian work itself, one on the agent Gabardine, and one on U.S. military research. Let's start with the Russian work."

"Okay, although there's not much to say. Basically, we've been unable to get any hard information. Within the last month they've sealed up their scientists and laboratory facilities to what appears to be level-five security. In the past this has corresponded to either the active production of weaponry or at least the beginning of test runs. At any rate, it's prevented us from getting any of our available agents into the installation. It would perhaps be worth discussing at this time whether we want to have a covert team attempt to infiltrate the installation."

"What about material and personnel flow? Aren't we monitoring that?"

"We are. There's been very little. But machinery and huge amounts of supplies aren't necessary to start stockpiling considerable amounts of a biological weapon, so the information is of little value."

"We don't even have a housekeeper inside?"

"No one. They've done a better job of picking their personnel than they usually do."

"Which doesn't bode well."

"Agreed."

"I suggest that we hold off on discussing whether we send in a team until we've heard all of the reports. If there aren't any objections, let's have the report on Gabardine."

(Pause)

"Okay. There were two reporters at the Asilomar meetings who, as of our last meeting, we had not been able to identify. The remaining people present seemed to be legitimate. Mohair, one of the two unknowns, has been identified as a reporter for the St. Louis *Post-Dispatch,* and he was clearly there reporting for the paper. He looks clean in every other respect, and so we have dropped our interest in him. The other was Gabardine, who, you'll remember, registered as a reporter from the Boston *Globe.* The name matched a reporter there, but photographs didn't. We had a plant talk to the actual reporter, and it's clear that either he has no knowledge at all that someone used his name there or he's covering for Gabardine. Since we couldn't tell which, we've got someone covering the reporter now."

"What about Gabardine? Any sign of him?"

"We're almost at the point where we can say that he's not a news reporter for a major paper or wire service. We've checked that out carefully. And it appears that we have spotted him again."

"Appears?"

"Right. Look at these photos. This one is from the Asilomar meetings, and it's Gabardine. This picture is of a person who was at the Squaw Valley meetings just a couple of weeks ago."

"That's supposed to be the same person?"

"Look carefully. Assume that he's wearing a wig and has darkened his complexion."

"Isn't that stretching it a bit?"

"Except—look at these. These are voice patterns that we got off tapes from the two meetings, and both are the same. Our experts say there's no question about it. He's got some peculiarity in his speech that sticks out."

"That one from Squaw looks beautiful. Did you stick a microphone in his mouth?"

"No, he was so kind as to get up and ask a question at one of the meetings. I'll come back to that. He registered under the name of Jim Karls, which sounds like a sloppy cover for a Communist. Anyhow, he registered as a free-lance newswriter. The address and everything he gave are blanks. He apparently rented an apartment for a month, got his registration mailed there, and that's it. Neighbors said they never saw him at all. Apartment was vacant all month."

"Did he talk to anyone?"

"That's a problem. He talked to lots of people. We've spoken to some who remember him. He was asking people what they thought about work reported at the meeting on inserting bacterial genes into human cells. Most of the people look clean."

"Most?"

"We've got one funny. A guy named John Darnle, from M.I.T. No such person at M.I.T. Apparently a lot of registrations got screwed up, though, so it might not be anything. We're trying to trace it down."

"I thought we had someone there who was going to try to trail Gabardine."

"We did, but it wasn't obvious at the time that Karls was Gabardine. The disguise was well done. But next time I think we'll be ready for him."

"What do we know about possible leaks in our security? Do we have any indications that the Russians are aware of our project or its progress?"

"No. We have no evidence of any leaks. But I can tell you right off that that doesn't mean much."

"Pearson, you mentioned that Johnson had originally gotten the idea for this project from someone in Boston . . ."

"Right. A guy named Lloyd Haenners. And the answer is no, Haenners shouldn't have any idea about the project. Johnson never let him know that he worked for the military. Haenners is a big liberal of some sort, and Johnson didn't want to ruin Haenner's image of him, so they didn't actually discuss much more than how nowadays you can pretty well do any gene transfer you want to in bacterial and viral systems.

"We don't have anyone in the lab, but we do keep close tabs on their work. It's sort of useful to us to know anything new they come up with, and based on surveillance reports, it seems very unlikely that they're suspicious about anything at all."

(Pause)

"Maybe we should go on to Johnson's work?"

Pearson fast-forwarded the machine past his presentation.

" . . . to the question of sending in a covert team to try to penetrate the Russian facilities."

"Is that appropriate now?"

"Is there something else you want to talk about first?"

"No, no—I mean is it appropriate to send in a team now? We don't have any evidence that things are far enough along to warrant the risk of losing a good team."

"I tend to agree. It doesn't seem that things have reached a panic point yet."

"Well, I disagree. First of all, I don't think it's necessary to reach a panic point before using our men for what they've been trained. I'd hate to lose them as much as anyone else, but they're useless if we're afraid to use them. Second, I'm not sure what more signs we could be looking for. We have indications that they're constructing and stockpiling whatever they've been working on . . ."

"Those indications are pretty weak . . ."

"I know, but in the past a level-five security . . ."

"Has been used for heavy-weapons research. Biological weaponry is completely different. With missiles, you don't have to worry about someone accidentally carrying one out on the bottom of his shoe."

"I'm not going to stand for a squabble here. I suggest that people be allowed to finish what they're saying before others speak."

"Thank you. Third, and last, depending on the sort of weaponry they're talking about, it isn't inconceivable that they've already struck us. Either a small tactical attack, just to test out the agent, or a serious tactical attack, like trying to hit Washington with a tumor-producing virus, or for all we know, they've already hit us with an agent that's sterilized everyone in the country! I think we have to know what's going on before we find ourselves completely defeated!"

"Okay, wait a minute. First of all, they haven't sterilized all the women in this country without our knowledge, and everyone in Washington isn't coming down with cancer."

"You don't know that for a fact!"

"Let him finish."

"Thanks. We can indeed say that. And in another week we'll be able to say that if they've tested anything, anywhere, that was supposed to significantly affect the health of the people, then the test was a failure."

"How?"

"Thank you. Over the last several years, we have had the government set up the national Epidemiological Survey Network, which has computerized the current data on things such as births, deaths, and the rates of every disease we know of. Although officially an HEW project—which means we didn't have to pay for it—the network was essentially designed by us and specifically for purposes like this. We've already carried out a nationwide scan for increases in major diseases, fertility, infertility, and the like, and there was absolutely nothing significant in the country. For the last month the computer has been combing all the data for every abnormality in its memory for increases in the last six months. If they've done anything, we'll catch it when that data is recovered."

"And we'll have that back in a week?"

"One or two. We're already using a huge share of the time, and we don't want to attract attention to what we're doing, so we have to go slowly."

"Perhaps, then, we can put off this decision until next month, when we have the results?"

"Unless something big shows up. Then I want an emergency meeting."

"Of course, of course."

Pearson turned off the recorder. No wonder he was on Johnson's back so much. If those damn Russians tried anything subtle, it would be next to impossible to prove. What we need, he thought, is an equivalent weapon, so we can show them that we're on to them, and ready for them, without coming out in the open. Well, with luck, they'd have it next month. Then they'd be ready!

Friday, November 13

Doc was just finishing with his last patient for the day when Beth came in. She noted the empty waiting room and sat down. He'd been unusually busy lately, and their dinner dates had often pushed at the closing time of restaurants. Besides, he was always just a little more grumpy when he had to work unusually late. Sharon waved a hello to Beth. "He'll be out in ten minutes. And no one else is expected, so you can probably have a regular old dinner, just like normal people."

"How'd the day go?" Beth asked.

"Not bad at all. It's funny how you get absolutely mobbed for four days, and then on Friday it's almost calm. I think people are afraid to get sick on Friday. Means they lose the weekend." She smiled. "Our friend Diederson pulled a surprise visit this afternoon."

"Again?" Beth asked. "I thought he was here yesterday."

"He was." Sharon smiled. "But he's so clever, he figured that we thought he was only coming once a week, so he was hoping to catch all those druggies rushing in on Friday, since it would be safe. It's really funny. He's not at all sure about Fred anymore, and he's even starting to seem just a bit embarrassed by the whole thing. But for all I know, it might be a front."

Doc came bouncing out of his inner office, and swinging an arm around Beth, he steered her toward the door. "Time's up. No more thinking about such nasty subjects." Turning to Sharon, he started to say something, but she anticipated the request.

135

"I'll lock it up tight as a drum and make sure everything's off."

"Thanks," Doc said, and he and Beth headed out to the parking lot.

Over a quiet dinner they talked about the day. "That woman Waterper called Charlie today," Beth told Doc. "She received a call from the computer place down in Washington. They're a little farther behind than usual, I guess, but hope to have the results back to her in two weeks. Charlie was disappointed. He had to wait a week to find that out, and I think he felt that should somehow count as part of the two weeks."

Doc laughed. "I've got to hand it to him. When he gets going on something, he's a whirlwind. I'm surprised he didn't call Washington to explain why he needed his results immediately."

"Don't joke. He told me that he wanted to, but Waterper assured him it wouldn't do any good. He almost apologized for not calling anyway." She shook her head. "He's certainly going after it, though, I must agree." She picked some more lobster out of the shell. "It's even better than usual," she said, indicating the lobster. "Want to try it?"

"Thanks, not tonight. If I eat any more, you'll have to roll me home." He wrapped his arms around his stomach and made impolite moaning sounds.

Beth kicked him under the table. "Shut up," she whispered. "You'll have everyone in the restaurant staring."

He let out a huge belch by way of a response.

"My, but we're in a good mood tonight," Beth commented. "I'll have to be careful."

Doc laughed. "I promise to give you a ten-second warning before jumping you." Turning more serious, he asked, "Is there anything new on the job scene?"

Looking unhappy, Beth answered, "Nope. Nothing new came in today. Oh, wait!" She suddenly perked up. "I almost forgot. Guess who got a job offer today."

He was confused. "Not you?"

"Nope." She smiled. "Bill Hebb."

"Bill Hebb?" Doc asked, unbelieving. "I didn't even know he was looking for a job."

"He wasn't," Beth answered. "Guess who offered it to him."

Doc shook his head.

"Crop Research Associates."

"The group that Tom Darnell works for?" he asked. "That's insane. I thought Darnell shared your opinion of Hebb."

"So did I. I mean, it was Tom who finally tried to talk to Lloyd about Bill's incompetence. Admittedly, he hasn't completely wrecked anyone's experiments in the last few months, but Tom and I have almost quarantined our lab." She laughed. "Which doesn't eliminate all problems. Poor Tom knocked over a flask with radioactive nutrients in it yesterday, and we spent all afternoon decontaminating the lab."

"What does Tom say about the job offer?" Doc asked. Judging from the description he had gotten from Beth, the only way Bill Hebb could ever get a job would be if everyone who knew him lied and the employer never met him. It seemed impossible that CRA would hire him if Darnell was working with Bill and was in any sort of communication with CRA.

"He actually seemed embarrassed," Beth said. "Basically, all he said was that he certainly hadn't recommended Bill to them. CRA apparently wants someone besides Tom from our lab. He said that they just decided that regardless of his qualifications, if he worked for Haenners, he couldn't be all bad."

"Which is actually probably true," Doc said.

"Well, if it is he's certainly fooled me and Tom," Beth insisted. "In a way I'm glad, since it means that he'll be getting out of the lab before too long, but at the same time I think I've been insulted."

"I don't understand."

"That's the job they offered me! I felt good that someone wanted to hire me, but then they go and take Hebb. I'm not so sure that the whole thing isn't an insult!"

Doc laughed. "Well, at least Darnell won't be hassling you about taking the job."

"I wish," Beth complained. "But he actually went

out of his way to assure me that their hiring Bill in no way meant that their offer to me was being retracted. I almost laughed. I said that if I'd taken the job, part of the reason would have been to get away from Bill. He just shrugged and repeated his statement that he had been opposed to their hiring Bill. I think he really was unhappy about it."

Doc smiled sympathetically. "So I guess we don't even know whether to score the whole incident in the plus or minus column." He ate a clam and continued. "Then I take it there's nothing new on the faculty market."

Beth's gloom returned. "No, nothing. I think Lloyd's even more surprised than I am. He takes it quite personally. Makes it look like he's lost his influence. The only place that's offered me a job is in California, and Lloyd didn't know anyone at all there.

"Actually," she went on, "there are a couple of rejections that I don't understand. In one case I'd talked to the department chairman and he made it sound as if he'd be more than happy to make me an offer. It's almost like I've got a social disease."

"Maybe they know you had an offer from industry, and that turned them off," Doc suggested facetiously.

But Beth obviously didn't find it funny.

"Well," Doc continued with a wink, "I could always use a little extra help around the office."

"It's not funny!" she replied, obviously upset. "It happens to be my whole life you're joking about. What do I do if the only job offers I get are from a shitty corporation that Bill Hebb's working for, located off in the middle of Iowa, or else in L.A., where you can't breathe the air? I don't plan to spend the rest of my life as a goddamn cocktail waitress or a doctor's mistress!" Angered and upset, she pushed back her chair and stormed out of the restaurant.

Friday, November 20

Kip greeted Beth at the door. The babble of voices behind him told her that most of the people were already there. She smiled a greeting and gave Kip her coat. He lived in a typical Cambridgeport three-decker located on Brookline Avenue just off Central Square. The apartment was in a slightly decrepit state, but Kip had done a miraculous job of making the best of it. Holes in the plaster were covered with posters, and a brightly colored Chinese lantern shaded the bare bulb that hung from the living room ceiling. She peered into the room, her eyes adjusting to the dim light. "Doc with you?" Kip asked, still standing at the door.

"No," Beth said. "It was too confusing to make connections ahead of time, so we decided to get here by ourselves." She had been hoping that he was already there. They had only seen each other once since the incident at the restaurant a week ago, and that meeting had, of necessity, been brief. It was sniffles time in Boston, and Doc was swamped with patients.

Seeing Beth in the hallway, Ann rose and went to greet her. She was well into the third trimester and would enter her eighth month in just over a week. Her walk had begun to develop that characteristic waddle, and she was loving every minute of her pregnancy.

"Ann, you're looking great!" Beth said. "How're you feeling?"

"Fantastic," she answered, "although I must admit

that I'm starting to get just a little bit tired around evening time."

"I can believe it," Beth said, "what with carrying around that extra weight."

"Thirty-three pounds," Ann said. "Charlie says that after Disney's born I have to start carrying bigger packs when we go backpacking. I'm sure glad I'm not working now."

"I guess that forty years ago you'd have been advised to stay in bed from here on out."

Ann smiled. "And ten years ago I would have been told to keep my weight gain down to twenty pounds for the whole pregnancy. If I was doing that, I'd probably be in bed!" She laughed and they both headed into the living room. "I'm really glad you came," Ann said quietly. She and Charlie were the only ones who knew about her quarrel with Doc. "I'm tired of the woman always being excluded from the group when a couple has a fight. Let Doc stay home!"

"I thought he was coming," Beth asked. "Did he say something about not coming?"

Ann looked surprised. "I guess I'm not sure. Warren mentioned having seen Doc and that he said he wasn't sure if he'd make it." She seemed embarrassed. "Look, don't worry about it. He'll probably show if you think he will. I think you know him better than Warren does."

Beth tried to smile as they sat down on the couch.

"Hi, Beth," Justine called from a huge overstuffed chair across the room. "You should have been here ten minutes ago. Charlie was singing your praise."

"Oh?" Beth asked. "Have I done something I don't know about?"

"If you have," Kip said, "I doubt that Charlie'd know about it. He's just been filling me in on the ghoul story." Kip had been out of town touring for the last week and had only returned to Boston the day before. "Hey," he said, "Beth, you tell me what the survey said. I can't figure it out when Charlie explains it."

Beth laughed. "The reason you can't understand Charlie's explanation is because he doesn't want to admit that the data make no sense. First of all, since the ghoul picked seven of the top ten towns, he must have known they were in the top ten before he picked them, and hence, they must have been in the top ten for at least six months. So it would seem that they were in the top ten before the acid came to town. But Warren says he has a friend in Middletown, which was number three, who also had Gloryhits, and that suggests that there is a connection between the high rates and the acid. Which contradicts point one. So we're left with a paradox, which Charlie doesn't like." She smiled at Charlie, expecting a rebuttal.

"So," Charlie said, as if continuing for Beth, "instead of just going to parties and arguing about it incessantly, I decided that we should actually check and see how long the rates have been this high."

"Wait a minute," Kip interrupted. "I'm confused. How do we know that the other towns didn't get Gloryhits earlier than we did? Wouldn't that make sense?"

There was a moment's silence, and then Charlie said, "That would explain it all, except for us, because we didn't have it any earlier—we know that. But one town by chance is easier than seven. If the other towns got it early enough, then it might have shown up in the statistics before the ghoul picked his towns."

"Meaning," asked Ann, "that now we're saying that the acid did cause the increase in all these towns?"

Warren started to say something but was interrupted by Doc's entry. "Are you all still talking about that?" he complained. "I thought if I got here late enough you'd be done with it." He paused to give Beth a big hug. "Hi," he said to her, "sorry I'm late."

"I thought you weren't going to come," she whispered, relieved at his arrival. He kissed the back of her neck.

"None of that," Kip warned. "We're rewriting our theory."

For Doc's benefit, they went through the explanation again.

"So," Doc said, "when the results of the new survey

come back, we'll know in fact whether the rates were higher that far back, and we don't have anything more to say on the subject until then."

"Wait a minute," Warren complained. "You-all won't give me a chance to interrupt."

Everyone quieted down, and Warren said, "I don't think Tony said anything about their getting the acid in Middletown before Boston. In fact, I seem to remember us figuring that we got them a couple of days before he did."

"Haven't you gotten in touch with him yet?" Ann asked.

"No, but someone answered his phone last Tuesday when I tried calling and told me he should be back either this weekend or early next week."

"My, my," Doc said. "More progress. Will wonders never cease! So that's another part of the mystery that we don't have to talk about anymore tonight."

Charlie laughed. "Except, Warren, be sure to find out when Tony thinks they first showed up in Middletown, not just when *he* got them."

Warren agreed. "And now, for Doc's sake, I promise to say nothing more about it tonight."

A voice issued from the depths of the armchair. "Beth, how's the job market going? Or shouldn't I ask?"

"Shouldn't ask, Justine. It's really going sluggishly. Kind of depressing."

There was a moment of embarrassed silence. "Well," Kip finally said, "my week of touring wasn't a disaster at all, so there!" He pulled his guitar case out from under the couch and opened it. "And as a reward to all you hard-working scientists and amateur detectives, I shall now strum a few songs." And as everyone settled back and relaxed, he began to play.

Friday, November 27

A week later Charlie finally got the call from Barbara Waterper. The results of his search were in. Picking up Beth across the hall, he headed out across the courtyard to Waterper's lab. There was just the faintest touch of snow in the air, but Beth doubted that Charlie was even aware of it. He was in one of his hyper moods and was only aware of what his mind was set on—The Survey.

Up in her lab, Waterper handed him the envelope. "It came in the afternoon mail, and I haven't even opened it. I can't talk about it now—I'm in the middle of things." She was rushing from one bench to another, obviously in the middle of a harried experiment. "Give me a call tomorrow. I'm curious about what you got."

"Definitely," Charlie replied, tearing open the envelope.

Beth grabbed it from his hands. "I need some coffee," she announced. "You can look at it when we get to the cafeteria."

"Come on," Charlie pleaded, "lemme look at it while we walk over."

"No way," she replied, heading out the door ahead of him.

Charlie followed after her, complaining all the way to the cafeteria. Finally, after she was seated at a table, coffee in front of her, she opened the envelope, and Charlie pulled his seat around next to hers. For several minutes they just looked at the data, trying to comprehend it fully.

"When did Greene start collecting?" Beth asked.

"A year ago last December."

They just stared at the data, confused. "But until just this last June, the towns he was collecting from were right down there near the average. In fact, two of them were still below average in June."

Charlie stared at the data. "Meaning that the increases occurred after he started collecting. When he picked them, they were just average towns, with basically normal rates of spontaneous abortion."

"But every town he picked showed a huge increase in the rate of miscarriages," Beth said, "six months after he picked them?"

"I don't know," Charlie answered. "It certainly looks that way. No, wait," he said, changing his mind. "We only know about the towns that were in the top ten for July through September. He might have been looking at other towns, too, where there wasn't an increase."

"Oh, yeah, but come on," Beth insisted, "how many towns could he be monitoring? Ten? Fifteen? Greene has got to be connected to the Gloryhits."

"But how? You're right about the towns. I doubt that they'd try looking at more than ten, which makes his success at predicting increases rather remarkable." He thought for a minute. "Doc hasn't heard anything from them? No response to his note last month?"

Beth shook her head. "Nothing. And why are you dismissing the idea of a connection between Greene and the Gloryhits?"

"They should at least be willing to tell us which towns they picked and how they selected them," Charlie insisted. "I'd sure like to know that, at least, before dreaming up some outlandish conspiracy. I'm as paranoid about things as the next guy, but something like you're suggesting is just too bizarre."

Beth shrugged. "But there doesn't seem to be anything we can do, short of going to New York and trying to track Greene down."

Charlie nodded, then changed the subject. "By the way, did you hear about Warren?"

"No," Beth replied resignedly, giving up on her idea.

"He got in touch with that guy Tony Belvedere.

They did get the Gloryhits the same time as we did, which, given the data we just got, still fits. And only one shipment. Their rate increased about four months after the Gloryhits came to town, which is about when you'd expect to see it. Looks like Doc's hunch was right after all."

"You don't look too pleased," Beth observed.

Charlie frowned. "I'm starting to agree with you and Doc. It is scary. And it's terrible to think of all those people losing their kids just because someone made up a bad batch of acid. It makes me realize how close Ann and I came to losing Disney."

Beth nodded. "One person out there somewhere, being sloppy in making it, and tragic results. I hate people like that."

"Speaking of which," Charlie said, trying to change the subject again, "what's the word with Bill and the job offer? Is he taking it?"

Beth's expression turned sour. "Yes, he took the job. 'Jumped at it' would be more accurate. Went around just ecstatic over the salary. The guy doesn't even pretend that he's taking the offer for any other reason."

"Well, at least he should be out of the lab soon," Charlie said. "How soon do they want him to start?"

"That's the worst of it," she complained. "They've already put him on salary, but suggested that he stay here for a few more months. They want him to try getting some virus growing in tissue culture here, where Lloyd already has the culture conditions working well. They're afraid that if he moves down there right now, he might have trouble getting things growing and all."

"What's Lloyd's reaction to this?" Charlie asked.

"Lloyd?" Beth asked, laughing. "Tom went and talked to him. He asked Lloyd to clear it as a personal favor to him. Bill would be off payroll, so it wouldn't cost Lloyd anything except supplies, and Tom suggested that something could be arranged, like around ten thousand dollars in supply money."

Charlie whistled. "That's a lot of support money for just a couple of months. Would he really spend that much?"

"Don't be silly," Beth said. "It's just a stupid bribe

from CRA. And Lloyd's not proud. He jumped at it."

Charlie was sympathetic. "So it looks like you'll have old Bill Hebb around a little longer. Well, it shouldn't be any worse than before."

"You're wrong," Beth insisted, "because now he's going to be working with some cell types that none of us use. We'll have to worry about contamination, and I'm terrified at the thought of his bringing a virus in here. I even mentioned it to Lloyd, because Bill is such a slob. But Lloyd said that Tom would be supervising his work carefully, so I shouldn't worry. Well, maybe he's not worried, but I'm terrified."

Charlie smiled. "Still, sloppy as he is, it's not very likely that he'd do anything horrendous in just a couple of months."

"You don't know him," Beth insisted. "He can mess things up faster than the human mind can comprehend!"

"Well, we'll see. Maybe you and Doc can run off for a vacation or something. Get away from the lab for a week or so."

Beth frowned. "I don't know."

Charlie's eyebrows rose. "Things not so good?"

"Oh, I can't tell," she admitted, exasperated. "It's all messed up with this job thing. The only offer I've received is one from the West Coast. Fred doesn't want me to leave the area, and I guess I'd just as soon not leave, but the situation is getting bleak. Now he's suggesting that maybe I could stay on with Lloyd until I find something in the area. But how can I do that? I can't turn down my career just to stay around here."

"Is the relationship that serious?" Charlie asked.

"I don't know, and Fred doesn't either. I know that he's not ready to adapt to my plans if they mean leaving Boston. And I have no intention of running my life around a man, no matter how serious the relationship is."

Charlie replied sympathetically, "I don't know what to tell you, Beth. I hope something turns up around here."

"All I know," Beth answered, staring into her coffee

cup, "is that my decision has to be based on what's best for me, and for my career. Not what's best for Fred, or me and Fred. I *know* I want a career, and I'm not so sure about him."

Wednesday, December 2

Charlie sat at his desk. The arrival of December had brought a psychological increase in the pressure from teaching. Finals would be in three weeks, and in addition to squeezing into the next two weeks all the material he had somehow failed to get in earlier, he also had to prepare a final exam. The students felt the approach of finals, too, and there was generally more tension in the classroom.

His work in the lab had again dropped to near zero. At least he wouldn't be teaching next semester. That would give him a chance to get things moving a little. He shuffled through some of the papers on his desk. Shit, he thought, all I've done since lunch is shuffle papers. Irritated, he pulled out the results of the epidemiological survey. Since they'd come back last week, he'd avoided looking at them again. They seemed to be a dead end until Greene could be contacted. He hadn't made his November pickup, and Doc was worried about it. He had even gone so far as to check with the Boston University student employment office to see if Greene had tried to hire someone again. But there had been no such request.

He looked at the data. As far as they knew, only Boston and Middletown had gotten the acid. And both had shown a jump in the rate of miscarriages about

four months later. How had Greene picked the towns?
All seven that he'd picked were normal when he started
collecting, and they all increased around June or July.
How had he known? Suddenly connections closed in
Charlie's mind. They'd *all* increased in June or July,
not just Boston and Middletown. And that suggested
that they'd all gotten the Gloryhits! A cold shock
swept his body.

He needed more information. That was all there was
to it, and suddenly he needed the data fast. He looked
over the list. New Haven. If Gloryhits had come to
New Haven, Terry Bernett might either know or be
able to find out. Charlie dug through a pile of papers
on his desk until he found his phone list. Bernett, a
friend from graduate school, was at Yale now, in the
biology department. He dialed the number and waited
impatiently for someone to answer.

"Dr. Bernett's office." It was his secretary.

"This is Charlie Cotten calling. I'd like to speak with
Dr. Bernett."

"I'm sorry," she said, "but he's taken the afternoon
off. Could I take a message?"

He made up his mind in an instant. "No, thanks,
I'll get in touch with him later." Hanging up, he started
gathering his notes on the results of the last survey,
then pulled those on the first one out of his files. If he
left now, he could be at Terry's house by four. The
trip would possibly be worth the drive if only to have
someone new look over the data.

Calling Ann at home, he explained what he was
doing. She didn't like the idea, but Charlie was adamant. He was out of the door within two minutes of
hanging up.

Traffic around Boston was slow, and it was past two
before Charlie was out of the city area and traveling
west on the tollway. Driving at a steady seventy, he
tried to put all the pieces together, but they still
wouldn't fit. It was frustrating to the point of irritation. Highway 86 down through Connecticut was
empty. A vast expanse of concrete, stretching to the
horizon, it ran through forests and fields, an incongru-

ous artificial fault line, cutting across nature. He pushed the old Volvo just a bit, trying to get down to New Haven before traffic within the city got too painfully congested. It had become almost impassable a few years back, before they had instituted a major mass-transit program, and it was moving back toward that state again.

He reached the city limits at four-thirty and spent a half hour creeping through the streets to Terry's house. Finally finding a parking space, he walked the five blocks back to the house and rang the bell. Suddenly feeling a bit foolish, he imagined Terry out for the evening. He hadn't even thought about such a possibility, which surprised him. It wasn't typical of his approach to things.

But after a few moments the door opened on a woman in her early twenties. She was unfamiliar to Charlie. "Hi," he said, "I'm looking for Terry Bernett."

Smiling, she opened the door wider to let him in. "He's hiding upstairs in his study. Don't take it personally if he throws you out—he's trying to finish writing a paper that was supposed to have been in the mail last Monday."

Charlie walked in. He hadn't seen Terry or his house in two years. The house looked less neat but at the same time more comfortable, and it was almost overcrowded with furniture. He could hear voices coming from the kitchen.

"Do you know the way up?" she asked. She was quite pleasant, Charlie noted. Basically average looking, with eyes that appeared intensely alert and seemed to take in everything about him.

"No, thanks, I've been here before," he answered, and headed up the stairs. Stopping at the closed study door, he knocked gently.

"Go away!" a gruff voice answered. "Crime and pestilence are rampant in here."

Charlie opened the door and stuck his head in. "So how's that different from the rest of the East Coast?"

Terry looked up to see who the intruder was. His hair was longer than Charlie had remembered, and he was starting to bald on top. Terry was tall and muscular, with an intensity about him that made one expect to see a hawk casually land on his shoulder. Under the wrong circumstances, he could be terribly intimidating.

"Charlie!" he cried, his stern, disapproving glare dissolving into a smile. "Where'd you come from?" He rose from his desk and charged across the room. Pumping Charlie's hand, he asked, "How long are you staying? Can you join us for dinner?" He looked back at his desk. "You picked a perfectly shitty time to arrive, but come on downstairs and tell me what you've been doing with yourself lately. I heard from Steve Mills that you were coming out to Boston, but I just haven't had time to look you up yet." Retracing Charlie's steps, they went down to the living room. The woman who had let Charlie in was now curled in a chair reading what looked like a medical text. She looked up, surprised.

"Margie, this is Charlie Cotten, an old friend from graduate school days."

She smiled at Charlie. "We've already sort of met," she explained. "I told him you'd probably kick him out."

"Naw," Terry said. "Decided I'd take a little time off instead."

Margie looked at him disapprovingly. "You're going to be lucky if that paper gets out this week at all."

"Nope," Terry insisted, "two more hours work is all I've got left. Unless Charlie's nice enough to stay over with us, I'll get it done tonight."

"We'll see," Charlie replied. "I might take you up and stay, but I can hide if it will make it easier for you to work."

"He'll stop writing for the most pathetic excuses you can imagine," Margie said. "He'd love to have you stay all week."

Charlie smiled. "Looks as though he's turning out like everyone else."

"Well," Margie said, rising from her chair, "I've retained a little discipline, so I'm going upstairs until dinner time. If Charlie's staying for dinner, you should tell Michael and Allison. I think they've already started."

"You'll stay?" Terry asked.

"Sure," Charlie agreed easily. "I was sort of counting on an invite."

Terry took him out to the kitchen and briefly introduced him to the two people working on dinner, explaining that Charlie would be joining them.

Back in the living room he explained, "We have people over unexpectedly so often that we almost automatically cook for one extra."

"Margie and the two in the kitchen live here, I take it?"

"Sure," Terry said. "It's a huge place, and I got bored living the exotic life of a bachelor. It's so much nicer having other people you like around. Some of the faculty think I'm a little strange for having a bunch of housemates. But screw 'em! It's my choice." He laughed heartily. "But tell me about yourself. How've you been? Ann still with you?"

"Very much so," he answered. "It's incredible how times have changed. Nowadays whenever you meet someone you haven't seen in a long time, you don't ask them how their husband or wife is, you ask if they're still together."

Terry shrugged. "What can you do?" he asked. "After you've blundered through asking half a dozen divorced people how their spouses are, you get a bit more cautious. I almost said I'd be surprised if you and Ann had broken up, but actually, I've given up trying to guess which relationships are stable and which aren't. There's no way to tell."

"It's true," Charlie agreed. "I do the same thing. But we're very much together. In fact, we're even in the family way."

Terry looked delighted. "Fantastic! It's about time some good people started having kids. I was starting to worry that the world was going to the dogs, just on the basis of relative reproductive rates. When is she due?"

"February seventh, plus or minus a couple of weeks," he answered.

"That's great," Terry said.

For the next hour they talked about the last two

years, discussing the similarities and differences in their experiences. Terry had been on the faculty at Yale for two years and was getting used to the concept. "I'm not crazy about New Haven," he admitted, "but I'm happy with the lab and the department I'm in."

They were interrupted by a whistle from the kitchen. "That means it's time for dinner," he explained, and they went into the dining room.

"What brings you down from Boston, Charlie?" Allison asked when they were seated.

"Actually, that's a very complicated question. The answer's a mystery. I mean it's a mystery that brought me down here."

Everyone looked appropriately interested.

"You've become a better storyteller," Terry commented.

"Well," Charlie said, "it's not so simple to explain." He tried to figure out how to start. "Say," he decided, "have any of you heard of some acid called Gloryhits?"

Michael looked up. The answer was obvious before he spoke. "Do you have an in to some?" he asked. "It's the nicest acid we've ever seen around here. Lots of people would like some more."

Charlie realized that he was upset. The whole scene reminded him of the party he had thrown when they had first moved into their new home. Kip had shown the same interest when he had mentioned the Gloryhits. Now he would get to play the role of Doc. "No, I haven't heard any news of any around in a long time. When did people around here get it?"

"It was a long time ago," Michael replied. "Last winter, wasn't it?"

"No," Allison said. "Wasn't it spring?"

"No, I'm right," Michael insisted. "It was at the tail end of winter, around the end of February. I remember because there was the issue of whether to wait until after exams to drop it."

Terry agreed. "You're right. It was around the twentieth, because, Michael, you complained that it came right after the Portrell concert, and that was on the fifteenth."

They all agreed. "That seems to be about when it showed up in other places, too," Charlie confirmed.

"Just that one shipment?" Michael asked. "We never saw it around here again. It's surprising, because it was good shit, and there was a market for it."

"There was only one shipment in Boston that we know of," Charlie answered, "and it's the same story in Middletown—just once around the middle of February."

"You seem to be an expert on the subject," Terry said.

Charlie frowned. "It's starting to look that way. Not that I'm particularly pleased with the status."

Terry looked confused. "I take it this is part of the mystery you alluded to?"

Charlie nodded and began to explain.

"Hold it," Margie objected fifteen minutes later. "It's making less and less sense. What are you suggesting this second survey indicates?"

Charlie held up his hands. "Wait a minute. I'm not getting a chance to eat. Wait till after dinner, and we can go over the survey results themselves. I brought them with me to show Terry. In the meantime, someone else talk so I can catch up on dinner."

Agreeing with him, the others turned the conversation to other topics while Charlie ate ferociously. Between the drive and the discussion, he found himself ravenous.

After dinner they spread out the computer results on the cleaned table and looked them over. "Let me see if I understand," Terry said. "First, there are these seven towns from which this guy Greene is collecting fetuses. There may be other towns, but these seven are in the top ten in frequency of spontaneous abortions at three to five months. Two, when he began collecting fetuses, none of the seven towns were showing unusually high rates of spontaneous abortions."

Allison spoke up. "Number three is that at least three of the seven had Gloryhits around late last winter."

"And we don't know about the other four," Charlie pointed out.

"But you also don't know how many other places around here had Gloryhits but didn't have high rates of abortion," Terry objected. "If Gloryhits were sold in a hundred towns up and down the coast, it's not surprising that you'd find it reflected in these three towns, too."

"Except," Michael objected, "that we called people in a dozen places trying to get our hands on some more, and no one had even heard of them."

"Wait a minute!" Allison said. "That's not true. Someone had heard of them but had been unable to get their hands on any. Who was it?"

"You're right," Michael said. "I remember that. But I can't remember who it was."

"I know!" Allison said. "Ursula Stringer, in Providence, said that there had been a bunch in town, but she'd been away when it came in, and it was all gone by the time she got back."

Charlie looked at their list of towns. It checked. "Well," he said, "change that to four out of seven. It's looking more and more likely to me."

"You mean that all seven got Gloryhits?" Margie asked.

"Wait a minute!" Terry insisted. "I want to get straight what we know first, then we can go on to what we think, or think we think." He paused. "Number three was that, let me correct it, that four of the seven towns, at least, had Gloryhits sold late last winter. Allison, your friend in Providence said it was about the same time?"

"I'm sure," she replied. "Within a few weeks, at the worst."

"Okay," Terry continued. "That's number three. Number four is that in Boston there was a high correlation between taking the acid and these miscarriages."

"With the acid being taken before conception," Charlie pointed out. "That's one of the hookers. It can't be a teratogenic agent."

"Right," Terry said, writing it down. "And then number five is that in at least three cases, the aborted fetuses had grossly enlarged heads, which means it couldn't just be a simple mutagenic agent, either."

"That's it," Charlie said. "I think we've hit them all."

They all sat quietly for a few seconds, trying to think if they had forgotten anything. "Well, then," Margie said, "we're left with two questions. First, what's with the acid? And second, what's with this Greene character?" She looked from one to another of them, hoping someone would have an idea.

"Obviously," Michael said, "you'd guess that there's a connection between Greene and the acid, that he knew ahead of time that it was going to increase the abortion rate."

"But that doesn't make any sense at all!" Charlie insisted. "Someone back in Boston suggested that, too, and it just doesn't make any sense."

"Why not?" Allison asked. "Maybe he wanted to see if acid had any effects on fetuses in humans."

"No, that clearly doesn't make any sense," Terry said. "Because then it would be critically important for him to know who'd taken the acid and who hadn't and, especially, when it was taken. Otherwise, you'd never be able to do anything with the data. Besides, why would he be so secretive about it? He could just ask the obstetricians to try to find out whether the patients had taken LSD, and if so, when. That wouldn't be so hard to do."

"But how else can you explain it?" Allison insisted.

"That," said Charlie, "is the mystery."

They all sat around quietly for a few minutes, looking at the computerized results of the searches, reading and rereading Terry's list of knowns.

"I'm trying to decide," Margie said, "whether more data would be of any use."

"More data?" Michael asked.

"Sure," she explained. "Like whether there really were Gloryhits sold in the other three towns and whether there's this correlation between the acid and the miscarriages that they found in Boston. I mean, if it's just in Boston that the correlation exists, it might be explained in other ways."

"You're right," Charlie said. "In fact, if it doesn't correlate in the other towns, then probably it isn't due to the acid at all."

"So we want more data," Terry concluded. "Let's get it!"

"How?" Charlie asked, confused by the sudden turn to action.

"How do you think?" Terry asked, pulling the telephone in from the kitchen on a long cord. "Find people who know."

They spent the rest of the evening on the phone. Finally, at midnight, they called it quits. Their results were fantastic. Or terrible, depending on the point of view. People in two of the three remaining towns verified the fact that Gloryhits had been around the previous February, making six out of the ghoul's seven towns. And in New Haven and Providence they traced down cases of people who had taken the Gloryhits shortly before conceiving a child and then had spontaneous abortions at three or five months.

Charlie had never felt the contradiction between the scientist and the humanist more sharply. Margie summed it up. "Christ, here I am feeling elated at our having done such a great job of building up a good, sound data base, and at the same time I feel like I want to be sick. The whole thing is so depressing."

"But where do we go from here?" Charlie wondered out loud.

"It's too bad you don't have more of the stuff," Margie lamented. "If you did, you could do laboratory tests."

"You'd need hundreds of hits to get any reasonable data anyhow," Allison pointed out.

"Not at all," Terry said. "If you used rats, one hit would be good for fifty to a hundred rats, on a weight basis, and that's how you do those experiments."

"Of course!" Charlie shouted. "I've been working so close to it that I never thought of that. Help me design the experiments, and I can start them as soon as I get back to Boston."

"So what?" Margie said. "There's not a chance of your finding any Gloryhits now."

"But I have some," Charlie insisted. "I've got seven hits stashed away in my freezer!"

All hell broke loose. When calm finally returned, they were all exhausted. It was nearly two in the morning. "I don't believe it," Charlie said, looking over the plans for the experiments that they'd drawn up. "I've gotten more done tonight than we did back in Boston during the last two months."

"I think you were all pretty much burned out up there," Terry said. "Half the reason you came here was to get a fresh opinion."

"It's true," Charlie agreed. "I just never thought it would be so useful."

Margie yawned loudly. "Well," she said, "I don't know about the rest of you, but I'm going to bed."

Charlie looked at his watch. "Oh, Christ!" He thought for a minute. "Terry, I think I'm going to head back tonight. I had planned to sleep here and leave at six this morning, but that'd be even worse." He started gathering up all his papers.

"Are you sure? It's a mean drive when you're sleepy."

Charlie shook his head. "I'll fill up on coffee and just think about the experiments."

"Leave a window down," Michael suggested. "That air will keep you awake."

Charlie promised. Putting on his coat, he thanked them all again. "I'll keep in touch. I really appreciate your help." They all said good-bye.

As he walked to his car, the cold winter air stung his face. But somehow it wasn't quite sufficient to remove the feeling of unreality that hung around the evening's events. It would take a while for him to soak it all up.

Thursday, December 3

An hour out of New Haven it began to snow. Not hard, but enough to make driving treacherous and to add an hour and a half to the driving time. He arrived home at six-thirty. Climbing into bed, he tried not to awaken Ann.

"Charlie?" she mumbled, half asleep.

"Hi, go back to sleep."

"Wha' time is it?"

"It's late, go to sleep," he whispered. She rolled over and fell asleep. Full as his mind was, he soon followed suit.

Ann woke him at nine.

"Lemme sleep," he complained.

"Come on, your class is in an hour," she said, opening the curtains to let the sunlight in. "What time did you get home? I didn't hear you."

He pulled the blankets over his head. "Six-thirty."

"When?" she asked, pulling the covers back.

"Six-thirty! Lemme sleep!" But he was slowly waking up. His head felt like a Chinese gong ringing in the New Year. "Oh, Christ," he complained, "I'm such a wreck, I don't believe it. Teaching that class is really going to hurt."

And it did.

But at eleven-fifteen, half asleep, he was trying to go over the previous night's events with Beth. Finally she laughed. "Charlie, go back to bed. I can't understand half the things you're saying. Much as I'm interested, let's talk tomorrow."

Mumbling a mild objection, he stumbled back to his

158

lab, grabbed his coat, and drove home to his warm bed.

Charlie was his normal self on Friday, and he went over the ideas for the experiments with Beth. Rats were ordered, and they'd be starting the experiments on Monday. On Saturday evening they filled the rest of the crew in on the details of Charlie's visit. They had gotten together at Doc's apartment.

"The rat experiments might be the most important," Beth agreed. "We can start to find out what it is we're dealing with, at least in terms of the effect if not the agent."

Ann had joined them late. "Can you give me a simple synopsis of what's being planned?"

"Sure," Charlie said, "love to."

"Simple, short, I mean," she warned.

"Okay," Charlie complained jokingly. "One-minute summary: We'll take a single hit of acid and dissolve it in water. We know from the analysis we made when we bought the acid that'll be equivalent to seventy-five hits for a rat. So we've got a hundred and twenty female rats coming in tomorrow at the lab. We'll give the acid to eighty-five of them and then induce ovulation in all of them with hormones. Within a couple of days they should all go into heat, and by supplying them with mates, we should get around a hundred pregnant. The normal gestation period is only twenty-one days in rats, so everything happens a lot faster. What we plan to do is carry out Caesarean sections at different ages to look at the development of the fetuses —see if they're deformed or not, see if they're dying, and that sort of stuff. And we'll also let a whole batch of them go normally to see if any are born, or what. Presumably some will be unaffected, but we'll have to see. There, that only took a minute."

"So you're just going to confirm in rats what we know is happening in humans?" she asked, somewhat confused. "I don't see how you're learning anything from that. And besides, how do you know that it'll work the same in both the rats and people? I've never understood how scientists make that leap of faith."

"It's not just confirming what we know is happening in humans," Charlie explained. "It's proving it. We don't know that it was the Gloryhits that caused the problem with the patients that Doc's run across. The odds are good, especially in light of the news from New Haven, Middletown, and Providence, but that doesn't prove it. This way we can. We can say that the rats that received this acid had miscarriages, or smaller litters, or deformed offspring, while the controls didn't. Then we know that it was the acid that did it, and that's what's important. In fact, I'm not sure that we have enough, but we could try to isolate the active factor in the acid, assuming that it's not the LSD itself."

"And that's just part of it," he continued. "In addition, if we do get deformed fetuses, we can look more closely at the nature of the deformities. A lot of the information we were trying to get from Greene we can probably get from the rat embryos. Especially if we see this thing with the enlarged heads, then we could do some dissections and see what we find."

"Another thing," Beth added, "although it's probably more difficult to extrapolate to humans, would be to look at the frequency of the deformity. We know from your case, Ann, that not everyone who takes the acid must have a fetus abort at three to five months. With the rats we can see how often they go to term and whether they're normal or not. But as I said, I'm not sure how well we can extrapolate the number. However, when you ask whether or not it causes deformities and miscarriages, you're dealing with an all-or-none phenomenon, so if we get an answer of yes, we can be pretty sure that it's what we think. If the heads are enlarged, we can also assume that it's for the same reason as for the human fetuses."

Ann wasn't listening. "What do you mean, see if they're normal? The ones that are born?"

There was a sudden silence as the others realized what Ann was asking. Doc finally answered. "You would have to say that there's a possibility that a deformed fetus could go to term. But so far we've had absolutely no indication that that can happen." He tried to say it as gently as possible.

"I—I guess I hadn't thought of that," she said, biting back tears. She turned to Charlie for help.

Coming to her side, he put his arms around her. "It's only a theoretical possibility," he insisted. "There's no reason at all to think that it might actually happen."

She bit her lip nervously. Looking at the others, she tried to smile. "I think I'd like to get some air," she said. Charlie helped her up and got their coats. She was past seven months, and very pregnant.

"We'll be back in a while," Charlie said, and they headed out the front door.

Doc shook his head. "I told him to tell her that four months ago. It's going to be a lot harder to deal with now."

"I hope it doesn't screw things up for the next two months," Justine commented.

"Well, if it does," Doc charged, "it's Charlie's fault. He knew he was hiding it from her."

"I feel shitty about having brought it up," Beth said. "If I hadn't been so dense . . ."

"Bullshit!" Doc exploded. "Charlie can't go out and lie by omission, and then expect the rest of the world to cover for him, when they don't even know what the lie was."

"I know," Beth muttered, "but I still feel shitty about it."

Doc put an arm around her. "Nobody's glad it happened."

They sat there, imagining Ann's anguish. Finally, changing the subject, Kip turned to Beth. "I hear you're having some problems of your own at work."

"Oh?" Beth asked. "Which ones?"

Kip laughed. "Charlie started telling me something about this guy Bill—I don't remember his last name."

"Oh, yeah," Beth said. "Bill Hebb. I'm not exactly having trouble with him; I'm just expecting it." She explained about Bill's new job.

"When does he start working with this virus?" Justine asked.

"Any day, I guess. Some tissue cell lines came to-day, along with what I think was a frozen stock of the virus. I guess he'll start working on getting the cells to grow first."

"Isn't Tom Darnell working with him?" Doc asked.

"He will be," Beth affirmed, "but he's on one of his reporting trips now, so until he gets back the middle of next week, Bill's on his own."

"What are these trips?" Doc hadn't heard of them.

"Oh, every month or so they fly him back to their headquarters in Iowa—so he can report on his work, I guess, and talk to some of the researchers there about their work. He's some sort of big shot in their re-search division. Hopefully, he'll get the story about this stuff that Bill's trying to work with at the same time. I think I'll feel better about it after that."

"It's some sort of plant virus?" Kip asked.

"I assume," Beth said. "I can't imagine what else they'd be working on. Christ, I hope it is." She laughed. "But I doubt that even Tom in his present double role would let Bill toy with anything dangerous. Bill's so sloppy!"

"He won't just be working on the same cell line that you are?" Justine asked.

"No, I'm using this line because I'm working on the corn-blight problem. Presumably Bill will be working on some other problem. I know there's been a lot of talk about a fungal infection that's begun to hit the soybean crop and that could really be disastrous if it spread. He's probably working on something like that."

Just then the door opened, and Charlie and Ann entered. Ann's face was ashen, and she turned toward the kitchen without coming into the living room. Char-lie came in. "Ann's sort of tired," he explained lamely. "I think we're going to head home."

After the others had left, Beth still felt bad. "It was such a stupid thing to say," she complained to Doc.

Doc just sat quietly in his chair.

Monday, December 7

1

In Washington, personnel from Military Intelligence had gathered quickly for an urgent meeting.

"Gentlemen, I'd like to start off by apologizing for the sudden change in the date of this meeting. Moving it forward from next Friday to this Monday was necessitated by some developments at the tail end of last week and over the weekend. I have also jumbled up the agenda, for reasons that should become clear. Pearson, would you start?"

"Certainly. You all have folios containing Johnson's most recent report, which we received here on Friday. You should also have my summary, attached at the back of his report. In short, Johnson has tested the efficacy of his newly constructed 'influenza botulinum' strains, and has isolated six lines of virus, each containing a distinct mutator attached to the attenuated botulinum toxin gene. They have been named with suffixes describing the effectiveness of the virus kill. I'd like to spend a moment on them. You'll remember from when I spoke to you about the mutators last September that the virus's kill potential was expressed in terms of the number of people in a city of one million who would be killed if one hundred people were initially infected. The suffix employed in our nomenclature is that number divided by one hundred—that is, the number of people killed for each individual in the initial one hundred infected. Thus, if there was no spread of infectivity, the suffix would be one, and if

163

there was one-hundred-percent stability of the botulinum genes, then the suffix would be ten thousand. Based on the studies in tissue culture, the six strains are numbered 1.25, 3, 10, 78, and 4250. What this means is that we have strains of the virus that will kill, at the least, one extra person for each four initially infected and, at the most, half the population in a city of one million. In the former case, one could assume no spread to other cities, and no ability to isolate the active botulinum virus on the part of the enemy. In the latter case, both of these events should be expected. Obviously, their uses differ."

"How close to a production stage are they?"

"The project has been moving with amazing speed. I would say that it would be possible to start the production of the virus for deployment immediately. On the other hand, the speed with which this project has moved has disallowed much of the rehashing and reevaluation that would normally have occurred during the course of its development. In some ways, the project has proceeded at a reckless pace. On at least one occasion it was quite clear that Johnson had let the project develop so quickly that even the most basic precautionary measures for protecting those working within the laboratory were temporarily forgotten. To me this is not a good sign, and I would recommend that a six-month moratorium on all further work be imposed, so we can think about everything that's been done."

"While the Russians move on?"

"Gentlemen. I would like to get all of the reports out before we get into a debate. Are there any more questions of a factual nature?"

"I take it that we now have a virus strain which could be deployed almost instantly, would kill only a small number of people, would not involve the risk of a significant spread, and yet would make it clear to the authorities in the area that something very unusual, shall we say, was occurring?"

"I think that strain 1.25 would make clear to the Russians what we had."

"Thank you. That was beautifully blunt."

"Are there further questions? Then let's move on to Gabardine."

"Agent Gabardine was spotted at the meetings of the Federation of Societies of Experimental Biology in Atlantic City last week. Your folders include photographs. You'll see that he has once again switched wigs. His facial tone is the same as it was at Squaw Valley. He was spotted on the last day, and to our knowledge he made contact with no one at the meetings. A tail was put on him, and he was followed back to New York City, where he checked into the Biltmore. On Saturday he made contact with one Ralph Masco, who lives by himself in an apartment on Cathedral Parkway. He spent an hour and a half in Masco's apartment, while we tried ineffectively to get a bug on them. At one point their voices could be heard in the hall, and they were clearly arguing. No words could be understood. After that, he returned to the Biltmore and took the elevator up to fourteen, or so we think. We never saw him again."

"Did he spot the tail?"

"It doesn't seem likely. The agent who was on him at Atlantic City said that Gabardine just seemed to assume he was being followed. He's clearly well trained."

"What about Masco?"

"We're doing everything we can. His apartment is totally bugged now, and as soon as we know his movements better, we'll try to place some on his clothing. But that takes a while. We've moved an agent in down the hall, and she'll do what she can to get to know him. Unless he's funny, it shouldn't take long. She's good."

"Anything about what the guy does with himself?"

"He deals dope."

"What?"

"He sells drugs. Mostly around Columbia University. Soft stuff—grass, LSD, amphetamines. As far as we've been able to tell, no heroin or the like. He's got a large amount of LSD in his apartment, but we couldn't find any evidence of narcotics. No setups or anything."

"Do you think Gabardine's visit might have been for pleasure?"

"Doubtful, if he was still assuming a possible tail. Presumably he wouldn't make any unnecessary contacts under the conditions."

"I'm not so sure. Oh, well, this is not a debate; it can wait."

"There's just one more thing that may or may not fit anywhere. He was first spotted at a session on DNA excision enzymes, which we had predicted he would attend if he came to the FASEB meetings at all. But when followed, he spent the afternoon at a symposium on the genetics of human intelligence. Our current hypothesis is that he was either laying a false trail or expecting to meet someone who never showed."

"I know this question is out of place, but may I assume that appropriate steps will be taken to see that if he's spotted again he won't be lost so easily?"

"We weren't expecting someone quite this professional. There was no way we could have known ahead of time. Don't worry. We won't lose him again."

"Are there any factual questions?"

"Have you considered getting information from this Masco guy? If he's in the drug subculture, we might be able to work him with truth serum without his even being aware that that's what hit him."

"We have considered that, and we'll discuss it later."

"Very good."

"Any others? Then, Cortman, give your report on the epidemiological survey."

"Right. We may, and we may not, have turned up something. It's not totally clear, but there are definitely strange things going on. Along the New England corridor we've picked up eight towns, or districts, where there has been a sudden and dramatic increase in the rate of spontaneous abortions in women during their second trimester, a normally safe period of pregnancy. All eight towns have increased from relatively average rates last February, March, and April to rates that put them among the twelve New England districts with the highest rates of second-trimester miscarriages during the months of June, July, and August. We are in the process of determining statistically how likely or unlikely it is that a concerted jump could occur just by chance. But there's another factor that makes it clear that this phenomenon is not purely chance. Someone has been collecting all spontaneously aborted fetuses from those eight districts, and four others, since last December. We're in the process of trying to trace this person and find out what his game is, but that'll take a while."

"Nothing unusual about the other four towns?"

"Not that we've been able to tell. They might just be controls."

"I'm not quite sure what we're supposed to make of this. Is this some sort of Russian attack?"

"I'm not sure if you mean that question seriously or not."

"Neither am I."

"We are considering the possibility that the Russians are testing out an aborting agent, either chemical or biological. But it'll take a lot of tracking down to find out anything about it. Our best hope now is to locate the guy who's been collecting the fetuses."

"I take it he's doing it openly?"

"At least in Providence, where we made contact with an obstetrician. He picks them up once a month, somewhere around the twenty-fourth. We're checking the other towns to see if we might be able to put a tail on him sooner than that. The twenty-fourth is almost three weeks away."

"What about the women who had the abortions? Anything in common?"

"Haven't had time to look at it yet, but we're working on it."

"What might we be dealing with here, at the worst?"

"At the worst? An infectious agent that causes abortions, perhaps much the same as German measles causes deformities. But perhaps it's something without any other symptoms, so that it would take twenty years to isolate it and prepare an immunization against it, during which time there would be no children born in the U.S. At the worst, it's very bad."

"Are you suggesting that conceivably such an attack could already have been launched?"

"No, not in these towns. There has been absolutely no spread, and in fact, there are indications that the rates may be dropping back, suggesting that it was a single-hit event. But it could have been a test. The collecting of the fetuses suggests something like that."

"What do you think the odds are for something like that going on?"

"It seems clear to me that someone is testing something and that the something is not very pleasant."

"Pearson, do you still feel that strongly about a six-month moratorium?"

"What can I say? Given the new information, I would support a move to stockpile virus, but I still want a moratorium on deployment. You have to understand that this is a whole new field, and it could be catastrophic if something went wrong."

"Wouldn't it be rather catastrophic if there were no births in this country for the next twenty years?"

"Don't be an ass. I'm saying that there isn't any clear need to act this month, or next month."

"Except to warn the Russians not to start something, perhaps?"

"But what's to keep them from interpreting our move as an attack, as opposed to a warning?"

"Could we talk about stockpiling, gentlemen, rather than deployment? Am I correct in perceiving that there is a consensus that stockpiling would be appropriate at this time? I ask because, as you all know, it would be in violation of international treaty, and it might take a while to convince certain parties of its necessity."

"Is anyone opposed to a request for authority to stockpile?"

No one spoke.

"Then I shall request that authority immediately."

2

Beth arrived at the lab at a quarter to nine on Monday morning. She and Charlie had agreed to start at nine sharp. Even so, it would be a long day. The rats had arrived at eight, so Beth began sorting them out into cages of three, labeling those that would be controls, those scheduled for Caesareans, and so on. By the time she got them all set up, it was a quarter to ten and there was no sign of Charlie. Irritated, she decided to start setting up the paperwork. The most critical part of the day's work would be seeing that the rats got the right doses, that the experimental and control rats were kept separated, and that accurate records were kept of everything done. So she spent just over an hour tediously setting up a data sheet for each rat, with places to record daily weight, observations, reports on when the rats got or would get the hormone injections, when they went into heat, when mated, and so on. She was annoyed with having to do it all herself, as she had expected Charlie at nine. It was eleven when she finished. No longer willing to work by herself, she grabbed a journal and sat down to read.

Finally, at noon, she called Charlie at home. Ann answered.

"Hi, Ann, this is Beth. How are you?"

"Feeling better, thanks. What can I do for you?"

"Is Charlie still there? I was expecting him at nine."

"He just left two minutes ago." Ann sounded apologetic. "It's my fault he's late. I guess I'm still a bit shook up about Saturday night, and I made him stay around until I was feeling better."

"Oh," Beth insisted, "that's okay. I just thought maybe he forgot or something, and I figured I'd call to remind him."

"No, he remembered." Ann sounded depressed.

"Ann, I'm really sorry about Saturday night. It was a stupid thing for me to have said like that."

"Why?" Ann asked. "Because you wanted to protect me from the truth, too? I mean, I'm not happy about the news, but at least someone finally told me what everyone else seemed to know." It didn't sound as if she and Charlie had had a totally supportive morning.

"I don't know what I mean," Beth said, confused. "I guess I'm just sorry that it came out in front of so many people, and so bluntly."

Ann laughed. "Well, I admit, it did hit rather hard." She paused for a moment before going on. "Beth, if I ask you a question, will you answer it honestly? If you can't promise, I don't want to ask."

She took a deep breath. "Go ahead."

"What else don't I know?" Ann asked.

She let the breath out. "Nothing. Nothing that I know about. Except that there isn't absolutely no reason to worry about the birth, as Charlie suggested. I really think, and Fred agrees, that the fact that you've taken something that we think can cause miscarriages or deformed fetuses makes it more likely than usual that there will be a problem. But there's really no way to guess the likelihood of it, and it may be next to nothing."

"So what do you recommend?"

"Well, first of all, I wouldn't recommend an abortion. I don't think the risk is that great. But besides that, it's impossible now. It wouldn't be an abortion; it would be a premature delivery." She paused for a minute. "Have you talked to your obstetrician?"

"About what?"

"Well, sometimes newborns die, when they medically could have been kept alive but when there's a clear sign of severe deformity or retardation."

"You mean, kill it?"

Beth went cold all over. "I'm sorry. It's just something you should think about, if it's obviously badly deformed."

"I guess I should." Ann's voice was cold. "Thanks," she said curtly, and hung up the phone.

Beth was sitting there, not knowing what to do, when Charlie walked in.

"Hi!" he called, his voice sounding cheery. "Sorry I'm so late. I won't even try to make excuses." He looked around at the rat cages and the record sheets Beth had set up. "You started without me. That was very noble of you." He smiled at her, and suddenly noticed her look.

"I called your house," she explained, "to see where you were. I talked to Ann." She tried to make it matter-of-fact, but her voice came out absolutely flat and emotionless.

"Oh." Charlie's effervescence evaporated instantly. "It was a rough weekend."

Beth nodded. "If you've got the acid, we can dissolve it and start the force-feeding. I've got the buffer made up, and everybody's labeled and ready to go." The excitement she had felt at nine seemed to have totally drained away.

He took a vial out of his pocket. "Here's the acid." He passed it to Beth. "But I haven't eaten anything today. Would you join me downstairs for lunch, or have you eaten?"

Hunger was far from Beth's thoughts, but she was relieved to leave the lab for a while. She accompanied Charlie out the door.

Downstairs, they ate quietly within the noise of the cafeteria. Finally Beth said, "Charlie, I'm sorry about Saturday night. I didn't realize . . ."

"That I had kept it from her?" Charlie laughed ruefully. "Well, I've paid for it now, and I'm just sorry that you had to be a part of it. You didn't do anything wrong. You just assumed that I was the nice, honest person I pretend to be."

She put her hands over Charlie's. "Come on. Maybe you were wrong to not tell her, but you don't have to start hating yourself about it. That doesn't help anything."

"It's just that I feel so goddamn trapped, like I just have to sit with my hands folded in my lap, waiting to see what kind of kid I get." He was near tears.

"Well, maybe we'll know more in a couple of weeks," Beth suggested. "The rat experiments have to give us some of the information we want."

"I know," he said. "It's just that I can't figure out that acid at all. If I could only find out where it came from or something. It dawned on me last night that maybe the reason that there was only that one shipment of it was because someone discovered what was wrong with it. If we could trace it back . . ." He was totally depressed. "But the guy disappeared months

ago. It's just another goddam dead end, like everything else we've tried."

But Beth wasn't put off by Charlie's depression. She
asked doggedly, "What about Warren's friend? Or your
friends in New Haven? Have you asked them yet?"

Charlie's voice was low and depressed. "No, I
haven't. I suppose I should get on the phone, though."
He laughed ruefully. "We'll probably find out that
everyone who dealt the acid has disappeared."

3

At home that evening, worn-out from force-feeding
eighty-five rats, Charlie doggedly hit the telephone.
Beth had begged off, feeling uncomfortable about
seeing Ann. So, alone in his study, Charlie began his
job. He started with Kip.

"That's right," Kip said. "His name was Larry Seigal.
Did you ever meet him?"

"Name's not familiar," Charlie said.

"Short guy, Jewish. Sort of heavyset, with a big nose
and long black hair. Has a nasty scar sort of like a
W on his right cheek."

"No," Charlie said, "definitely never met him."

"He used to stop through periodically," Kip explained. "I'm not sure if he lives around here or not.
Anyhow, I haven't seen him in the last six months, so
I'm not sure that I'm actually of any help. Has Warren
tried his friend yet?"

"Next on my list," replied Charlie. "I'll talk to you
later." He hung up and let out a deep sigh. It never
comes easily, he thought.

He called Warren next. "Sure," Warren offered.
"I'll call him and get right back to you."

"Great. I'm going to call Terry Bernett down in New
Haven and see what he can find out for me. One of his
roommates knew people in a bunch of other towns who
got the acid, too, so hopefully he'll be able to turn
something up."

Charlie put down the phone and decided to take a
break before calling. In the kitchen he found Ann,
eating a huge salad. "Hi," he smiled.

She reached out and put an arm around his waist. "How's it coming?"

"Slow," he said, "and I've got a long way to go. Thought I'd grab a cup of coffee."

"Lucky you," she pouted. She was avoiding coffee, not wanting the caffeine. She stuffed a huge piece of lettuce into her mouth. "All I get to eat is healthy foods."

"And as punishment, you'll live longer, too," Charlie teased. "Feeling better?"

She shrugged. "I feel as though it's just slipping into a back corner of my mind, where I'll be able to avoid it."

"There's not much else we can do," Charlie said.

Ann looked up at him. "Did you put that idea into Beth's mind?"

Charlie looked surprised. "What idea?"

"About talking to the obstetrician?"

"No. I don't know what you mean."

"Okay, I believe you."

"Well, wait—what did she say?"

Ann shrugged. "Nothing."

Charlie was irritated. "No, come on, what did Beth say?"

"Not now, Charlie, please," she begged. "I'm tired."

"Okay." He hugged her, then picked up his coffee and sipped it gently.

"You go back to work," she said. "I want to do some reading."

He bent over and kissed her, then retreated to the study. Sitting down, he looked through his notebook for Terry's home number and dialed.

Terry answered. "Glad you've called," he said. "We've been wondering how things were going."

"Pretty good," Charlie answered. "We force-fed the acid to eighty-five female rats today and will be injecting hormones tomorrow to induce ovulation."

"Anything new on that guy who's been collecting the fetuses?"

"Nothing," Charlie admitted. "I guess we're just going to sit and see if he comes this month. Otherwise, maybe we'll truck down to New York and try to locate him. It'd be a pain in the ass."

"Look," Terry suggested, "we're a lot closer to New York. Maybe we could do a little looking for you. People here go into the city a lot."

Charlie was delighted. "Hey, maybe we'll take you up on that. Let me talk around up here and see how people feel. But look, there is some help I'd like from you right now, if you've got some time."

"Shoot."

"I'm trying to track down those Gloryhits—see if I can't find out something about where they came from or why they stopped coming. We think maybe they only came once because someone realized what was happening. I'd like to see if I could find those people."

Terry let out a low whistle. "That could be tricky. But hold on a sec." Putting a hand over the phone, he shouted downstairs, "Michael? Can you pick up that phone down there?"

Michael got on the extension. "Hello?"

"Michael," Terry explained, "Charlie Cotten's on the phone. He's trying to find out who you got those Gloryhits from. He wants to try to trace them down."

"Hey," Michael said, "not a bad idea. I got them from Mario Caletti."

"Who?" Charlie asked.

"Mario Caletti."

"Tell me about him."

"Let's see," Michael said. "Short guy. Italian, with a big nose and long black hair. Sort of chubby." He paused, then added, "Oh, one more thing. He has a big scar on his cheek."

"Wait a minute," Charlie said. "A scar shaped like a W?"

"Yeah, I guess," Michael agreed. "You know the guy?"

"Apparently," Charlie said, rather confused. "But his name was Larry Seigal, and he was Jewish."

Michael laughed. "I believe it. The guy's as phony as a three-dollar bill. Is this Seigal guy the one you got the acid from?"

"Yeah."

"Well," Terry said, "there can't be too many acid pushers who fit that description."

"Look," Charlie said, "I don't care what his name is, is he around New Haven?"

Terry thought. "I haven't seen him since the acid."

Downstairs, Michael turned to Allison. "Have you seen Mario Caletti around?"

"No," she said. "Didn't he split right after Sally Carter had her miscarriage?"

"Could you have her speak louder or get on the phone?" Charlie asked.

Michael explained. "It seems Caletti split right after a woman we know had a miscarriage. Do you remember, Terry? She'd taken the Gloryhits and aborted three months later."

"I know who you mean," Terry said. "But what do you mean, 'right after' she aborted?"

"Oh, a bunch of us were at Morty's Tavern—I don't think you were there that time, were you, Terry?"

"Which time?"

"When Steve came in and told us about Sally?"

"No, but I remember you came home and told us."

"Yeah. Well, anyhow, Steve came in and sat down, obviously all upset. He told us that he'd just dropped Sally off at the emergency room, that she'd had a miscarriage. Well, Mario, or whatever his real name is, got all freaked out. I remember it, because he didn't seem to have been a friend of hers. He turned sort of pale, and after a couple of minutes he just up and left. I don't think anyone in town saw him after that."

Charlie took a deep breath and let it out slowly. "Sounds like Mario knew what was going on."

"Or was guessing pretty fast," Terry suggested.

"God, what a fool I am," Michael apologized. "I should have thought of that last week."

"Forget it," Charlie said. "It's soon enough. Look, could you check with those other people you knew in the other towns and see if they all got it from this guy?"

"Sure," Terry agreed. "We can do it right now."

"Make sure you get physical descriptions," Charlie

warned. "It's obvious that the name's not of much value."

"Will do," Terry promised. "And we'll try to get a lead on where he is."

"Thanks," Charlie said. "If I don't hear from you by midnight, okay if I call back to see what you've got?"

"Don't worry," Terry said. "We'll call by then."

"Great. Thanks."

Charlie hung up. I should call Warren, he thought, and have him get a physical description from the people in Middletown. God knows how many names this character might have been using. He tried to imagine the life of a roving dope peddler. He decided that Seigal must have only suspected what the acid was doing. Otherwise, why the surprise? But he would have had to have seen a lot of cases to make the connection. He tried to remember when Kip said he'd last seen Seigal around Boston. Was it after the abortions began? He wasn't sure. But if that was why he had left, he was going to be hard to find.

The phone rang and Charlie picked it up.

"Hello?" he answered.

"This is secret agent 047, reporting from Middletown."

"That you, Warren?" Charlie asked.

"Aw, there you've gone and blown my cover," he complained. "I talked to the people in Middletown, and it's a different pusher—guy by the name of Mario Caletti."

"Same person," Charlie said.

"What?"

Charlie explained his call to New Haven.

"Well, then this fits right in. He was last seen around there in late May or early June; they weren't sure. No idea where he's split to."

"Okay," Charlie sighed. He wrote "Mario—late May, early June" opposite Middletown on his list. "I guess I wait for further word from New Haven now."

"Good enough," Warren agreed. "If anything exciting turns up and it's not too late, let me know."

"Will do," Charlie promised. Hanging up the phone, he looked at a stack of unread journals on the corner of his desk and shrugged his shoulders. Might as well do some reading until they call, he thought, and picked one up at random.

He was on the third journal when the phone rang at a quarter to twelve. He caught it on the second ring.

"We may have something," Terry said. "First of all, it's the same guy in all three towns. He's Larry Seigal in two of them and Mario in the third."

"That jives," Charlie said. "He's Mario in Middletown."

"So that covers all of them, right?"

"Right. But it doesn't give us much of a lead. Is he still hanging around any of the places you've been in touch with?"

"No," Michael said from Terry's other phone. "He definitely cleared out of the whole area around June first. No one's seen him since."

"Any idea where he went?"

"Not really," Michael admitted. "Someone said they thought he used to hang out around Columbia."

"That's not much help," Charlie said.

"I know," Michael agreed. "Cuts it down to about a million people, if he's still there. But I just thought, maybe with that scar, someone we knew down there might have noticed him."

"I guess that's true," Charlie said, "and we could check out the two names, too."

"But it's kind of late to do any more tonight, I think."

"Oh, for sure," Charlie said. "Did you tell the people you talked to to keep an eye out for him?"

"Yeah. If anyone hears anything about him, we should know it right away."

"Great," Charlie said. "I'll try calling some people at Columbia tomorrow. I don't think I know anyone there who's into the drug scene, but I'll try to dig up somebody. I'll get back to you if I find out anything."

"Okay," Michael said. "We'll do the same from here."

"Good enough," Charlie said, yawning unconsciously. "I'll be in touch in a while either way."

They exchanged good-byes, and Charlie hung up

the phone. Exhausted, he went down the hall to the
bedroom, where Ann was already sound asleep. Ann
and Disney, both.

Thursday, December 17

The search at Columbia turned up nothing. Between
Charlie and all the crew in Boston, and Terry and his
friends in New Haven, they called some thirty people
at Columbia. None of the New Yorkers recognized the
names, and only one seemed to recognize the description. But in the end, even that drew a blank.

So Charlie concentrated his attention on the rat experiments. Daily it was becoming clearer that they
were seeing the same pattern as Doc had observed in
his patients. By the second week, Beth and Charlie had
enlisted the help of Barbara Waterper to examine the
fetuses.

On Thursday of the second week they stopped to
reconnoiter. Greene was due any day, and should he
show up, they wanted some data to hit him with.
"Where should we start?" Charlie asked.

"At the beginning?" Waterper suggested facetiously.
"How about dosages, hormone levels, efficiency of
mating, just stuff like that?"

Beth went to the blackboard. "I've got that data,"
she said. "We got two hits of the acid assayed, and
they contained one hundred and twenty-five micrograms LSD each, corresponding to a dose of about two
micrograms per kilogram body weight. As for con-
taminants, we don't know how much is there, but we
assumed that the dose was for a sixty-kilogram person.

So we gave about one-hundredth of a hit to each rat. They were starved overnight and then force-fed the acid in sugar water. All of them received hormones to induce ovulation on the same day they received the acid. All were mated with normal adult males. Both the controls and the rats that got acid showed about an eighty-percent success in getting pregnant, so it didn't seem to prevent conception or mating. So that part is very straightforward." She finished writing the details on the board. "Do you want me to give litter sizes, or should you, Charlie?"

Charlie was copying down Beth's notes. "No, go ahead. You're doing fine."

She nodded. Turning to Barbara, she gave some background. "What we want to know is about miscarriages, like the ones we saw with humans. With humans, they tended to cluster at three and five months, which corresponds to approximately seven and eleven days in the rat. But that's only approximate. So far, we've only gotten to nine days. With rats, you don't look for miscarriages, because that's not what they do. Instead, the fetuses are reabsorbed by the mother, sort of cannibalized, once they've died for other reasons. So what we've done is to look at how many fetuses each mother was carrying at different stages of gestation." She drew a table on the blackboard. "First let me give you the numbers per litter on the average, for both with and without acid." She filled in the numbers.

| Days gestation | Average Number per Litter | |
	Received acid	No acid
4	11.5	11
5	9.5	12
6	8.0	11.5
7	8.5	11
8	8.0	11.5
9	7.5	12

"So the rats that received the acid before they became pregnant are definitely showing loss of fetuses, starting around five days. I should point out that years ago it was shown that pure LSD, given before the rats became pregnant, didn't cause this kind of effect. So presumably we're seeing the effect of some contaminant in the acid."

"Those figures are misleading, though," Charlie said. "Because there's clearly a bimodal distribution in the treated rats."

"I was just getting to that," Beth replied. "It's clear that some of the rats are being affected and some are not. For example . . ." She dug out a sheet from her notebook. "At nine days, we examined four rats that had been given acid and two that had not. The two controls had eleven and thirteen fetuses, which is about normal. But the ones that had been given acid had four, five, ten, and eleven. Two of them were just about normal, while the other two had less than half the normal number. And that's the way it looks at all the ages. So it looks as though the size of some of the litters is affected while the size of others is not. If you leave out the mothers with ten or more fetuses, then the data, starting at day six, look like this." She copied her notes onto the blackboard.

Days gestation	6	7	8	9
Avg. litter, affected rats	6.5	6.0	6.0	4.5
Avg. litter, controls	11.5	11.0	11.5	12.0

"So in the affected litters, the number drops to about half by six days. I don't know if it's starting to drop again at nine days or not. That's just two rats, and they might be unusually low. We'll have to wait and see."

"But more significantly, we've begun to see the characteristic deformed head in the fetuses," Charlie said. Beth put down the chalk and sat down. Charlie stopped. "I'm sorry, Beth—I didn't mean to cut you off."

She shrugged. "That's all I have to say. The rest of the data is on the deformities, and that's your bag, and Barbara's."

"Well, okay," said Charlie. "Why don't I give some information on that, and then, Barbara, I want to hear what you have to say."

"Fine," she agreed.

"Good." He got up and went to the blackboard. "I won't talk about the nature of the deformities, just the numbers. What we did was to take each fetus and put it into a jar of formaldehyde, and we gave each one a code number. One of us would put it in the jar, and the other would score it for plus or minus deformity. That way, when we scored it, all we knew was its code number. We didn't know which mother it came from. That eliminated the possibility of our becoming biased from the results. Then we put the data into a table, giving the percent deformed in the controls, in the affected experimentals, and in the unaffected experimentals." He drew a grid on the blackboard, next to Beth's. "The numbers look like this."

Days gestation	4	5	6	7	8	9
Percent deformed, small ("affected") litters	10	35	75	91	83	89
Percent deformed, large ("unaffected") litters	0	0	5	10	5	20
Percent deformed, controls	0	0	4	0	0	0

"That 'four percent' in the controls was due to a single fetus. I don't know—I looked at it again, and it was a questionable one. But I scored it as deformed, so it goes on the table."

"What about the unaffected?" Barbara asked. "Do you think that's real?"

"Oh, yeah," Beth answered. "There were maybe ten altogether, and that's too many to be chance."

Barbara wrote a note next to the data.

"Something else you should remember," Charlie pointed out, "is that in the data for affected litters, those figures don't include the fetuses that presumably have died and been reabsorbed. If you assume that those were deformed, the numbers are appropriately higher."

Barbara frowned. "By seven days it doesn't look as if they could get much higher."

Charlie nodded. "I think that in actuality by seven days the figure might be right near one hundred percent, all totaled."

Barbara looked at the data. It was the first time she'd

seen it summarized and tabulated. "What do you think about the unaffected litters, where there doesn't seem to be any fetal loss, yet there are definitely some deformities?"

Again, they had no good idea. "Presumably," Charlie said, "they'll abort at the later stage, the one equivalent to five months. That's also what we assume will happen with the deformed ones in the affected class."

"But basically, we just have to wait and see," Beth concluded.

Barbara nodded. "Another few days should give us most of what we want. What do we have, twelve days to term?"

"Right," Charlie affirmed. "A week from next Tuesday."

"I guess that's all we have, isn't it, Charlie?" Beth asked.

"That's all I can think of. Barbara, why don't you go over your results?"

"Fine. I won't need the blackboard." She thumbed through some of her papers. "When you called a fetus deformed, you were always talking about this one specific deformity, the enlarged head. The first thing I wanted to see was whether there were any other abnormalities that I could detect. I worked mainly with the eight- and nine-day-old fetuses—the others are too small to do much with. But I did look at some of the younger ones, too. In a word, I found nothing. There was an abnormality here and there, but I found them in both the control and the experimental rats, and in frequencies similar to what you normally see. So when we talk about defects caused by this acid, or the contaminant in it, we are indeed talking only about the enlarged head.

"It's a general telencephalic enlargement—an enlargement of the front part of the brain. It almost looks as if the whole population of nerve cells in the telencephalon has just about doubled in size. In a couple of days, when we've got older embryos, I'm going to have a neuroanatomist look at it more closely, but that's approximately what it is."

Barbara smiled. "Well, there's not much more. Mostly what I have left to say is what the deformity isn't. It isn't anything like anyone I've talked to has ever seen or heard of. It's not a tumor, it's not a general disorganization of the cells, it's not a general neuronal dysfunction. The telencephalon has its normal patterns of cell types, layers, and divisions. It's just that for some reason there are more cells in every layer than there should be. I'm not a developmental biologist, but it looks as though all the cells just divided one time more than usual before stopping, if that makes any sense. Even the eyes were larger."

"The eyes?" Beth asked. "I thought it was just the telencephalon."

"That's part of it," Charlie explained. "The eye is just a bump on the forebrain that reaches out to the surface of the head. Vision is not like hearing and smelling, where peripheral cells send information to the brain; the eyes are actually an integral part of the brain."

Beth shrugged. "Okay."

Barbara sat down again. "That's it."

They all sat there for a minute. Beth looked at Barbara and Charlie. "Does it seem reasonable to just keep going the way we have been? Are there any changes that we should make in light of any of this?"

They were interrupted by a knock at the door. Bill Hebb stuck his head in. "Hi, Charlie, is Beth around?" He looked around the room and spotted her. "You busy right now?" he asked.

Beth looked irritated. "Yeah."

Bill shrugged. "Well, when you're finished, could you show me how to use that vertical flow hood?"

Barbara looked confused. "A vertical flow hood?"

Bill grimaced. "They make us use it when we work with these viruses, despite the fact that the viruses are harmless." He obviously was displeased with the requirement.

"They're filters," Beth explained, totally ignoring Bill's comment. "By working inside them, you insure that any viruses that might escape from your flasks and test tubes are captured and don't get out into the environment."

Bill turned toward the door. "Well, I'll be working in my lab until you've got time." He started to back out the door.

"Wait a minute!" Beth roared. "What are you going to be doing until then?"

He shrugged again. "Starting on those viruses CRA sent up. The cells are growing well enough."

Beth jumped from her chair. "You're just going to start with the viruses on your benchtop?"

"Sure, why not?"

Beth was furious. Turning to Barbara and Charlie, she said, "You two just go on and finish without me. This is going to take a while, I can tell." She stormed out of the office, Bill Hebb trailing behind.

Across the hall, she went to Tom Darnell's lab and found him writing at his desk. "Talk time," she said, pulling a seat over to his desk.

Tom looked up, surprised at Beth's tone. Bill stood a small distance away. "What's up?" Tom asked.

"My dander," Beth retorted. "I thought you were going to be directing Bill's work insofar as it was connected with the CRA stuff."

"I am," he replied calmly.

"Does that include his working with this virus on his benchtop?"

Tom turned to Bill. "I thought you were going to use the vertical flow hood, to make sure that no stray viruses were released into the air." There was just a hint of bite in the question.

Bill shrugged. "I was. I was just waiting for Beth to show me how to use it."

Tom looked at Beth. "But he was going to use his benchtop until I had time to show him!" she exploded.

Bill looked from one to the other, clearly not interested in the argument. "Look, I can wait until you show me if you want."

Beth sputtered. "If I want! Unbelievable—just unbelievable! Have you been working with the cell line, getting it to grow, on your benchtop all this time?"

"Of course," he said. "Where else?"

She looked at Bill, standing calmly before her rage. "I'll come and get you when I've time to show you how. Just don't go opening up any goddamn virus capsules beforehand. Do you understand?"

Bill turned to leave. "Yes, I understand," he repeated mockingly.

Beth waited for him to leave the room before turning to Tom. "This cannot be allowed to continue," she stated. "Did you know that he was working without the safeguard of a hood?"

Tom answered cautiously. "I knew he was doing some of the work without a hood."

"But how much do you know about the cell line he's using? Whether it has any viruses in it, any plasmids? It's really stupid to use those kinds of cells outside a safety hood unless you've spent a lot of time making sure you really know what's in the cells!"

"Then maybe it would be more appropriate to ask me if the cells have been tested, rather than jumping down my throat like this," he answered evenly.

Beth was taken aback. "You mean they have been checked out? To standards that Lloyd would be willing to accept?" She didn't want just industry's stamp of certification. They were often motivated by forces other than the public safety.

"I mean that in a civil lab, where people are trying to remain on friendly terms with one another, it might be wise to ascertain whether there is a problem at all before launching into an all-out assault." He was clearly upset. "All of these experiments have been discussed with Lloyd, and he has approved them all. I wouldn't think of acting otherwise."

Beth didn't know what to say. "But what about Bill's working with the virus on an open bench? Come on, that's dangerous."

"Whether or not it's dangerous depends on the nature of the virus, clearly. But I agree that he shouldn't, and I told him not to. I appreciate your bringing the discrepancy to my attention, and I will be more careful in my monitoring of him in the future." He sounded like an administration spokesman.

Beth was at a loss. Nastily she asked, "How much longer is he going to be working around here?"

"Probably until mid-March. That's our current estimate of when he'll finish up here."

Beth got up and left. "The sooner the better!" she shouted back over her shoulder.

Charlie and Barbara were just coming out of his lab. They looked surprised at her outburst.

"Grrr!" she muttered. "Things are reaching a breaking point over there."

"I don't think I followed all that," Charlie said. "Join us downstairs for coffee?"

"I'll join you," Beth answered, "but I think I need a sedative more than coffee." On the way down she explained what had happened.

"You seem to be getting everybody over there upset," Charlie said. "I thought Darnell was a reasonable guy."

"Well, so did I," Beth said. "But I think he's starting to put his corporate ties above the public safety."

"I thought there were pretty strict guidelines for that sort of research," Barbara asked.

"Oh, there are," Beth agreed. "But absolutely no enforcement procedures. Scientists are very good people; they don't have to be patrolled, you know. They would never do anything that was wrong."

Charlie objected. "Come on, that's not fair. There's constant peer pressure to force compliance, just like what you did right there. And although there isn't any punishment for noncompliance, there is a standing committee that will investigate complaints, if it were to ever come to that."

"Sure," Beth agreed, "but in all this time I don't think the committee has ever done a thing."

"Which means no complaints," Charlie insisted.

"Which doesn't mean a damn thing, except that scientists don't tattle on each other."

"Maybe," Charlie conceded.

Saturday, December 19

Ralph Masco lay on his side, running a finger gently up and down the backs of her thighs. She squirmed closer to him. "It tickles." He pulled her against him and kissed her. Two hours ago she had been a stranger in his apartment-house elevator. She had moved into the vacant apartment down the hall from his a couple of weeks ago, and he liked it that way. She was in her late twenties, her body still nearly perfect, and she had learned a lot in her years.

"You got any dope?" she asked, running a finger up and down his spine.

"What would you like?" he asked.

"Just some real mellow grass."

"Just a sec." He rose and padded barefoot into the other room. A minute later he returned with a baggie full of grass and a pipe. She sat up on the bed, legs folded in front of her. They smoked for a while in silence.

"Mmmm . . ." She smiled lazily. "This is really nice. I was afraid to bring any on the plane with me and haven't been able to find any since I got here."

He handed her the baggie. "It's yours."

"Really?"

"Call it a housewarming gift."

She leaned forward and nipped at his neck. "Thanks."

They smoked some more, made love again. "This is really fine weed," she said. "Not too much like it down in Norfolk."

Ralph laughed. "I can believe it."

She traced the outline of the scar on his cheek. "How'd you get this?"

"From a broken bottle," he answered.

She shuddered, images of streetfighting in her mind. "It was a long time ago," he said.

"Do you know where I could get some acid?" she asked.

He smiled. "I think you've found a pretty good source for just about anything you need," he answered.

"Oh, really?" she asked, smiling. "How convenient." She snuggled up closer. "Do you traffic much?"

He wrapped a leg around her. "Enough to keep me going. I'm not greedy."

"Good," she replied. "I don't like people who are greedy. Not about money, anyhow." She smiled at her joke. "I bet that guy a couple of weeks ago didn't buy much. He didn't look the type."

He looked confused. "What guy?"

"You know . . . When was it? Two weeks ago today. That's right—it was Saturday morning, I remember. He was dressed up all straight, with a coat and tie and polished black leather shoes. Didn't look like a druggie."

Masco fingered his scar nervously. "I don't know who you're talking about. Maybe it was someone else in the hall, not me."

"Oh, yes," she insisted. "I'm sure, because that's when I first decided you looked so nice."

"Way back then?" he asked. "Where've you been?"

She rolled over, away from him. "Trying to figure out who that guy was." She frowned at him, unhappy.

"Forget it," he said. "He was a nobody. Doesn't make any difference to anything."

"Well, you don't have to shout!" she complained.

He smiled. "You're right. I'm sorry." He pulled her back to him. "I'll make it up to you real nice."

She pulled away again. "No. Not until you tell me who he was. Now I want to know. Was he a cop or something?"

He got out of bed. "Quit with the third degree, all right? The guy's a nobody, that's all. If he's so important to you, go find him instead. I don't want to talk about him." He paced around the room.

She rose from the bed and went over to him, wrapping herself around him. "Come back," she said gently. "I don't have to know. I was just curious."

He stroked her hair. "Well, forget it. For now and for always. He's a real bad scene. I wish I'd never met him."

She pulled him back to bed.

Not far away, the tape recorders whirred quietly.

Monday, December 21

The phone jarred Charlie out of an unpleasant dream. He looked at the clock. It was two A.M. A typical ending to a Monday, he thought. Reaching around in the dark, he found the phone and dragged the receiver over to him.

"Hello?"

"Charlie, that you?"

"Yeah. Who is this?"

"It's Kip. I'm in New York. You awake?"

Charlie swung his feet over the side of the bed and sat up. "I guess. It's the middle of the night, you know."

"Yeah, I know. Sorry about that, but musicians live lousy hours."

"Well, what the hell do you want? If you just called to chat, I'll kill you."

"I've found him."

"Who?"

"Larry Seigal, Mario Caletti. Down here he's Ralph Masco."

"You've got him?"

"A friend of mine knows him. Has to be the same guy. Fits the description to a T, including the W scar. And, to top it all off, he moved in around the first of June."

Charlie was wide-awake. "Look, I'll catch the first train down tomorrow. Can we talk to him then?"

"Take your time. My friend works. We can go see him tomorrow evening. Be here at five."

"Where at?"

"Four-forty West End. Apartment seven A."

"I'll be there."

Friday, December 25

It drizzled in Washington on Christmas. Late in the afternoon, Pearson found himself back in his office, trying hard to decide where he stood on the issue of Gabardine. The agent assigned to Ralph Masco had done remarkably well. He marveled at her talents. Right there, at the last possible moment, she had pulled out that statement. He picked up the transcript. "He's a real bad scene. I wish I'd never met him." What was he doing with a drug peddler? Christ, if they'd only had bugs planted on him or something. Did Gabardine have anything to do with this acid business? He started up the tape recorder for the tenth time.

"I'm coming, I'm coming. Who is it?"

(unintelligible)

"Hey, Tommy, come on in. Who are your friends?"

"Hi, Ralph. This is Charlie, and Kip here I think you know."

"Oh, yeah. How ya doing, Kip?"

"Good . . . Ralph. How are you?"

"Oh, gettin' along. Staying pretty much down around the city lately. Guess I haven't been up your way in a while now."

"No, not since June."

"Yeah, well, I guess it's just the city, man. I just love it here."

"Looks like you're set up pretty good here."

"It's okay. I'm hustling enough to keep alive."

"Well, we miss you up in Boston, you know. Everybody up there still remembers those Gloryhits you brought in. They'd love more of them if you've got any around."

"Oh, yeah? I didn't like them too much. Some people I gave 'em to said they were too speedy, so I cut them out."

"Really?"

"Gee, that's too bad, because they liked them in Providence, too."

"Oh, yeah? Did they get them in Providence?"

"And in Middletown, and New Haven . . ."

"Say, what is this?"

"We just liked the acid, that's all. It was a shame you left town when you did. You could have made a fortune on that acid."

"Yeah, well, maybe I should have stayed. I never was much of a businessperson. That's how come I live in this apartment."

"Heard much from Sally Carter lately?"

"Who?"

"Sally Carter, in New Haven. Remember, she had a miscarriage just before you split town."

"Oh, yeah, I remember her. No, I never hear anything from her. Hardly knew her more than to say hello."

"But you took it awful hard when she lost the kid."

"Yeah, well, that was just real bum luck."

"Luck?"

"Yeah, that she lost it."

"I think you know as well as I do that it wasn't luck."

"Hey, Tommy, what's with your friends here? I mean, is this any way for them to act in someone else's place?"

"They want to know where the Gloryhits came from, Ralph. They figured out that that's why Sally and a lot of other women lost their kids. And they know that you figured it out, too. No one's blaming you, but we want to know where that acid came from."

"Oh, come on, Tommy, that was over a year ago. Some cat blew into town with some good acid cheap. So I bought in."

"Who else bought?"

"Oh, Christ, I don't know. There were a bunch of guys there. I don't know who bought and who didn't."

"What was the name of the guy who sold it?"

"Shit, man! I can't remember that kind of thing."

"Ralph, cut it out. You've shown me that book of yours. You write down every purchase and sale you make."

"Yeah, but it's not in there."

"Bullshit."

"No, man, it's true. I'll show you . . . Here, look for yourself. Tommy, you bought it in February. So look. Here's December—just some Blotter. January, some Chuckles; February nothing. Not a thing. I didn't even write down the sales. See? Nothing in Boston. Nothing in New Haven. It's just not in the book."

"Why not?"

"I don't know, I got sloppy. Just forgot . . . Honest. I just forgot. Look, man, I don't know where I got it! Lay off, will ya?"

"For chrissake, Ralph, you've got *liar* written all over your face. I've never seen you lie like this! Who you trying to protect, huh? Why are you covering for bad acid? You can get a real bad rep that way, and fast."

"Come on, you guys, will ya? It's my skin. I can't tell you. You can beat the shit out of me, but I can't tell you."

"You talking about the Mafia?"

"Yeah, it's the Mafia . . . Hell, no. I don't know who they are; I only know a contact. Look, I'll try to get in touch with them, okay? I'll try to find out what was in it. Maybe they know. Maybe they'll tell me. Gimme a week. I'll see what I can find. But that's all. If they say no go, I can't tell you a thing."

"What do you think?"

"There's no use pushing him."

"Then let's come back in a week."

"You'll be here?"

"What'm I gonna say? No? I ain't gonna hide from you."

"Okay."

"Sorry we had to be like this, Ralph, but you know, that was just real bad acid."

"I know, man, I know. Ya think I moved here for fun? I never want to hear about that shit again."

Pearson turned off the tape recorder. His hands were sweaty. Boston, New Haven, Middletown: three of the towns that had shown up on the survey. Did the acid cause the miscarriages? Researchers had looked into that question before and never observed anything this obvious. Why this batch in particular? And what was Gabardine's or Jim Karls's connection with it? There was an obvious interpretation sitting in front of him, and it didn't make for a very pleasant Christmas.

Monday, December 28

1

Ann and Charlie had a beautiful, snow-covered Christmas. Disney was due in six weeks, and it became
harder and harder for them to believe that there could
be anything wrong with their child. Or maybe they
just worked harder and harder at not believing it. At
any rate, it was far from their minds, and the six
weeks ahead looked wonderful. Disney kicked and
punched and rolled from side to side. Sometimes it
would beat out a staccato rhythm on Ann's belly.
With stethoscopes that Charlie had borrowed, they
would lie in bed and listen to the strong, steady
heartbeat. They were going to have a baby.

On Monday, Kip and Charlie drove back to New
York, hoping to find out something about the acid.
Larry Seigal, alias Ralph Masco, had had his week
to dig something up. Neither Kip nor Charlie knew
exactly what they would do if he had nothing to say.

When they arrived, there was no sign of him. They
were waiting in the hall, hoping for his return, when
an attractive woman in her late twenties came up.
"Hi, can I help you guys?"

"We're trying to find Ralph Masco. Do you know
if he's around?" Kip was surprised. It was the first
time someone in New York City had offered to help
him.

"I don't think he's been around the last few days.
Thought maybe he went off somewhere for Christmas
or something. You two friends of his?"

194

"Sort of," Charlie hedged. "He was going to try to find something out for us."

She smiled. "I understand."

Charlie realized that she must have thought he meant drugs.

"You want to leave a message?" she suggested. "I see him when he's around."

"No, that's okay," Kip answered. "We'll stop back in a few days."

She shrugged. "Okay. See you around."

Riding down in the elevator, Charlie asked, "What do you think?"

Kip rode quietly until they reached the lobby. "I guess we should come back next week again."

"No, but what do you think about where he is?" Charlie persisted.

"Look," Kip said, "you're the scientist, you make predictions. I'm a musician, I just play along. Maybe he went somewhere for Christmas, maybe he split. We'll know better in a week."

"What about your friend Tommy?" Charlie asked. "You think he might know something?"

"He, I know, is out of town for Christmas. Told me last week he would be." Kip headed toward the subway. "Want to find Greene?"

"What?"

"Well, we've got a post office box number, so we should be able to find out who's renting it." The smile on Kip's face showed his pleasure at outthinking Charlie.

Charlie laughed and slapped him on the back. "Lead on, Sherlock."

Kip hit Charlie for twenty cents and stopped at a phone booth. After a brief discussion with the information operator, he led Charlie into the subway station.

"Getting around in New York is an art," he said as they let a local go by. "A mere two transfers and twenty minutes should get us there." They bounced and jostled their way through the New York underground, finally reemerging into the world of light twenty-five minutes later. "Missed our train," Kip explained. "That's why it took five extra minutes."

The man behind the counter was a caricature of a post office clerk—short, heavyset, with glasses slipping down his nose. "You got some sort of complaint with these people?" he asked, looking through a pile of blank forms.

"Oh, no," Charlie answered. "Just want to talk with them."

"Sent in money for something and it never came?" he asked. "Because that's mail fraud, and we've got inspectors that'll look into it. Usually it's just a mistake, or they're behind in filling orders. But sometimes it's out-and-out fraud."

"Oh," Charlie replied.

"Well, is it?" the agent repeated. "That's a special form."

"Oh, no, no. We just want to talk to them."

"It broke, huh? Or never worked? Them are a lot harder."

"No," Charlie insisted, "we didn't buy anything from them. It's not that kind of thing. They're collecting . . ." Kip kicked him hard in the ankle. "They're collecting information on some stuff, and we're curious what their results have been." His voice trailed off uncertainly.

The agent just looked at him, then shook his head and went back to the forms. "Well, if you just want to know who's renting it, there's a form for that somewhere in here."

"We could just give you the box number," Charlie suggested. "Couldn't you just look it up?"

"Just look it up?" the agent asked. He snorted. "Just look it up! Hah! This, sonny, is the United States Post Office." He jabbed a pencil eraser at Charlie. "We handle millions of pieces of paper every day. We love 'em." Finally he pulled a form out of the stack. "Ah, here it is. Yessir, we love them. Get more every chance we can. You want to use the washroom?"

Charlie was lost. "No."

"Hah!" cried the agent triumphantly. "Everything

else in here, you gotta fill out a form." He chuckled to himself and handed a form to Charlie. "If you mail it right here, you don't even need a stamp."

Charlie was still confused. "But can't I just give it to you, and you fill in the bottom?"

The agent shook his head and turned to Kip. "Your buddy a slow learner?"

"He's from out of town," Kip explained. "How long's it gonna take?"

"A week, ten days," the agent replied. "Except that we're still digging out from Christmas—might take two weeks." He looked at the return address. It was Doc's. "Boston, huh? They'll probably lose it."

"What!" Charlie cried.

"A joke." He smiled. Pulling down the "Closed" sign, he addressed the woman behind them. "I'm closed now. Use the next window."

Charlie and Kip left the woman shouting at the empty window.

Outside, Kip began laughing hysterically. "Charlie, you just witnessed a rare sight."

"You mean a postman going mad?"

"No, in a good mood. A rare sight indeed."

"He was crazy," Charlie insisted.

Kip continued laughing. "Well, maybe. In New York City the standards of sanity are a little lower than elsewhere." He led Charlie back to the subway. "Well, don't feel terrible. At least we got the forms filed. We'll have the information soon enough."

"A waste," Charlie muttered. "A total waste."

But Kip disagreed. "Look, at least we got the form filed on Greene. That has to show up something. We drew bad luck on Masco, but we met someone who appears to keep tabs on him."

"Except, who knows where she can be found?" Charlie was depressed.

"Shame on you," Kip chided. "Twelve K."

"Huh?"

"Twelve K. She unlocked the door and went in while we were waiting for the elevator. For a scientist, you're not too observant." Kip was in splendid form.

"You seem to blossom in New York," Charlie commented, mildly humored by Kip's cleverness. They rode out to Pelham Bay Parkway on the subway, talking of the city and its mood. Finally they recovered their car and headed back to Boston. They weren't five minutes out when, muttering to himself, Charlie pulled off and into a gas station.

"The car?" Kip asked apprehensively. He never believed that the old Volvo still ran, let alone held together.

"No," Charlie replied, "my brain." He got out of the car. "I promised Doc I'd call as soon as we found out anything." He headed over to a pay phone. Chunking in dimes and quarters, he dialed Doc's office.

"Dr. Blake's office." It was Sharon, his secretary.

"Hi, Sharon. Charlie Cotten. I'm calling long distance. Can I talk to Doc?"

"Well, he's with someone," she said. "Let me see how long it'll take." She put him on hold, while Charlie pulled more change out of his pocket.

"Hi—Charlie?" It was Doc.

"Yeah, hi. Look, this is long distance, so I'll be brief. Ralph Masco wasn't there. A woman who knows him says he hasn't been around for a while, thinks maybe he went home for Christmas or something. So that's deadend for a while. Kip and I'll try again next week. But we also filed for the name and address of the owner of Greene's post office box, so that'll give us a lead on them. But it'll take the post office a couple of weeks to process the goddamn form, so that's at a standstill, too."

"Doesn't sound like it was a very profitable trip," Doc commented.

"No, not really," Charlie admitted, "although it seems to have boosted my feelings anyhow. I guess I feel that at least we're trying harder now."

"Maybe. Hey, have you talked with Beth?"

"Not since yesterday. Why?"

"She called around noon. Wants to talk to you, wouldn't tell me what about. Sounded absolutely mysterious. Anyhow, she says she'll be at your lab until she makes contact with you, so maybe you should call her there."

"Okay, will do. Maybe Ann and I'll stop by this evening. She's been complaining that she never sees you."

"I'll be home."

"Good. Talk to you later." He hung up and dialed the operator, calling his own lab collect. Beth answered and accepted the charges.

"Hi, Charlie, I've been trying to get in touch with you." She sounded tense.

"I know. I just talked with Doc, and he said to call you. What's up?"

She paused before answering. "How fast can you get to the lab?" she asked.

"Four, five hours," he said. "I'm just barely out of New York City. It'll be more like five, because I'm going to hit traffic around New Haven."

He could hear her take a deep breath. "Charlie, some of the treated rats gave birth today."

"And?"

"And some of them were deformed."

Charlie froze. "Dead?"

"No. They seem perfectly healthy."

"They're nursing and all?"

"Charlie, they're acting perfectly normally!"

"How many?"

"I don't know. Three—no, four: two in one litter, and one in each of two others."

"What size litters?" The questions seemed to be coming out by themselves while he listened passively.

"The two were from a normal-sized litter, twelve all together. But the one's with just one, they were the only ones in the litter. Charlie, I haven't told anyone, not even Doc!"

He tried to regain some control over his racing mind. "Look," he finally suggested, "why don't you go home? I'll pick you up when I get back, and we can go to the lab. No use your sitting around there."

"No," she whispered. "I can't. I have to see if they survive, or if more are born. I'll be in the lab."

"Beth, you're just wearing yourself out!"

"For chrissake, Charlie, don't argue. I'll see you when you get back." She hung up.

Charlie stood there with the receiver in his hand, as if expecting something to happen. Finally he hung up the phone and rubbed his face, trying to clear away the confusion. But it didn't help. After a minute he got up and went back to the car.

Without saying a word, he got in and started the car.

"What happened?" Kip asked.

"Nothing," Charlie replied in a monotone. "Talked to Doc about the day." He pulled onto the expressway.

"Charlie! You look half dead. Is something the matter?"

He shook his head. "Just tired from the day, I guess."

"You want me to drive?" Kip asked apprehensively. Charlie was obviously not himself.

Charlie shrugged, then pulled over onto the side of the road. "Why don't you?" he said, getting out to let Kip slide over. Back on the road, Charlie fell into a half sleep, frantically trying to escape from reality.

2

Peter Alder watched in silence while Greene paced back and forth in the small room. The television set blared as a hockey game went unnoticed. After forty years, he thought, we still use baseball games and running water as the best defense against snoopers.

Greene turned toward him defiantly. "I'm telling you, it's too dangerous to continue! Maybe in some of the other towns, but Boston has got to be dropped. And I'm not too happy about that damn answering service, either. That gives them a tie to us that shouldn't be there anymore. Alder, if this gets out, the repercussions will go clear around the world!"

Alder calmly pulled on a cigarette. He'd been expecting something like this ever since the reports from Boston started coming in. And things certainly hadn't gotten any better when Patterson blew his end of it. He looked intently at Greene, trying to gauge his precise mood. "Greene, if you'd just calm down, maybe we can work something out that would be mutually satisfactory. But not unless you pull yourself together! Now, sit down. 'Repercussions.' Christ, you've got a fine sense of understatement! I doubt that our own government has much more than an idea of what we're doing, and we haven't trusted the army with so much as a hint, for fear of leaks. But we've been in a lot tighter places than this, and there's no need for panicking now."

Greene dropped into a chair. "I'm not panicking, all right? Basically, I just feel that you should be able to get those people off my back."

"We've got people working on that. In fact, if they hadn't blown the job, the problem would be over. We had an agent try to take the good Doctor Blake out of the picture, but he blew it.

"I'm not telling you this to have someone to share my problems with, but to point out to you that we need you in Boston. Not only are you getting us those fetuses, and that would be enough, but right now you're one of our best links to what those bastards are doing."

"Well, I still think this bit about using random people out there was stupid." He gestured vaguely out the window at uptown Manhattan. "It would have been so much easier if we had tried it out on our own people."

Alder sighed. He would just as soon have told Greene nothing. "You say we should try it on our own people?" he asked Greene. "Why?"

Greene looked confused. "Why, because we can trust them, of course!"

"Trust them to what?"

"Not to blab about it."

"About what?" The questions were coming out in a monotone.

"About the miscarriages. Why, they wouldn't even have to know about the deformities."

Alder shook his head. "You actually think we could find trustworthy women who would be willing to carry a child for three to five months, knowing that they would lose them?"

Greene stuck out his chin. "Yes! For their country,

they'd do it. We train our people well. To strengthen their country, they'd do it." Irritation flashed across his face. "But instead, we come here and try it on these hippies—in America, no less! Better in the jungles of South America!"

Alder stared at him sullenly. "But if we'd used our own people and they knew about it—that was your suggestion—what if the pregnancies went to term?"

"You mean if the experiment failed?"

Alder leaned forward in his chair. "No, I mean if it succeeded."

Greene looked blank. "I don't follow you."

"I know," Alder sighed, leaning back in his chair, "which is why I'm here and you're out in the field. Because you don't know what's going on!" He leaned forward again. "I'll say it again: The miscarriages are *failures!* It's live births we're after, and that's just the start. How would you keep the children secret for the next ten years? How would you keep people from noticing that a number of our operatives had slightly but consistently deformed children? No, it couldn't be someone connected with us. Because even if they didn't understand it at first, it would be seen, and eventually understood.

"Why drug users? Why in America? Because we have agents here, thousands of them, who could keep tabs on those children no matter where they went. And people like you, who can collect the fetuses that abort. We don't even have to know who took that acid. We'll know the results when we see them. But more important than that, who would wonder? Who would suspect? A bunch of druggies have spontaneous abortions, deformed offspring. Who would look any further for an explanation? 'Bad drugs,' they'd say. 'Serves them right.' And that would be the end of it."

"Except," muttered Greene, "that's not what they said, and the end's not in sight. I'm damned if I'm going back to Boston!"

Alder set his cigarette down in an ashtray and looked out the window. "We've made it this far; we'll make it to the end." He turned to face Greene. "One more month is all we need. Get us that, and keep everyone out of our hair while we dismantle our apparatus here, and then we can all disappear with the wind." He sat quietly, thinking for a minute, expecting a response from Greene. When none came, he continued. "Greene, listen to me. We've got seventy-five people on this project, of whom exactly three have the entire picture. That number cannot, and will not, get any larger. But I can say this much. First, as I just told you, the abortions are failures. But we expected them. We saw them in preliminary studies with rats and monkeys. Your job is to get us those fetuses, so we can compare the human abortants with the animal ones. It's critical to this project that we know that relationship. That's why we've got ten people at our Jersey lab analyzing every one you bring in. And without them, we won't know whether we've succeeded or not. But I can make you this promise. If we find that it works in people the same as it does in rats and monkeys, then—and only then—we'll use it on our own people!"

3

Charlie got to the lab around eight that evening, calling Ann to say he'd be working late. Beth was distraught. "Fred called just a little while after you did."

"About what?"

"The obstetricians around town got letters from Greene today."

"Saying?"

"Saying thanks, the experiment's over."

"You mean he's finished?" Charlie exclaimed. "He's not even going to pick up the fetuses that were collected?"

"He asked people to send what they had to that post office box, assuring that he'd reimburse them for postage. That's all. Doc was pretty upset about it."

Charlie stomped angrily around the lab. "Well, this has been a fantastic day all around!"

"He said you got some sort of lead on where Greene is?"

"Oh, shit. We filed a goddamn form to find out who rented the post office box and where they live. But that's going to take two weeks. The bastard had the information in a file right behind him, but insisted on all this formality shit. So we get to just sit and wait for that."

"Well, there's been one more born since you called. We've got five now, all as healthy as can be. Want to see?"

Charlie hesitated. "Yeah, come on. Show me."

She led him back to the animal quarters, where the shelves of rat cages were kept. Four of the tags had big red X's on them. She pulled them out and put them on the table.

"The new one's in a normal-size litter," she told him. Charlie just nodded.

Finally he leaned over and looked into one of the cages. Beth removed the metal grating from the top. It was a normal-size litter, the pups fighting frantically for access to the teats. The mother looked up lazily at Charlie and then laid her head back down. He couldn't make out the deformed ones.

Beth picked the mother up by the tail and gently shook off the babies. "They're always the last to come loose," she whispered. Sure enough, after all but two were off, Charlie could clearly see the swollen heads. He felt sick. Putting down the rat, Beth pulled out a chair for him. "Sit down," she said. "That's what happened to me, too." She put the cover on the cage. "The deformed ones are all just like that. Healthy as can be."

Charlie folded his arms on the table and put his head down on them. It all seemed like a bad dream. "Why are they alive?" he asked, not lifting his head.

Beth just shook her head. "They're so goddamn healthy, Charlie! I suppose they could fall over dead at any moment, but right now they're so healthy. Sometimes I just watch them for half an hour. They always have a teat. They're stronger than the others."

There was a tremor in Charlie's voice. "Now what?"

"We sit and watch, I guess. I've been checking every half hour or so, looking for more, looking for dead ones. I guess there's no real need for both of us to stay, but I can't sleep tonight, I know that."

"No," Charlie agreed, "I'll stay, too. Lemme call Ann." He got up to call.

"Charlie, are you going to tell her?"

He stopped dead in his tracks. Turning to her, he said, "No, not yet." Beth nodded, offering no argument. Thankful for that, he turned back and walked to his office. It's like an acid trip, he thought. Your body goes on acting perfectly normally while your mind is screaming out because it doesn't understand what's happening. His hand picked up the phone and dialed, his mouth gave some explanation to Ann, and his mind screamed out in pain and confusion. Hanging up the phone, he sunk into his chair. Beth came in, and without saying a word sat down in the other chair.

During the night two more came, alive and healthy. In the morning they had seven live, healthy, deformed pups. The light of day somehow added just a touch of reality to the events of the night.

In the cafeteria, drinking coffee, they looked over the results. "You know what?" Beth said. "They all came a day early."

"What?" They were both half asleep.

"Well, look," she insisted, turning the logbook toward Charlie. "We don't expect any litters until sometime today. The ones born yesterday were a day early."

Charlie shrugged. "They come a day early lots of time. About twenty percent, I think."

"Yeah," she muttered, "I guess you're right."

But by Wednesday it was clear that he wasn't. In all there were twelve live, deformed rats, some two days old now, and all were thriving. And all had been born a day early. The other litters, born on time, were full of normal rats.

Barbara Waterper, knowing nothing about Ann or Disney, was confused by their depression. "Personally, I don't know why you're both so unhappy or why you think the results aren't clear." She thumbed through the logbook. "We know two things now. First, fifteen percent of the pups born of rats given the acid are deformed but healthy. Second, the presence of a deformed pup in a litter means the litter will be born a day early."

"But what about humans?" Charlie asked.

"Oh," she said. "That's right. I'd forgotten that there are humans who've taken the drug. You mean there might be some women carrying live, deformed fetuses. I guess that's possible." She wasn't happy with the thought. "That would be really sad."

Charlie couldn't take it. He got up from his chair and walked out of the office. "Tell her!" he shouted back at Beth as he left the lab.

He wandered up and down the hall, trying to untie some of the knots in his stomach, but failing. Somewhere a flask fell and broke, setting his nerves off again. Someone else was having a good day. He walked down to the drinking fountain and took a long drink he didn't really want. He felt as if he were on the edge of cracking up. He hadn't told Ann or Doc or anyone else yet. Beth had kept the confidence. Wandering back down the hall, he peered into Lloyd Haenners's lab. Bill Hebb was wiping up a puddle on the floor, broken glass still in evidence. Charlie smiled. "Lose an experiment?" he asked.

Bill looked up, faintly annoyed. "These flasks are so slippery, they slide right out of your hand!" He got up and rinsed a sponge out in the sink, then dropped it onto the floor again. He pushed it around with his foot, getting up the last of the puddle. Bending over, he picked it up and rinsed it out again. "That was half of my whole virus stock," he commented. "Lucky I had it in two flasks."

"Lucky, indeed," Charlie said. Hebb would never change. Feeling just a little better, he wandered back into his office.

Barbara came over and took his hand. "Charlie, I'm sorry. I had no idea."

Charlie smiled faintly. "We're all learning to live with it. Just don't spread it around." It didn't hurt anymore; he was numb for now. Turning to Beth, he commented, "Bill just lost half his virus stock. That's the flask you heard smashing out there."

Beth's face paled. "Where'd he break it?" she asked urgently.

"In his lab," Charlie answered. "He was mopping it up with a sponge . . ." He was suddenly struck by the realization of what had happened. Following Beth out of the lab, he shouted, "The bastard just washed it down the sink!"

When they got to Bill's lab, they discovered the cold water turned on full and gushing into the sink. "You idiot!" Beth shouted. She had hoped that he had just poured it in and left it. Then most would have been caught in the trap. Now it was hopeless. She stared at Bill's confused face. "You stupid idiot!"

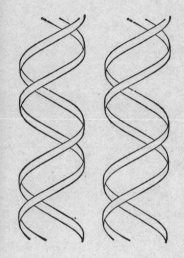

PART
III

Friday, January 1

New Year's Eve came with no celebration planned. Kip was out of town playing a big concert, and Warren and Justine were not back from visiting her parents in Vermont. Finally Ann called Doc and demanded that he and Beth join them for the evening, and between the two of them, they managed to drag both Beth and Charlie out of the lab.

It was a quiet evening. Ann was due in five weeks. Her feet had swollen just enough to make standing for long periods painful, and she tired easily now. But she was basically in a jubilant mood, happy with her "condition." Disney was kicking with a passion, and she was convinced that she was getting black and blue on the inside.

It was a strangely peaceful evening. Without anyone's saying a word, they had all agreed not to bring up Greene, or Bill Hebb, or the rat experiments, or anything remotely related to them. It reminded Charlie of a time that seemed years in the past, when life had been simpler.

But Friday, January first, saw both Beth and Charlie back in the lab. The rat experiment had been finished for a couple of days, and a new batch of rats were in, to be used for a repeat experiment. Beth was sitting in Charlie's chair when he came in. She spun it around when he entered. "You get the guest chair," she said. "I'm too pooped to get up."

Charlie dropped into the other chair. "How much sleep did you finally get?"

"Not enough," she complained. "Fred was all hyped up about his letter."

"Letter?" Charlie asked. "What letter is this?"

"Oh, didn't he tell you? He finally got mad enough yesterday to send a registered letter to Greene, care of the post office box, saying if he wasn't contacted within a week about the data he wanted, he was instituting court action immediately. I read it before he sent it off. It was full of legalese. He'd called a lawyer friend to get the proper phrasing. I think he actually expects to hear something now."

Charlie was impressed. "Maybe he will. God knows, nothing else has worked. Is he really ready to bring suit if nothing happens?"

Beth shrugged. "He's not sure. It would bring the whole thing into the open, and it could be messy in terms of both publicity and legality, since possession of acid is illegal. I think he wants to talk to you about it, too."

Charlie nodded. "We should probably all sit down and talk about it sometime this week. Hopefully we won't have to go that route, but I'm not overly impressed with Greene's cooperation." He yawned. "I didn't get all that much sleep, either," he admitted.

"What's happening with the spill?" he asked. "Anything new?"

"Not much," Beth replied. "Tom's off skiing for a week, and no one knows where. We've tried getting in touch with Crop Research Associates, but no one ever seems to be there. Maybe the whole damn place took off for the holidays."

"Did you talk to Lloyd about it?"

"Oh, Lloyd's such an ass!" she complained. "Yes, I talked to him, and he called Bill in, and they had a, quote, long, serious talk, unquote. But Lloyd insists that there's nothing to be done until either Tom gets back or we contact CRA. Basically, he says it's too late to do anything about it and it's probably harmless anyway." She was obviously irritated with Lloyd's response.

"What did it turn out to be?" Charlie asked.

"Can you believe that Lloyd doesn't know?" Beth asked. "He agrees to let Bill do these experiments without knowing what the cell line is or what the virus is! And Bill doesn't know, either! It's an absolute farce."

Charlie was amazed. "But how can he work on them without knowing what they are?"

"Oh," Beth explained casually, "they sent him the nutrients for the cells and everything. The only thing new he's trying is to use our techniques for getting the virus into the cells, and then to check and make sure that they're in. For all he knows, they could be cancer cells and a black-plague virus."

Charlie smiled. "Black plague is bacterial, and you know it."

"I know," she complained. "At least they're obviously plant cells and viruses, but I still worry that they somehow can interfere with animal cells. I don't have any idea what the virus is or whether it's been contaminated with anything else. Some virus preparations can be really dirty."

Charlie agreed. "That was brought up at the second Asilomar convention—how important it is to have a pure virus stock before you relax your safety procedures. I'm surprised that Lloyd responded so calmly."

"Oh, he didn't respond calmly. He got very upset, as he should. It's just that in the end he didn't do a damn thing about it."

"Although," Charlie pointed out, "there isn't all that much that one could do."

"For a start," Beth pointed out, "he could have thrown Hebb out of the lab!"

"Come on," Charlie remonstrated with a smile, "that's kind of extreme."

"Charlie," she complained, "don't go getting like Lloyd on me. Bill's been screwing everything up around here for two years, with absolutely no interest in or concern for the effects of it. And Tom's not much better. For all his care and concern, he just wasn't doing his job of watching Bill. When do you draw the line and say 'Enough'? Bill couldn't do much worse than he did last week."

He gave Beth a quizzical look. "You want to check out this virus?"

"What do you mean?"

He gestured to the next room and the rats waiting for the acid experiment. "Come on, we don't need all of them for the acid. Let's give the virus to some of them. In fact, we could give them the virus and then mate them. If the virus survives, we can check its effects on the fetuses as well as the mothers. Aren't there places to keep them where it would be safe?"

Beth nodded. "Up on the fourth floor they keep animals with dangerous viruses and infections. I don't think they're anywhere near full up. They just finished building the setup last year, so it's got room for a lot of expansion." She got up from his chair. "Come on, let's go check it out."

An hour later they had finished the grand tour of the new facility with its director and were moving their animals upstairs, along with a vial of the virus. The director was serious about his job, and he stayed with them throughout the process of giving the virus to the rats, moving the rats to their housing area, and cleaning up. "You had no right to expect to find me here today," he joked. "New Year's Day is supposed to be a holiday. But nobody ever told these animals that."

Charlie laughed. "Well, we appreciate your help, walking us through the whole procedure the first time. There seem to be a lot of places where one could slip up."

He nodded. "Keeping viruses contained isn't an easy job, but I'd hate to see some of them get out. It's my personal policy to walk everyone through the first time. Can you imagine what could happen if someone got sloppy and let some of these viruses out?"

Sunday, January 3

Patterson looked out the window of the thirtieth-floor apartment at the evening traffic creeping through downtown Manhattan. "I don't like it," he said. "Those bugs look like military hardware, and if the army's got him bugged, they must be on to something." He dropped the photos on the table.

Alder thought for a moment. "Does he know the place is bugged?"

"Of course not!" Patterson gruffed. "He doesn't even know about *our* bugs. Speaking of which, are they still operative?"

Alder nodded. "But that doesn't mean they weren't spotted. I didn't inactivate any of theirs, except the phone bug, and that one will look like an accident."

Patterson sank into a chair. "So whoever has the other bugs presumably has a tape of the meeting with those three guys, Tommy, Charlie, and—who?"

Alder crushed out his cigarette. "Kip. The third one was Kip, whoever the hell they are. Sure, if the other bugs were there early enough, they got the conversation, too." He lit another cigarette. "Not to mention my own little chat with him."

"Which brings up the question of the woman who asked about you," Patterson pointed out.

Alder nodded. "We've got someone on her now, but she's clean as far as we can tell. But it bodes no good. All of a sudden there's too much focus on him. Washington's not too happy, either. They don't want any interference from the military and are pressing hard to keep them in the dark on the whole thing.

215

Meanwhile, they want us to try to tidy things up at this end."

Patterson frowned. "Well, I guess we'd better get on with it."

Tuesday, January 5

Beth quietly watched Tom's face as he responded to the news of the spill. She suddenly realized that Darnell was a more complicated person than she had assumed. In one moment she saw several emotions flicker across his face, and then it returned to its usual calm expression.

"I can't believe that Bill could be so stupid. Was anything done about it?"

"Oh," Beth replied casually, "he'd washed it all down with lots of water, so it was altogether too late by the time I got there. I mean, I shouted at him, and Lloyd shouted at him, but that's all. Bill, of course, didn't understand why we were all upset about a corn virus."

The emotions flickered across Tom's face again at the mention of Lloyd. "How did Lloyd find out?" he asked.

"I told him," Beth replied, challenging him to object.

"Well," he replied cautiously, "that was probably the best thing to do. It's too bad I was out of town."

"Why?" she insisted. "What would you have done?"

He wasn't happy with the challenge. "I don't know," he dodged. "Maybe watched him more closely, caught him just before he threw it out."

Beth shrugged. Somehow he dodged all the questions. "But the point is that we shouldn't have to watch him all the time. What use is that?"

Tom frowned. "It wasn't me that picked him, you know. But CRA is determined to have someone with a lot of experience in Lloyd's lab, seeing as how he's got the best techniques for this sort of work. Myself, I would have been much happier with our first choice." He smiled at her. "Made any decisions since I saw you last?"

Beth shook her head. "I'm still holding out for something around here." But she snapped back to the issue. "Tom, what is the virus that Bill spilled?"

"I'm not sure of its exact name, but it's something they're working on at CRA."

"Come on, Tom! That doesn't tell me anything. Is it a dangerous plant virus? Does it have some recombined DNA in it? What sort of thing is it?"

But Tom wouldn't budge. "Beth, I honestly don't know the details. Some of this stuff gets locked up as industrial secrets, and they don't tell more people than need to know."

"Well, don't you think that we need to know now?" she insisted.

"Maybe," he said, "maybe we do." He seemed to be deciding. "Look, I'm going out to Iowa, probably this Thursday. I'll try to find out then. I'm sure I can get the information we need."

"Again so soon?" Beth asked. "Weren't you there just a couple of weeks ago?"

"Well, things are at a funny point," he said, "and there are a lot of major decisions to be made that they'd like my opinion on."

Beth gave up. "Okay, then, but you promise you'll find out about the virus?"

"Promise."

"And the cell line, too?"

"The cell line, too."

Beth smiled thinly. "Thanks. If I see Bill come in, should I tell him you want to talk to him?"

Tom frowned. "No, I'll find him myself. Otherwise he'll walk in when I'm in the middle of something and can't possibly talk. He does that somehow."

She wandered across the hall, wanting to talk to Charlie about Tom's reluctance to discuss the spill. He was on the phone when she walked in. He looked up and pointed to a chair for her. He seemed upset.

"Patterson?" he asked into the phone. "The same one?" She could hear someone talking at the other end but couldn't make out any words.

"So did you find out anything? . . . No, that was probably the best thing to do. Okay, I'll talk to you when you get back. Beth's sitting here right now. Look, what about your friend Tommy? . . . What about twelve K? . . . Okay, it sounds like you've done all you could. Call me as soon as you get back? . . . Thanks. Bye."

He hung up the phone and stared at it. Finally he looked up. "That was Kip," he explained. "He was down in New York, looking for Ralph Masco."

"The pusher?" Beth asked. "The one who sold the Gloryhits?"

"Yeah," Charlie said. "He's dead."

Beth froze in the chair. "Dead?" There was a touch of fear in her voice. "Murdered?"

"Probably," Charlie explained. "It was a hit-and-run driver. There was a witness, about a block away, who said it looked intentional. It's not at all clear.

"Apparently, when the police checked out his apartment, they discovered a huge supply of dope. That's when they decided to bring in the homicide squad."

"You got this from the police?" she asked.

"No. When Kip and I were down there the second time we met this woman who knew Masco, so he checked with her. She was totally freaked. Apparently he had come in earlier that evening and told her that he had to break a date with her so he could go meet some guy. He never made it."

Beth's face was pale. "Do they have any leads?"

"Kip didn't know. This woman didn't know of any, and Kip decided that there was no need to interact with the police, who undoubtedly would want to know who he was and whatnot."

"What did I hear you saying about Patterson?" she asked.

Charlie frowned. "Apparently the police—I mean the city police—have been more or less pushed out of the picture. It's not clear who is investigating, but there was a guy named Patterson in charge. Kip got a pretty good description, and I'm supposed to check with Doc to see if it's the same guy that was in on the bust."

"You mean you think they're connected? How could they be?"

"Well," Charlie said, "if Doc's bust was connected with the Gloryhits somehow, then that could be a link." He was playing scientist. "But it would be hard to imagine who would have known that Doc was involved with Gloryhits, or even that Masco was."

"Maybe Patterson's a federal narcotics agent," Beth suggested. "I mean, Doc was being busted for a huge amount of heroin, and God knows what they found at Masco's place."

"That's certainly a simpler explanation," he admitted.

"And as a scientist . . ."

"I have to accept the simplest explanation." Charlie finished the sentence for her and laughed for a second. "You win."

But the good mood quickly disappeared. "I guess I should call Doc," he said. "He's not going to be happy about this. Our leads seem to dry up real fast in this business."

"Maybe it really isn't as easy as it seems in the movies," Beth suggested. "But don't bother to call. Doc should be here in ten minutes anyhow. We're going out to dinner, and it's his turn to drive."

"An egalitarian relationship," Charlie commented, a smile on his face.

Beth smiled back. "If you want to pay gas and maintenance, I'll be happy to drive. But a dollar ten a gallon is getting kind of steep."

Charlie put a hand up in defense. "I'm sorry, I'm sorry. I take it back. Stupid comment."

Beth accepted his apologies. They sat quietly for a minute, thinking about Masco.

Beth changed the subject. "What's happening with the virus-treated rats? They should be getting on now."

Charlie shrugged. "It's only been four days. That's not very pregnant."

Beth apologized. "Time seems to be going slowly again. What do you plan to do with them?"

"Not much. I'm going to put most of my effort into repeating the acid study. I think I'll just let the rats with the virus go to term, see if litter sizes are normal or what."

"No Caesareans at all?" Beth asked, somewhat surprised.

Charlie let out a long sigh. "Oh, Christ, I don't know. Maybe we could do some around fifteen days. I just feel so wound up with all this acid stuff, I don't have much energy for anything else." He thought for a second. "Sure, what the hell. We can do a few Caesareans. They won't take any time at all."

"Now, that's the kind of enthusiasm I like," Doc boomed, coming into Charlie's office. "Sure, we can knock off a few Caesareans, and maybe an appendectomy or two before lunch, too. I know surgeons like that. You two'll be rich in no time."

Beth smiled. "It's an unusual day that brings you here early."

He laughed. "Some days actually end on time. There's nothing we can do about it." Turning to Charlie, he asked, "How's it going?"

The smile left Charlie's face. "Bad news," he said. "Masco's dead, probably murdered."

"What? You're joking!"

Charlie shook his head. "I wish I were," he said. "Kip just called from New York." He went through the story again.

"That sounds like the same Patterson," Doc said when Charlie had finished. "But Christ, it describes half of America, and ninety-nine percent of all plain-clothes cops."

"But Kip said he didn't think the guy was a cop, didn't act like it at all."

Doc nodded. "I got the same impression. Hell, I'm sure it's the same one." He frowned. "You think he's just a roving narc?"

"Or?" Charlie asked.

Doc shook his head. "All this stuff reminds me of Peter Alder."

"Who?" Beth asked.

"A pig," Doc explained. "Back—what, almost ten years ago—when Charlie and I were getting into politics together, there was this guy Peter Alder who turned out to be a provocateur. Got a bunch of people set up for some sabotage work and then informed on them. Busted up a pretty good science research group that had been investigating military uses of scientific research. Anyhow, it ended up being so blatant that they all got off on entrapment. Alder left town real quick, right after the trial."

"He was a police agent?" Beth asked.

Charlie shook his head and frowned. "No, he wasn't that. He was too smart for that. At first we thought he must have been just a science freak who got busted for drugs or something and then was used by the police."

"But then," Doc added, "we decided that wasn't right, either. Because he so obviously was pushing for the prosecution."

"I know," Charlie said. "I was going to say that." He turned to Beth. "In the end we decided that he was FBI or CIA or something like that."

"Oh," Doc said, "you mean you never heard?"

"About what?" Charlie asked.

"The results of Kip's search."

"No, I never even heard of Kip's search. What is it?"

Doc explained. "When the federal government passed the revised freedom of information act, Kip decided to go back and try to dig out the story of Peter Alder. He was down in Washington doing a gig, and spent a couple of days poring through old FBI memos. There was one memo saying that they were unable to find out anything about the background of Peter Alder. That was from before he turned informer. Then there was another, dated after the bust, intimating that Alder had CIA ties. They referred to his being attached to a 'separate agency.' Kip thought they must have been referring to the CIA."

"You never saw him again after that?" Beth asked.

Doc shook his head. "Never. I'm sure the CIA just pulled him out of Boston and resettled him somewhere else with a new name and a new job. Too many people around here knew him. He couldn't have hung around."

"Well, poor Masco probably wasn't a CIA agent. It sounds as though he was closer to the Mafia," said Beth.

"The CIA isn't much nicer," Doc pointed out.

"Well, anyhow," Charlie said, "we've reached a dead end on the source of the acid. What's happening with you and Greene?"

Doc shrugged. "It's only been four days, so I'm not too worried yet." He paused, a frown on his face. "I don't know what to do next if he refuses. If we go to court over it, it's going to be in all the papers."

"Well?" Beth asked. "If that's what you have to do, why not? It's obviously important to get the information, and maybe there are Gloryhits kicking around somewhere else in the country. It wouldn't hurt to get the word out."

"Nonsense," Charlie objected. "Pushers would just start calling it something else. That's all."

"But still," Beth said, "maybe a little publicity is what we need."

"Anyhow," Charlie pointed out, "the week isn't up yet."

Thursday, January 7

Two days later, an excited Doc telephoned Charlie. "Greene called!" he announced.

"Fantastic!" Charlie exclaimed. "What happened?"

"It was great," Doc replied. "He was all sweetness and light. Said he meant to get back to me, but had gotten bogged down in some other stuff. Apologized profusely and all that."

"But did he agree?" Charlie demanded.

"Completely. He said he was a little upset about the tone of the letter, and that I should send him a detailed statement of what I want, just so he would be covered. He promised that I'd have the data in my hands within a week of when he got my letter."

Charlie let out a whoop of delight. "Incredible! Have you sent it yet?"

"Have I sent it? The bastard only hung up two minutes ago. I haven't even sat down yet."

"He was a little upset about the tone of the letter, eh?" Charlie laughed.

"I'd say so," Doc snorted. "It's obvious I'd never have heard from him again otherwise."

"Of course not. Have you told Beth? Or do I get to?"

"No, I haven't, but let me call her. I want to hear her reaction."

"Are you going to call right now?"

"Yeah."

"Okay, then I'll walk across the hall, so I can at least watch. Talk to you later."

"Right. Hey, listen, can we get together this evening and talk about what goes into that letter?"

"Sure. After dinner? Ann said she'd cook tonight, and I don't want to burden her with extra work."

"Fine. How is she?"

"Tired," Charlie answered. "What is today, the seventh? She's due four weeks from today, which means we're almost at the 'any time now' stage. No more trips to New York for me."

"Just tired, though?"

"Oh, yeah, nothing serious at all. The swelling in her legs has gone away, and she's walking around easily now. She's just carrying an extra thirty pounds around with her all the time, and it's hard."

"Well, it sounds as though she's doing great," Doc said. "Tell her I'm looking forward to seeing her tonight."

"Will do." Charlie hung up the phone and went over to Beth's lab.

She was sitting at her desk, reading a book. She smiled at Charlie.

"Hey," he said, "that's fiction you're reading. Not allowed."

She made a face. "Tom's flown off to Iowa, and I'm not going to give Hebb enough time to himself to do anything stupid again. Right now I'm waiting for him to get back from a leisurely lunch. But I'm not going to try to do any experiments until Tom gets back. I'm serious about watching Bill."

They were interrupted by the phone. Charlie watched with delight as Beth heard the news. She turned to him.

"I know," he said. "I've already talked to him."

Turning back to the phone, she said, "Fred, this is so great. I never really thought that a threat would do any good, but you sure called it right . . . Okay, I'll see you later."

Hanging up the phone, she turned to Charlie. "That's fantastic!"

"I know." He grinned. "I came over to watch your reaction. Maybe we're finally going to get a real break." But Beth frowned. "Did I say something wrong?" he asked.

"No," she replied, shaking her head. "I was just thinking that our last lead was when we located Ralph Masco." They were both quiet for a moment. "Have you heard any more about it?"

"Kip tried calling his friend, to see if he'd heard anything, but couldn't reach him. I don't know if he's tried again."

"That still has me upset," she said, "even though I never knew him. I wish I could believe it was just an accident."

"But it looks as if it wasn't," Charlie said. "And it would have to have been the person who called him that same evening."

"Why?" Beth asked.

"Because they'd have to set him up—get him to walk to some place where they could run him down without much risk of a witness."

She shuddered. "So Masco must have known him."

Charlie agreed. Looking out the door, he saw Bill Hebb returning to work. "Your nemesis is back."

"Yep," she sighed. "I'll give him a couple of minutes to get started messing things up before I wander over."

"Is Darnell going to be gone long?"

"I don't know. He left all of a sudden. I'm pretty sure it's because of the spill, but he insists it's not. Normally he wouldn't be going for at least a couple of weeks, but he said something came up. He's acting more and more like somebody's lackey. I'm really starting to dislike him."

Charlie nodded. "I know. I tried to talk to him about the spill, and he was really slippery. I couldn't even get the type of virus out of him."

"He claims he doesn't know," Beth explained, "but he's promised to 'look into the matter,' as he put it, on this trip. So, hopefully, we should know more in a few days."

"Does he know about our experiments?" he asked.

"No. I wouldn't say I'm hiding the fact from him, but I'm not going to start offering up information if he's not."

"Sounds like a friendship on the wane."

"Christ, Charlie, I've got to get out of this place,"

she complained. "I'm just about ready to accept that offer from Los Angeles."

"No news on the job front?" he asked.

"As of now, I've nothing left. Lloyd is absolutely up a wall. He's starting to think it's because he hasn't been pushy enough."

"Say," Charlie said, "have you tried Sid Cramer's department?"

"At MIT?" Beth asked. "I was told he didn't have any openings."

"He didn't, but I was talking to him yesterday, and he was griping that one of his young faculty members had decided to move, sort of unexpectedly, and would be leaving in a few months. So that space should be open."

Beth was excited. "I'll get a letter together right away. I would have written him the first time around, but Lloyd said there weren't any openings."

"And I'll give a call," Charlie added. "Maybe it would help."

Beth agreed. "I think Lloyd knows him pretty well, too, so maybe we'll finally get somewhere!"

Friday, January 8

"You should have come over last night," Charlie said. "We wrote the letter to Greene, and even Ann got into the act. It's a beautiful letter."

"Now he won't answer," Beth complained.

"Not a chance. We've got him beat, and he's admitted it. It's a fine letter. We're demanding data on specific fetuses and a Xerox of their notes on the fetuses. We're also demanding information on similar deformities in the other six towns. That was Ann's idea. It should really blow Greene's mind, since he has no idea that Doc's aware of the other towns being studied."

Beth frowned. "I hope we don't push him too far."

"Look, if we get a quarter of what we're demanding, we'll have all we need. Besides, you keep forgetting, it doesn't really matter to Greene whether he gives us the information or not."

Beth shrugged. "So now we can try the same stunt with the damn virus that Bill spilled."

"What's the story on that?" he asked.

"Oh, Tom's not back yet. He's due back today, I guess." Frustrated, she complained, "Those bastards are getting off way too easily. Look at us, big hot-shit radical scientists, and we just sit around with our mouths open over this spill."

"So what do you want, we should shoot Bill dead?"

A look of delight came into Beth's face. "I'll tell you what we should do. In fact, I can thank you for the idea."

"Well, go on," Charlie insisted.

"Look, remember you mentioned that there's a federal panel set up to investigate things like noncompliance with the Asilomar guidelines?"

"Yes," Charlie responded slowly.

"Let's report the spill."

"But we don't know that it's recombinant DNA."

"And neither do Bill and Tom, or they didn't when the spill occurred. Charlie, it's a perfect case. They didn't even know what they were working with! They had no way to know if even the levels of protection they were pretending to use were good enough."

Charlie wasn't happy. "That's going to cause havoc around here . . ."

"Charlie, don't go liberal on me now. When I said that scientists were too elitist to report each other, you denied it. Well, now it's a challenge. Report it."

He was furious. Furious that she thought him a

hypocrite, furious that she was putting him in the role
of the establishment man, but most furious at how
close to home her accusations came. Even so, he was
hesitant. "Wait for the results of the rat experiments."

"Why?"

"Well, because they might tell us something. If we
get any indication of the virus causing any abnormalities, I'll feel a lot better about making a big
fuss about it, and they'll be forced to move faster on
it."

"And it'll make it easier for you to face Lloyd?" she
suggested.

"Yes, dammit, that too. But I'll file the complaint
either way." There. He'd taken the plunge. It felt
good—he was back in the thick of it again. "Should we
tell Lloyd?" he asked.

"No."

Realizing that they'd been talking rather loudly, Beth
suddenly felt nervous and stuck her head out into the
hall.

"Hi, Beth. I've been looking for you." It was Tom
Darnell.

"Hi," she replied nervously. He would have been
able to hear them from the hall. Maybe even clearly.
"When did you get back into town?"

"Just this morning. I wanted to tell you that I
talked to my boss about the virus, and he convinced
me that it's perfectly safe. They've checked the cell
line for any viruses that might be in them, and there
aren't any. The virus can only infect the plant cells,
and, in addition, it's not even a very healthy virus.
They've mutated it some, just like you've done with
yours. Which doesn't excuse Bill for spilling it, or
me for not supervising him more closely. They almost
took my scalp for that, and they're starting to think
they should have paid more attention to my opinion
of Bill. But Lloyd apparently wrote him a pretty nice
recommendation, and that convinced them."

Beth frowned. "I don't understand how Lloyd could
do that."

"Maybe he should spend more time in the lab,"
Tom joked. "But I have to go talk to Bill. There was

some discussion about his coming out to Iowa sooner than we'd been planning."

"The sooner the better," Beth retorted.

Tom smiled. "I'll see you later."

She went back into Charlie's office.

"I take it Tom's back?" he asked.

"Yeah."

"You just bumped into him walking in?"

She frowned. "No, he was just outside the door."

"Do you think he heard anything?" He didn't like the idea.

"He acted as if he didn't even know I was in here."

"Woosh," Charlie said. "That's a relief."

"I don't know," Beth said. "I went out there because I realized that I was sort of shouting. There's really no way he couldn't have heard us."

"Unless he had only just walked up," Charlie suggested.

"It was kind of weird. He was just leaning against the wall outside your door." She seemed puzzled.

"Obviously eavesdropping," Charlie laughed. "Come on, you've got conspiracy on your mind."

"Well, what about telling Lloyd?" Beth asked, bringing the discussion back to where they'd left it.

"I feel that we ought to," said Charlie.

"But you don't want to have to do it," Beth finished.

He laughed. "Fair enough. I don't want to."

She shrugged. "Look, as long as we're putting off filing a complaint until the rat experiments are done, let's put this off, too. If we get a result, like you said, it'd be easier to justify to him." Smiling, she added, "I don't particularly relish the idea of telling him myself. After all, who are we complaining about?"

"What do you mean?"

"Well, we talk as though it's just Bill and Tom that we're complaining about."

"Isn't it?"

"No, it isn't. This is Lloyd's lab, and he's in charge of it. That's the way he wants it, and that's the way it is. So that makes him primarily responsible for what happens in it."

"Oh, come on," Charlie said. "He was just letting Bill use the space, that's all."

"What do you mean, that's all? You let a drunk borrow your car, and he goes out and kills someone with it, you don't have any blame?"

"I doubt that you do, legally," Charlie said.

"Oh, shit! Charlie, pretend it was someone you didn't know. Would you still act this way?"

"No," he realized. "I'd take the same position you are. You're right."

Beth sank back in her chair, exhausted. "Okay, let's wait for the results of the rat experiments."

Saturday, January 9

The next night, Charlie couldn't sleep. He and Ann had gone out to a movie, an old Saturday-night tradition which they had recently revived. Ann was exhausted when they got home, and had fallen asleep quickly. Finally Charlie gave up and got out of bed. It was almost two. He had spent some time on Friday drawing up a draft of the complaint but had forgotten to bring it home. Now he was irritated, because he'd decided that at least some time on Sunday should go into it. He decided to drive to the lab and get it.

The empty streets glistened with hard-packed snow, and the intersections seemed unnaturally quiet. He drove in silence, listening to the stillness of the normally busy city. He rode the elevator to the third floor. Wide awake, he hoped he would be able to sleep when he got back home.

His footsteps echoed loudly in the empty hall. Down at the end, he saw light coming from his lab. Beth, he thought. I'm not the world's only insomniac. But the person who stepped out of the lab wasn't Beth. At the distance he couldn't make out the stranger's features, beyond those of a male of rather normal build. Seeing Charlie, he turned the other way down the hall and walked to the staircase.

"Who the hell was that?" Charlie wondered, hurrying down the hall. Inside the door of the lab he was met by five crates of rats. Stealing rats? It was the craziest thing he'd ever heard of. Sure enough, the crates were full of pregnant rats. "Oh, shit," he moaned, "how am I ever going to get them sorted out?"

He walked into the animal room and turned on the light. What he saw only confused him more. There were no rats missing! Picking up the phone, he called the security office and had them send a man over.

"So I don't get it. You've got extra rats?"

"That's it," Charlie replied. "All I can figure is that they're stolen from someone else and whoever stole them had just gotten to my lab. Maybe he hadn't gotten enough or something."

The security officer scratched his head. "Doesn't make any sense, but I'll write it up."

"Maybe you should try to find out if any other rat rooms have been disturbed," Charlie suggested.

The security officer looked at his watch. "I go off at three, but maybe they'll have someone on the next shift check it." He pointed to the crates. "What do you want me to do with these?"

Charlie sighed. "I'll put them in my room here. They need food and water."

"Ugly things," the man said. "Can't imagine who'd want them."

Monday, January 11

1

On Monday, Charlie got a call from the security office. "We've checked with everyone who's running experiments with rats, and nobody's missing any."

"That can't be," Charlie insisted. "I've got them sitting in my lab right now. They didn't come out of the air."

"Look, Professor, I know you've got those five crates of rats; it's in the report. I'm just calling to tell you that they didn't come from any of the labs in this building."

"What about the biology building?" Charlie asked. "Or the physiology building?"

"Well, first of all," he answered, "we only run security for the medical center. You'd have to check with the security office on the main campus for that. But I don't see why someone stealing rats would lug them up to the third floor of the med center."

"Are you sure you didn't miss someone?" Charlie asked.

"Professor, I've been doing this job for fifteen years now, and I think I do a pretty decent job."

"Yeah, okay," Charlie conceded. "I just can't figure where they could have come from."

"Well, I guess they're yours if you want them."

Charlie laughed. "Thanks." He hung up the phone as Beth walked in.

"How's it going?" she asked. He had told her the story earlier in the day.

"Oh, that was the security office. They say nobody's missing any rats."

"But where could they be from?"

"I have no idea," Charlie admitted. "All I know is that I have twice as many pregnant rats as I have any use for." Beth laughed and was about to say something, when the phone rang.

Charlie picked it up. "Hello . . . Yes, it is . . . Okay." He turned to Beth. "A call from the president of the university." He made a face to show that he was suitably unimpressed.

"Hello, Dr. Cotten?"

"Yes."

"This is President Armstrong calling. I was wondering if you might have a minute?"

"Certainly. What can I do for you?" He saluted into the phone for Beth's benefit.

"I'm calling in connection with an accident that occurred in Dr. Haenners's laboratory a few days ago. I believe that you're aware of some material that was spilled?"

All the humor left Charlie's face. "Yes, I am," he replied curtly.

"Well, a rather unusual thing happened this morning. I received a call from Washington, from some government people . . ."

"Yes?"

"And they said that they had been informed of this spill, and that it isn't dangerous at all, but that it's part of a rather delicate project the government's working on. They wanted to make sure there wouldn't be any publicity over the matter." Armstrong paused, waiting for a response.

"I see," Charlie replied slowly. "However, it was my impression that this was part of an industrial research project."

"Well," Armstrong blustered, "the government is always farming little projects out to industry—and the university, too, I might add."

"Yes," Charlie said. "Am I to understand that this is some sort of secret research?"

"Oh, no," Armstrong insisted. "It's not classified

work at all. What the individual I spoke with said was that the project was involved in some aspects of a possible international agreement that's being negotiated."

"That isn't very specific," Charlie pointed out.

"I'm aware of that, Dr. Cotten, and I've already spoken with Dr. Haenners about it. We're still a bit sensitive about certain types of research being conducted at the university. In fact, I think Dr. Haenners had decided to terminate that work. The person doing it is apparently moving to the industry's facilities shortly anyhow."

"That was my impression," Charlie replied. "But I'm not quite sure why you're calling me. Did Dr. Haenners suggest it?"

"Oh, no. The person who called from Washington asked me to talk to you and Dr. Haenners, to see if I could establish an agreement that there would be no unusual to-do made about the spill."

"I see," Charlie said, "yes, I think I do. Dr. Haenners agreed, of course?"

"Yes, he did, wholeheartedly."

"Well," Charlie hedged, "I can assure you that I won't go spreading anything about without talking to you first."

The president was silent for a moment. "Is there some reason why you might?"

"Oh, no," Charlie said, trying to sound casual, "but I hate to make promises like that without thinking about it for a while."

"Oh—well, certainly. I don't mean to push you. Why don't you think it over for a few days and then call me back?"

"Yes," Charlie agreed slowly. "I'll do that."

"Fine, then, and thank you for your time."

"You're welcome." They both hung up.

"What was all that?" Beth asked.

"I think," Charlie said, still trying to decide, "I think our friend Tom did indeed overhear our conversation the other day."

"About filing a complaint? What does that have to do with President Armstrong?"

He explained the phone call to her.

She let out a low whistle; then, irritated, she demanded, "What the hell is going on around here?" Rising from her chair, she said, "I think we ought to have a little talk with Tom."

"Wait," Charlie said. "Maybe we should think a minute first. Tom must have contacted CRA after overhearing our conversation. That's the only way to explain why they wanted Armstrong to call me in addition to Lloyd."

"Obviously, but what's this government shit?"

Charlie shook his head. "Let's ask Lloyd." They crossed the hall.

Lloyd was in shock. "I'm totally baffled," he admitted. "And I don't like the feel of it at all. I've told Bill that he has to close down his bench by the first of next week. And I've told Tom that I want to know about everything he intends to do around here from now on. I'm really upset about this. Secret government research! I don't want any stuff like that going on here!" Charlie had never seen him so upset.

"Have you talked to the people at CRA, or to Tom, about it?"

"I've talked to Tom," Haenners answered, "but he doesn't seem to know very much. He's agreed to fly out to Iowa this weekend to try to find out for us exactly what the project is."

"But I thought he just did that," Charlie complained.

"Oh, no," Beth said sarcastically, "he only found out that there was nothing to worry about. He's about as easy with information as Greene."

"Who?" Haenners asked.

"Someone we know," Charlie said. "But why don't you call CRA and talk to them yourself? That would seem to make more sense."

Haenners looked exasperated. "Of course that would. But you haven't been dealing with them for five years. Not once have I been able to get anyone who knows anything on the phone out there. At best, you can get them to call back in a day or two. I talked to Tom, and we agreed that the best thing would be for him to go down there. I've stopped the project, so I don't feel as though there's any terrible rush now."

"Or by next week," Beth corrected him.

"Next Monday," Haenners said. "There's no reason to make him dump experiments he's in the middle of."

"Why, no, of course not," Beth replied tartly.

"What I don't understand—" Haenners began. "Oh, hell, I don't understand any of it, but I also don't understand why they called you about it."

"I don't get it, either," Beth said hurriedly, before Charlie could say anything. "But didn't they say when they called you?"

"No."

"Well," Charlie said, picking up on Beth's lead, "I guess that's the least of our worries." He rose to go. "Let me know if you find out anything, will you?" he asked.

"Definitely."

Beth got up to go. "Oh, I meant to ask you, Lloyd — Have you had a chance to talk with Sid Cramer?"

"Yes. In fact, I talked with him this morning, just before Armstrong called. He wants you to come visit sometime this week and bring along your curriculum vitae and reprints of your articles. You'll probably receive his letter tomorrow." Smiling, he added, "I think you've got this one."

Beth frowned. "I don't get my hopes up anymore. But we'll see." She and Charlie left the office.

Back in his office, Charlie looked at the draft of their complaint. "So, it looks as if we shelve this for a while."

"Just a while?" Beth asked.

"Well, if the rat experiments turn something up, I'm filing it."

She smiled. "Good for you." She sat down in the chair. "See what I mean about Lloyd being an ass?"

Charlie looked surprised. "What? I was thinking that he had actually done something good."

"Oh, sure. After the president of the university calls him personally to tell him that there's secret government research going on in his lab without his even knowing about it, and that it's been spilled and all,

then he gives Bill a week! Why a week? It's an
apology to Bill. It's Lloyd saying, 'Look, Bill, I hate
to do this, but I have to.' I think Hebb should have
been thrown right out on his ear. And Tom! The way
he's been acting. I think he could have spilled it as
easily as Bill!"

"Maybe so," Charlie conceded. "So Tom's going
out to Iowa again. He's becoming a regular commuter."

"I know," Beth said. "I'm getting funnier and funnier feelings about him. How come he's so calm about
this? And why does he still claim not to know anything about the virus except that CRA says it's safe?
I don't even know that I believe it."

"Well, maybe this trip will finally clear things up."

2

In Washington, Major Pearson stared at the obstetrician and thought grimly to himself, The bastards
have actually attacked us! All five were there, late
Tuesday night, at an emergency meeting.

"I think we can save our guesses for later. Do we
have any further questions to ask before we excuse
Dr. Muller?"

"It was your definite impression that he thought that
the fetus collector was blocking his investigation?"

Muller wasn't sure. "At times that was how it
sounded, but at other times he just seemed to see it as
colossal bad luck. But he has determined that there was
a particular batch of LSD in all of the towns where
Greene was collecting."

"Did he give the name of the pusher in New York?"
one of them asked.

"No," Muller replied. "He was clearly upset about
the fact that the guy had been murdered, or at least
killed."

"What do you mean, 'at least killed'?"

"Oh, I'm sorry." Muller had left out the details the
first time through. "Apparently he died in a hit-and-
run accident. A witness said it looked like the driver
was aiming for the guy, so I assume it was murder."

The other frowned. "That's Masco, all right."

They were all silent for a minute, trying to piece it all together, to decide if there were any other questions. "Look," Pearson finally asked, "all together, how many miscarriages would you say there were?"

Muller shrugged. "I could only guess," he said, trying to calculate in his head. "Maybe ten per town, maybe fifteen. It's surprising how much LSD gets used around there. So maybe seventy-five to a hundred all together."

"Well, if there are no other questions, perhaps we should go into session." There were no objections. "Thank you, Dr. Muller. I was wondering if we could ask you to wait in the adjoining room while we hold our session. We might want to call you back for more questions."

"Certainly," he said, rising to go.

"You should find the room quite comfortable."

"Thank you," Muller replied, and left. The door closed with a solid click.

They all looked at each other in silence. "Is there agreement, then, that we've been attacked?" No one objected.

"Could someone just list what we know for sure?" Pearson asked.

"I can do that. One, we know that Jim Karls is an alias for a person who has been attending meetings on recombinant DNA. He has taken steps to hide his identity. Two, the Russians are working on something that we can assume is a biological warfare project with recombinant DNA. Three, Karls made connection with a drug pusher in New York, who was subsequently murdered. Four, the pusher had sold a specific batch of LSD to people in eight towns, and the acid caused an unusually high rate of spontaneous abortion when taken prior to the time of conception. This is different from the action of LSD, so it was presumably caused by something added to the LSD. And five, someone has been collecting the aborted fetuses from all eight towns, and this person can no longer be found.

"The conclusion, if I may, is that Karls, as a Russian agent, has been doing two things: first, gathering information on American research into recombinant

DNA and, second, directing a covert testing program of a Russian-designed biowarfare weapon."

"I think that's the only possible explanation." The rest nodded in affirmation.

"In that case," Pearson said, "I would like to withdraw my request for a moratorium, and ask that this group inform the Joint Chiefs of Staff that we feel that some sort of reprisal, presumably with the botulinum influenza, should be launched immediately."

Tuesday, January 12

TOP SECRET!   EYES ONLY!

Effective this date, 12 January, authorization is given for deployment of agent Black, effective power 1.25 (one point two five), for initial infection of 100 (one hundred) persons per target, 8 (eight) targets, code numbers 62 (sixty-two) through 69 (sixty-nine), code sheet 142 (one hundred forty-two).

(signed) John Cordon
          for the Joint Chiefs of Staff

TOP SECRET   EYES ONLY

Stanley Johnson stared at the letter, then ripped it in half and threw it into the garbage. Somehow, he had never expected it to come to this. Westland had spoken to him on the phone yesterday, saying that a specific request for materials would be coming, but he hadn't made it any clearer than that. Except to make it absolutely clear that there were to be no questions asked and there would be no explanation given.

In the freezer were the frozen virus stocks, one hundred vials for each mutator stock. At least it was the 1.25 strain; that one had the least spread. Still, they were talking about killing a thousand people in the eight targets. He realized he didn't even know where the targets were. Russia? China? The Mideast? He didn't want to know. He withdrew eight vials, carefully checking and rechecking the labels. Each of them contained virus grown from a single virus. Each had been checked for the presence of the botulinum toxin. And each of the original eight viruses was grown from a single virus in which the speed of the mutator gene had been double checked at one and a quarter. Nothing else could have been done to insure that they were correct, except to check the mutators in each of the hundred vials individually, and there had been no time for that. He packed the vials in dry ice, and called for a military courier. Five minutes later, they were on their way.

Friday, January 15

On Friday, a rather puzzled Beth came into Charlie's lab. He was dissecting some of the acid rats—fourteen days pregnant—and the results were duplicating those of the previous test, with almost identical numbers of deformities. He looked up and noted her expression. "You look confused."

"I am," she replied. "I just got a bizarre phone call."

"Oh?" Charlie stopped working and asked about it.

"Some guy just called up and said he was a friend of Bill Hebb's, that Bill had left for Iowa, and could I clean up his bench for him."

Charlie laughed. "What's so strange about that? It sounds just like him to me."

"No, it doesn't," Beth insisted. "I was talking to him just yesterday, and he was upset about having to leave so soon. But he said he had a big experiment that he'd be able to finish just in time, like Sunday afternoon. As of quitting time yesterday, he was almost excited about it."

"So maybe he came in last night and found that the experiment had failed. That happens all the time, and I can see why he'd split after a big experiment failed."

"Yeah, that all makes sense," Beth said, "except that he never comes in at night. Even when he's running experiments that he's superexcited about, he'll skip points rather than come in after five to get them. Besides, I was here until one A.M." She paused for a minute. "And, Charlie, he'd never think to call and ask me to clean up after him. He'd never do anything like that. He'd just walk out and never be seen or heard from again."

Charlie shrugged his shoulders. "So what do you think?"

"I don't know. It's getting creepy with it's being secret government research and all."

"Maybe CRA convinced him to come right away. Lloyd mentioned something about everything being speeded up. Maybe they got him to move just like that, and then they called to tell us."

"I don't know," she repeated. "I just wish there were some way to get in touch with him."

"What about Tom? Did you ask him about it?"

"He left for Iowa this morning."

"Maybe Bill went with Tom," Charlie suggested. "Tom'll probably know when he gets back."

"I just wish Tom weren't the one holding all the cards," Beth muttered.

Monday, January 18

But on Monday, Tom's answers seemed too good to be true. "You have no idea how relieved I was to find out what it was," he said. "That bit about it being secret government research had me up a tree!" It was good old Tom, everybody's friend. "It turns out the government has come up with this supersoy, as they call it, that increases soy crop yields the way superrice increased rice production. But the hooker is that it's unusually sensitive to a lot of plant diseases. So what they've contracted with CRA to do, is to get into the plant a plasmid named PL142. The plasmid carries the genetic information for resistance to a large number of standard plant diseases. It's found in nature hooked to a virus, which also infects the soy plant. Apparently the virus likes the plasmid, because it keeps the plant from getting infected by anything else. So CRA is trying to get the virus into the plant cells, and then select cells in tissue culture which are resistant to the other diseases but not infected by the virus. That'll happen on occasion, when the virus separates from the plasmid. And that's the big supersecret research."

"Well," said Lloyd, "that makes me feel better! I was having nightmares that we were doing secret germ-warfare stuff." He laughed nervously. "But I shouldn't have had that going on in my lab without knowing more about it. That won't happen again."

"Doubtful," Beth murmured to Charlie. "Tom," she asked, "do you know anything about Bill's going to Iowa?"

"Has he left already?" Haenners asked, glancing at the mess on Bill's benchtop.

"Yes, he has," Tom said. "He actually ended up flying the last leg from Chicago with me. He'd flown out of Boston a couple of hours ahead of me, but planes to central Iowa aren't so frequent."

"What about all his stuff?" Charlie asked. "He didn't even take his books out of the lab."

"Oh, CRA will pay for movers, I'm sure," Tom said. "I don't know about this stuff in the lab—maybe we can get it all together, and I'll take it over to his apartment before the movers come."

Haenners frowned. "He sure left his bench a mess."

Tom looked at Beth. "He told me that he was having a friend call and ask you to clean up for him. He was apologetic about it, but I guess he decided to move rather suddenly."

"I'd say," Beth complained. "It's sort of late for him to ask a favor, after he's already left the lab. It's not as if I could have said no."

"Oh, we'll all help," Haenners suggested.

"Don't bother," Beth replied. "It'll be a pleasure removing the last traces of Bill from the lab."

Charlie laughed. "Isn't it a bit unusual for someone to move before the movers come?" he asked Tom. "I thought they wouldn't go into a house unless someone was there."

"Bill gave me his keys," Tom said, fishing them out of his pocket. "I said I'd go to the apartment when the movers came."

"Lucky for him you ran into each other in Chicago," Beth commented. She found it hard to believe that Bill was apologetic about anything.

Tom was about to reply when the phone rang. Picking it up, he said hello, then passed it to Beth. "It's for you."

She spoke quietly into the phone. Her expression slowly changed to delight. "Sure, something like that sounds fine . . . That sounds great. I'll talk it over with Dr. Haenners and get back to you later this week, when we've gotten a better estimate, but that does sound about right . . . Thank you—thanks a lot." Hanging up the phone, she turned to the curious audience. "Sid Cramer just gave me the job!"

Cheers broke out from Charlie and Lloyd. Charlie gave her a big hug. "Well, congratulations! You couldn't have done better."

Haenners shook her hand. "You had me worried there for a while, you know."

She smiled. "I know. Me too."

Tom offered his congratulations. "I must admit that in a way I'm sorry. But I suppose you'll be happier there than out in Iowa."

"Well," Beth said, "Sid Cramer chairs one of the top genetics departments in the country. I wouldn't have passed it up for anything."

"I didn't even know you'd applied for a job there," Tom commented.

"That's what you get for going to Iowa all the time," Beth teased.

"Maybe," he conceded with a smile. "Well, congratulations." He left the lab, leaving the others to celebrate in earnest.

Tuesday, January 19

On Tuesday, Doc and Beth went out to dinner to celebrate. "You know," he commented, "before all this started with the acid, and then the virus, I used to expect things to work out for the best. Maybe they still do in the end." He was almost as happy about her job as she was. Now she could stay in the Boston area without compromising her career.

"I don't know," she teased. "Back then I was positive that I was sick and tired of the East Coast and wanted to move to California."

"Naw," Doc said. "All people do out there is lie in the sun and bleach their brains out." He squeezed her hand. "I'm so happy that you'll be staying around for reasons other than me. I think that would have just had to cause problems."

Beth agreed. But as they talked, she became aware of an underlying tension in Doc. "What aren't you saying?" she finally asked apprehensively.

"Huh? Oh, just some more of that acid stuff. I promised myself I'd tell you about it tomorrow."

"Bad?" she asked.

"Later," he said. "Let's have our dinner."

"No, come on. What's up?"

He gave in. "Some interesting, some bad. Which do you want first?"

"Bad."

"Well, I don't know if you've noticed, but Greene's overdue with his response."

"He is? I didn't realize it. How far?"

"Not much," Doc said. "I mailed the letter to him

245

a week ago last Thursday, so I figure he got it a week ago yesterday. That would make it only one day late."

"That's so bad?"

"No. But rather than let it drag out, I thought I'd call that answering service and leave a message that I was getting anxious."

"And?"

"They're not taking calls for Greene anymore."

"When did that happen?"

"They stopped a week ago Monday, which would've been just when Greene got the letter."

Beth's cheerful expression was growing increasingly somber. "Can you still reach him by the post office box?"

"And that's the rest of it, I'm afraid. I got the form back from the post office on the box of his." He paused for a moment. "It's rented to a Felix Greene, at 540 Cathedral Parkway. But they noted that the box expired last week and hasn't been renewed. So I can't reach him that way, either."

"What about a home phone," Beth suggested, "now that you've got his name and address?"

"I tried that. No such listing. In fact, no Felix Greene at all." He frowned. "That's the bad news."

Beth stroked the back of his hand. "So we're not going to get anything from him."

"I don't know," Doc replied. "Kip's going down there tomorrow. Maybe I'll have him try to scare the guy up at home, see if he's even there still. I've got a sour feeling that he's up and split."

"But that's crazy," Beth objected. "The guy's got a home, and a job. If the box and all was in his name, he couldn't have been too small a fish. Where could he have gone? And where's this research institute he was working for?"

"Oh," Doc lamented, "I left that out. I was so wrapped up in trying to force the data from him that I never concerned myself with finding out what institute he was connected with. Today I called a half dozen obstetricians, and none of them knew. It isn't clear that Greene ever told anyone."

She shook her head sadly. "So there's almost no chance."

They were interrupted by the waitress bringing their food. Hungry, they ate in silence. After a while Doc said, "Anyhow, we're here to celebrate your new job, not to talk about the ghoul."

Beth smiled. "That's right. I'd actually forgotten." She squeezed his hand across the table. "What a rush that was."

They ate in pleasant silence, happy in the knowledge that she had a good job in town. "Mmmm," Beth said over a mouthful of food, "what was the interesting news? You said there were two things."

"Oh, that's right. I'd forgotten. I had a visit from an obstetrician in New Haven a while back. Studeman sent him to me."

"What about?"

"It turns out that he's on to the miscarriage thing, too, and came up to Boston to talk to some people at Harvard Med about it. Someone there suggested he talk to Studeman, and of course he referred the guy to me. Anyhow, after a while I told him about the acid and that I thought there was a case in New Haven, too. That was after I swore him to silence about the whole matter, at least until after Ann delivers. I don't think he's going to do much based on what I told him."

As Beth and Doc sat eating their dessert, their conversation drifted from her job to their relationship to the acid to the virus. Much as they preferred the first two topics, the others kept intruding. "What did this OB from New Haven think of the deformity?" she asked.

"I didn't tell him," Doc answered. Beth looked at him quizzically, and he explained. "I just didn't feel good about saying anything about that. In another two or three weeks you and Charlie will have repeated the experiments, Ann will have delivered, and we can figure out how to go about this. It was a risk talking with him about the Gloryhits, but at least we can substantiate that. I didn't want to take a chance on the question of the deformities blowing up right now."

Beth smiled. "That sounds reasonable. I think I might have done the same thing." She went back to her dessert, then said, "Fred, there's something that's really bothering me, and I want to talk about it. It's kind of weird. Promise you'll hear me out?"

Doc nodded in agreement.

"Fred," she asked, "describe the deformity to me."

Doc shrugged his shoulders. "The deformity is a general enlargement of the front part of the brain, accompanied by the necessary increase in skull size." He looked to her for an explanation of the question.

"Fred, do you remember who Jim Karls is?"

Doc shook his head. "Name's familiar, but I can't place it."

"Tom's friend at Squaw Valley."

"Oh, that's right. They saved you from the masses, as I recollect."

Beth nodded. "But do you remember my telling you about a question he asked at one of the sessions?"

Doc shook his head.

"He asked whether it was possible to transfer genes for increased cranial capacity and thereby increase the intelligence of the recipient."

Doc's face went blank. "You're not suggesting . . ."

"That he's not only developed the technique but field-tested it." She finished the sentence as a statement.

Doc sat for a moment in silence, then shook his head. "Preposterous," he said softly. "And Tom Darnell's working out the techniques in your lab, right?"

"Yes!" Beth shouted, her voice too loud for the restaurant. Then, more quietly, "Do you think Karls asked that question by accident? That he and Tom just happened to run into each other? That Tom just happened to hear us talking about publicizing the spill, which would have blown the whole thing wide open, and was able to get pressure applied from Washington to get the whole thing hushed up?"

Doc shrugged. "It's too weak, Beth. Why are you so adamant on its being a giant conspiracy?"

"But it fits together so well," she insisted.

"Except," Doc pointed out, "for why Tom is working on plant cells, and plant viruses, and how they could possibly be connected with the pusher, Masco, in New York. And where would Greene fit in?"

"Greene?" Beth asked. "Of course! Those fetuses were what they were after. And, Fred, the one you had, the one that disappeared? You told Greene about it!"

Doc thought for a minute. "But you're saying that they wanted live ones, supergeniuses— Isn't that what you're suggesting?"

"Yes," Beth admitted. "Maybe they just wanted the aborted fetuses out of the way, so no one would notice. Or maybe this is their first test in humans and it doesn't work right all the time."

"That's sounding pretty farfetched," Doc said. "And you still don't have a role for Tom. He's the link that holds your whole idea together, and you don't have a function for him, except that he's working on recombinant DNA. If he was working with human cell lines, and human cell viruses, then maybe I'd believe it, but he's not."

"No, he isn't," Beth agreed, "but there's something funny about that supersoy stuff." She paused for a moment, then added, "If he was even telling the truth."

Doc let out a long sigh. "Come on," he said softly, "let's not fight tonight, okay?"

"Okay, but I still believe what I said."

He put a finger to her lips. "Not a single word more about it tonight, not from either of us."

She kissed his finger sadly.

Wednesday, January 20

1

Wednesday was frigidly cold, and Charlie spent half an hour getting the old Volvo started. He had wanted to take the subway rather than fight the car, but Ann had insisted. She was due in two weeks and could deliver any day now.

But Charlie was in no hurry. He had never told Ann about the fifteen percent of the rats born early—and deformed. One day early in a rat corresponded to two weeks early for a human, and he prayed that Disney would be late. The results from the repeat experiment should come tomorrow, but the data so far had been identical.

Ann kissed him good-bye. "Have a good day," she said, "and don't get involved in any more three-week experiments."

He smiled. "Tomorrow I finish up all my long-term experiments, and no more until Disney's got a new name."

"It'll be a beautiful month," she said.

He agreed. He was taking a full month's paternity leave, all he was allowed. "I'll see you this evening."

At the lab, he picked up his mail, then went to his office. As none of the mail looked interesting, he wandered back to inspect the rats. "What the hell?" He hurried from rack to rack. All the cages were empty. "Impossible!" he muttered. He looked around the room again. They were obviously gone.

250

He raced across the hall, hoping that Beth had done something with them. "Tom," he asked, "have you seen Beth around?"

"No," he replied, "she hasn't come in yet. Anything I can do?"

Charlie shook his head. "Someone's stolen my rats."

"Stolen them? Are you sure?"

Charlie shrugged. "Unless Beth did something with them."

"What was the experiment for? Is it going to be hard to repeat?"

"No, it was just an experiment I was doing for a friend," Charlie lied. "It can be repeated."

"Oh." Tom was clearly thinking about something, but it passed. "Well, I'll send Beth over as soon as she gets in," he offered.

"Thanks." Charlie headed back to his office. But in the hall he remembered that there were other rats, rats that couldn't be replaced. He hurried upstairs to the quarantine area. Since Darnell had destroyed all the virus in the lab, those experiments couldn't be repeated. He met the supervisor at the door.

"Those rats of yours look about ready to give birth," he commented.

"Have you seen them today?" Charlie asked.

"Yep, not twenty minutes ago. Some of them don't seem to be pregnant, but about half of them look pretty close to term."

Charlie let out a sigh of relief. "Yeah, they're due day after tomorrow." He remembered that he had meant to do some Caesareans last Monday. Maybe when Beth came in they'd do some. He headed back toward the lab.

"Did you want something?" the supervisor called after him.

"Oh, no, thanks," Charlie replied.

Back in his lab, he decided to call the security office. Maybe the rats had turned up somewhere else. But he was out of luck. "No, sir, no reports of extra rats. You're the one who got them last time, aren't you?"

"Yes," Charlie replied, irritated.

"Well, if anything turns up, we'll call you."

Muttering good-bye, Charlie carefully placed the phone back in its cradle. He found himself wondering if it was being tapped, and if so, by whom. He felt as though his grasp on reality was slowly slipping. Am I heading for a breakdown? he wondered. But no, dammit, it was the real world that was acting crazy, not him. Why the hell would anyone steal his rats? It made no sense at all.

"You're looking for me?" It was Beth.

Charlie frowned. "I don't suppose you did anything with the rats last night?" He knew the answer from her expression.

"No, why?"

"They're gone." He said it calmly, too tired to get upset.

Beth, apparently, was not. "Gone!" she shouted. "What do you mean, gone? Which rats?"

Charlie picked up a ruler and started playing with it, focusing his attention on it rather than Beth. "Oh, the virus rats are still upstairs. Only the acid rats are gone. Gone. Just plain gone." He said it like a weather forecast for more of the same.

"Did you tell Tom?" she asked.

"Yeah."

"Well, how did he respond?" she demanded.

"Sympathetically."

"Was he surprised, or did he seem to expect it?"

Charlie shrugged. "Beth, ask him yourself. I'm beat, just totally beat. I don't have any more energy to put into this, okay? Maybe after Disney comes, maybe then, again. But no more now, please?" He seemed totally lifeless, sitting in his chair, turning the ruler over and over.

Beth sputtered in anger. Was everyone going to desert her? "What about the virus rats? Are you just going to forget about them, too?" she demanded.

He took a deep breath and let it out slowly. Then, still looking at the ruler, he said, "No, we'll do those. There weren't any litters this morning, but I'll check again tomorrow and every day until they've all delivered. At the very least, I'll get a litter-size count and get half of them into formaldehyde. The other half have to wait until they're older."

"I know," she replied curtly. "I did help in the planning of the experiment." All her anger, frustration, and fear seemed to be coming to the surface. But there was nothing to do with it. She opened her mouth to say something, then turned and walked out.

Charlie put his head down on his desk, trying to think about it all and trying to forget about it at the same time. He was left with a dreamlike awareness of impending doom, and nothing else.

The phone woke him. He looked at his watch. More than an hour had passed. It rang again. Terrifying images of Ann, in labor two weeks early, raced through his still half-asleep mind. Bewildered, he picked up the phone.

"Hello?"

"Hi, Charlie, this is Kip."

"Oh." All the terror and confusion slipped from his mind as he finally came fully awake. "What's up?"

"I just stopped by to see Tommy, to find out if he discovered anything new."

"Anything new on Masco?" he asked, interested despite his exhaustion.

"Charlie, something weird's going on."

"That's for sure." Charlie felt the exhaustion creeping back, the desire to get out of the whole thing, to go home and just be with Ann. "Go on," he sighed. "What now?"

"I don't know," Kip said. "I went over to Tommy's place, and knocked. When he opened the door and saw me, he slammed it shut. I pounded again, and he told me to get the hell out of there or he'd call the police! When I shouted some more, he just stopped answering." He stopped, expecting a comment from Charlie. "Anyhow, I went to a pay phone and called him. When he heard my voice, he just hung up, and wouldn't answer when I called again!" Charlie said nothing. "Charlie, are you there?"

"Yeah, I'm here. So we got another blind alley— what's so surprising about that?"

Kip didn't know what to say. "Charlie, it doesn't make sense."

"None of it does!" Charlie retorted angrily. "But I can't do anything about it, okay?"

"Hey, what's the matter?"

"Nothing's the matter. I'm just a little bit tired, if that's okay with everybody. I'm tired of this whole mess."

"Charlie, has something happened?"

"No, nothing's happened— Oh, shit, yes, my rats are gone, but that's nothing, that's just the last straw. I'm fed up with this whole business, whatever it is. Everything just dead-ends, one thing after another. Maybe we should take a hint and just forget the whole thing."

"Charlie, have you talked to Beth about it?" Kip felt helpless, two hundred miles away.

"Yeah," Charlie answered, "and she's pissed at me, too. Look, I'm busy now. I'll talk to you later." He hung up the phone before Kip could reply and, grabbing his coat, stormed out of the building.

2

Across the hall, Beth saw him leave. Screw him, she thought. When it gets to be too much, good ol' Charlie Cotten just pulls out. He'll make a fine professor around here. She knew she didn't believe it, but she felt it. It was bad enough having Fred pooh-pooh her idea, but now Charlie had backed out on the feeble grounds that he was just too tired. She felt totally alone. Across the room, behind her back, she could hear Tom working quietly, steadily. Since the spill, he had been even more quiet, interacting with her less than before. It made her feel that she was working in the presence of some malevolent force.

Yet at the same time, part of her believed Doc's saying that she had conspiracy on the brain, and agreed with Charlie that they should all just let it ride for a while. It was a form of schizophrenia, she realized, not knowing whether or not to believe what she believed. Somehow, to not do so would be to deny her own reality. She sat at her desk, too frazzled to work. Needing something to do to distract her mind for a while, she decided to clean out Bill Hebb's room. There would be a certain pleasure in removing the last traces of the idiot. No, she thought, not idiot. Idiots can't be blamed for how they act.

She went next door and surveyed the place. It was a nightmare, lacking any semblance of order. How Tom had ever found the virus stocks was beyond her comprehension. But he had found them, and destroyed them, with unusual energy. Why did he want them gone so fast? She still didn't have Tom figured out.

She started at the end of the bench. There was no other order to work around, no organization of any sort. She couldn't even tell which glassware was clean and which dirty. Finally she decided that everything would have to be sterilized for safe measure. So, quietly, efficiently, she loaded containers full of she wasn't sure what onto the cart. She was amazed at how much had fit on his workbench.

When she couldn't fit any more on the cart, she wheeled it down to the autoclaves and loaded everything in. They would sterilize for half an hour—No, she thought, give them an hour—and then she'd take them to dishwashing. She turned the autoclaves on and returned to Hebb's lab.

In the corner of his room sat the incubator where he had grown his tissue cultures. I wonder if Tom left any, she thought. She went over to it and opened the door. He had. The incubator was full of dishes of cells. They would have to wait until the other glassware was sterilized, then she could do them. But it would be an hour, so she started back toward her own lab.

At the door she stopped, a smile on her face. She wondered what secret supersoy cells looked like, and tried to imagine TOP SECRET stamped on each cell by a government-employed cretin. Taking out a covered dish, she took it across the lab to the sterile hood where Bill was supposed to have done his work. Its cleanliness told a different story. Putting the dish under the microscope, she tried to focus in on the cells. "Oh, for chris'sake," she muttered. It was completely out of alignment. She spent the next ten minutes getting it

working, wondering how anyone could have gotten it
that badly misaligned, then laughing at herself. She
had forgotten that it was Bill Hebb she was talking
about. Finally the cells in the dish jumped into sharp
focus.

She sat silently, looking at the cells, hardly breathing at all. As if in a dream, she moved to the incubator and took out a whole stack of tissue dishes.
One by one, she looked at the cells in them. At the
end, tears fell onto the eyepieces, making it impossible
to go on. Where was Charlie, where was Fred, where
was anyone she could talk to? She took the dishes and
put them back in the incubator, wiped her face, and
went back to her own lab. She sat there, trying to
understand how it all fit together. They weren't plant
cells at all. They were nerve cells!

Behind her, she could hear Tom put something down
and then leave the lab. She followed the sound of his
footsteps down the hall, heard the opening and closing
of the door to Bill's former lab. A couple of minutes
later she heard it open and close again, and a cart
rattled down the hall. Smiling bitterly, she went next
door and checked. Tom had taken all the tissue culture
dishes from the incubator. Still in a half dream, she
went back to her lab and sat down. Tom glanced at
her when he came in again.

"Too late," she said with a pained smile.

He eyed her quizzically.

"I've already looked at them." Picking up her coat,
she walked out before he could reply.

3

The cold, damp air stung Beth's face as she left the
building. Her feet turned left, heading across the
campus, but she had no place to go. She felt nervous
and scared about her remark to Tom. Whatever it
was he was part of, it had already left at least Masco
dead. She didn't think she could face Tom again. There
had been a coldness to his face when she told him she
had seen the nerve cells, a coldness she had never seen
before. Why had she told him? It wasn't as if he were

a two-bit gangster of some kind, it was . . . She couldn't think of what.

She needed desperately to talk to someone, but who? She couldn't go to Charlie, not in the mood he was in. And Doc—would he just laugh again? She couldn't take that now. She suddenly realized it was Ann she wanted to talk to. Turning abruptly, she headed to a phone booth. But in the booth she stopped. They hadn't told Ann about the deformed rats being born, and she'd promised Charlie she wouldn't.

She felt terribly alone, cut off from all her friends, cut off by the very thing that she needed help with. She realized for the first time how much the issue of the acid had cut into every aspect of her life. She glanced suddenly over her shoulder, half expecting to see Darnell, but there was no one in sight. She hailed a cab and took it to the Common, watching for any sign of being followed. Was she cracking up? If her distress was paranoia, it was now complete. She realized she was fleeing from an unknown.

She walked the streets of downtown Boston, staying lost in crowds, wandering through bustling department stores, trying frantically to distract herself. Finally, in desperation, she went to a movie, wondering what the others in the theater were hiding from.

But by five o'clock she was exhausted. Not wanting to go to her apartment, she finally decided to call Doc. She was half convinced that she had gone a little crazy. Everyone was acting so nice, so normal. Except Ralph Masco, she thought. She needed to talk to someone, anyone. She called Doc at the office.

"Hi, Sharon, it's me. Can I talk to Fred?" Her voice sounded perfectly normal.

"He's not in," Sharon said. "He caught a plane to New York, to check out this guy Greene's address. He tried calling you, but you weren't in the lab or at home, he said."

"Oh, no. I wasn't. Did he say when he was coming back?"

"Later tonight, I think. He's got a normal schedule for tomorrow. Can I take a message?" she asked encouragingly.

"No, no, I'll talk to him later, I guess." She hung up the phone in confusion. Was his apartment safe? Patterson had been involved with Masco's death, too. She sat in the phone booth, staring out the window. She felt as if she wanted to stay in the protection of the booth.

Exhaustion washed over her, and a shiver of cold penetrated her body. She had to do something. Numbly she got up and went back into the cold, heading for Doc's apartment.

Heavy, wet snow had begun to fall as she walked the last few blocks to his apartment building, half expecting to be shot down from a passing car.

She unlocked the door to his apartment. It was empty, and warm, and just like it always was. She walked from room to room, touching things, as if to reassure herself that they were real. Everything was just like normal. Just like normal. She locked and double-locked the doors, checked the windows, and only then ate some dinner.

Afterward, in the back of her mind, she heard a pounding, demanding her attention. She opened her eyes to silence. The room was dark; she had fallen asleep. Then the pounding on the door began again. "Beth? Are you in there?" It was Doc's voice. She ran to the door, remembering that it was locked from the inside, and opened it wide. It was Doc, just like normal. Tears welled up in her eyes as she threw herself into his arms and finally let all the fear and anxiety flow out.

Later she told him of the events of the day: the missing rats, Charlie's withdrawal from the problem, the nerve-cell cultures, revealing her discovery to Tom, and her flight through the city. He listened in silence. "So that gives us the role for Tom," he said at last. He sat quietly, thinking about it all.

"What happened in New York?" Beth asked.

Doc frowned. "It was a front. I went to the address, and there was no Greene. Someone remembered that a Dr. Greene had rented an apartment for a month and then moved out. He apparently took it for just long enough to establish residence for the purpose of the post office box."

"So he's part of it?" she asked. "You do believe me, that something's going on?"

He smiled. "I believe you, and it looks as if Greene's part of it, too." It wasn't a happy smile. "But I doubt that you're in any danger. I doubt that they want to risk coming out into the open."

"Who?" Beth demanded. "Who are they?"

Doc shook his head. "I don't know. I just don't know."

Thursday, January 21

1

By morning eight inches of snow blanketed the ground, and there was no indication that it was letting up. Beth slogged through the snow to the bus stop with Doc, and then they separated. It would have been useless to try to drive. The bus struggled up and down the streets, slowly wending its way to the medical center. She dreaded facing Darnell, but she and Doc had agreed that Beth couldn't just hide. Worse, she knew that he would be all smiles, with some almost believable explanation of the nerve-cell cultures.

She walked up the stairs and right into the lab. He wasn't there. Breathing a sigh of relief, she crossed to her desk, hung up her coat, brushed off the snow, and sat down. In the middle of her desk was a note. "Beth," it began, "I looked at some of the plates, too, and I assure you that I'm as disturbed and confused as you are. I'm catching a morning flight to Iowa. We have to get to the bottom of this right away. Be back soon, Tom." Dropping the letter into the wastebasket, she laughed. His constant flights to Iowa were becoming farcical. Sometimes she thought he just went home and slept for a couple of days.

More relaxed, she decided to go see if Charlie was in a better mood. But as soon as she walked into his office she knew he wasn't.

"All right, all right, then," he complained into the phone. "So come over at eleven, but I don't know what there is to talk about with him." He muttered a good-bye and hung up. "Jesus Christ!" he said. "No one will leave me alone about this shit!"

"Who was that?" she asked.

He looked at the phone in disgust. "That was Kip. His friend Tommy, in New York, the one who knew Masco? He's come up to Boston and wants to talk with us."

"What do you mean, us?"

"That's the whole thing. He won't tell Kip. He wants to talk to us all. Kip, me, Doc, all the people involved. I haven't the foggiest notion what he's after, and I'm not particularly interested."

Beth was furious. "Well, that's too bad, Charlie, but the world still exists out there, you know. You just can't lock yourself up in your ivory tower! Now, shut up and listen a minute." She proceeded to fill him in on the events of the day before and Tom's note that morning. Then she launched into her explanation of the connections.

Charlie listened in silence. "But, then, what about the virus?" he asked.

Beth stopped cold. "I don't know," she replied, unsure of herself. "But maybe we should check out those rats. At least they weren't stolen."

Suddenly Charlie smiled. "You know what? I think they were supposed to have been stolen. Those were the experiments that couldn't be repeated, the ones that Tom so innocently asked about. If he overheard us talking about it . . ." He rose from his seat. "Let's go

see those rats!" As they rushed into the hall, they could
hear the phone ringing in Beth's lab. There was no one
else there.

"You go on up," she said. "I'll get the phone and be
up in a minute." She turned into the lab, and picked
up the phone.

It was a woman's voice. "May I speak with Dr.
Darnell, please?"

"I'm sorry," Beth replied carefully, "Dr. Darnell
isn't in right now. Could I take a message?"

"Well, yes, please," the woman said. "This is Ms.
Kling at the Copley Square Travel Agency, and I'm
calling to tell him that his eleven-thirty flight to Dulles
International has been canceled because of the snow.
If he—"

"To where?" Beth interrupted.

"Dulles International Airport, in Washington," she
replied.

"Are you sure?" Beth asked. "Is he making some
connections there?"

"Yes, I'm sure, ma'am, and no connecting flight. I've
booked him on this flight several times in the last few
weeks."

"And it's always been to Washington?"

"Yes, round trip to Washington."

Beth felt some more pieces clicking into place. "I'll
give him the message," she replied politely.

"Thank you."

Beth hung up the phone and then, suddenly coming
to life, rushed after Charlie.

2

Peter Alder drove hurriedly from the airport, ignoring the treacherous snow. Darnell had sounded close to
hysteria on the phone, and if he didn't catch him at
his apartment before he left for work, Darnell might
just blow the whole thing.

It was so unlike Darnell. He was one of their most
reliable, levelheaded agents, the one link Alder had
never worried about. But he had obviously been wrong
in putting that much trust in him. Alder suddenly

realized that Darnell had made three critical blunders. He ticked them off in his mind: first, not pulling off the first switch of rats; then, getting the rats out the second time but failing to get replacements in; and finally, letting that spill happen. My God, he thought, that spill was almost a month ago, and I still haven't done anything about it! The problem had him completely stymied.

He carefully drove past Darnell's apartment and parked around the corner. Sitting quietly in the car, he fought frantically to calm himself down enough not to be conspicuous. Finally, letting out a long, slow breath, he casually got out of the car, locked it, and walked back to Darnell's apartment building.

Upstairs, he knocked gently on Darnell's door. He waited, and then knocked again, barely restraining the urge to pound loudly. He glanced nervously up and down the hall, then pulled a passkey out of his pocket. It was crazy for him to be in Boston. There were people here who would remember him, and remember his connections. That would really do it. That would blow the whole thing wide open! He pushed the door open and stepped quickly inside.

Instinctively he sensed that Darnell had left. Frantic now, he hurried into the bedroom. He was right. Drawers were open and empty. He suddenly realized what had tipped him off in the living room, and rushing back out, he stooped at the fireplace, poking at the still-warm ashes. Darnell had been burning papers, he had left an empty can of lighter fluid on the floor.

He fought to get hold of himself. Now he would have to be doubly careful. Because not only was Darnell clearly running scared, but he himself was close to doing the same. As long as he stayed in Boston, both he and the project were in mortal danger. At least Darnell had had the sense to burn his papers. But would he have done the same at the lab? "Dammit," Alder muttered, "I'll have to make sure myself!"

3

Major Stanley Johnson stood before the Joint Chiefs of Staff. General Westland was there, and Pearson was there. Pearson read the report, half to the Joint Chiefs, half to Johnson. "In seven out of the eight towns, short outbursts of flu were accompanied by a total of between one hundred twenty and one hundred thirty-five deaths. All seven towns were quarantined shortly after the first deaths were detected, and there has been no evidence of spread.

"In the eighth town, there appeared to be no cases of influenza that did not result in death. In all, an estimated twenty-five hundred have died, with no stoppage of the spread indicated. In addition, we have reports of deaths in two neighboring towns. Clearly, an unidentified carrier has taken it out of the first town."

He turned to Johnson. "Major Johnson has an idea as to what has happened."

They all turned to Johnson. He shifted uneasily on his feet. "Well, it's only a guess," he began. "But basically, it looks as though the influenza virus has lost the mutator gene, without losing the botulinum genes. It's possible, but not very likely."

"How likely?" someone asked, angrily.

"One in a million," Johnson estimated.

"Bad luck, Johnson," someone muttered.

"What are the losses going to be?" another asked.

Johnson shrugged. "It depends on how well they can quarantine the infected people." He was frantically searching his mind for the way out, the solution.

"If the quarantine fails?"

Johnson shrugged. "Everybody who gets it."

"And no one has resistance to it? No one at all?" Westland was in shock. "At all?"

Johnson looked down at the floor. "Well, a couple of hundred people. We vaccinated the people in our labs, and . . ."

"No one!" Westland shouted. "For all practical purposes, no one in the whole world is immune to it?"

Stanley Johnson nodded without looking up.

4

Beth was out of breath when she finally caught up with Charlie in the animal rooms. "Charlie, he's been going to Washington. Darnell's been going to Washington, not Iowa!"

Charlie looked up from a rat cage he had been staring into. "What?" he asked, seemingly irritated at the interruption. "What are you shouting about?"

Beth tried to calm down, telling him the details of the phone call. "So you see? The whole thing with his going to Iowa is a sham. Whoever he's been going to see is in Washington!"

He seemed unaffected by her statement. "Charlie, doesn't that have any effect on you at all?"

"No," he replied, anger in his voice, "nothing surprises me anymore." He looked ready to lash out at anyone who crossed him. He pointed at the cages. "Look!"

Confused, she looked into the first two cages. They appeared to contain normal-size litters. But in the third cage there was a single newborn. "Oh, God, no!" She turned to Charlie. The pup had a deformed head.

Charlie silently removed the cover from the first cage and lifted the mother by the tail, shaking off the pups. Finally only two were left, both obviously deformed.

"But how?" Beth asked, her voice shaky with fear. "How can they be the same?"

"How?" Charlie asked. "Because the virus that Bill Hebb poured down the drain, out into the environment, is the same as the contaminant in the Gloryhits. The goddamn virus is what causes the deformity!"

"Oh, God," Beth whispered, "what does it mean?"

"Mean? Ask Darnell. How the hell should I know how infectious it is? For all I know, it'll be a long time before there are any normal babies being born around Boston!" He shoved the cages back on the rack.

"Come on, is there a chance that Darnell's coming back?" He rushed out of the lab, not waiting for an answer.

"I don't know," she said, running after him. "His flight's been canceled, so he might come in." But downstairs there was no Tom.

"Shit!" Charlie muttered. "I wouldn't be surprised if he was gone for good!" He looked around. "Don't tell anyone about those rats upstairs. We're going to blow this whole thing sky-high!"

"But, Charlie, who are they? Who is Darnell seeing in Washington?"

"How should I know," Charlie snarled. "Maybe the military, maybe the CIA. Hell, for all I know, he reports to the Russian Embassy." He paused, surprised by the idea. "In fact," he commented, "I wouldn't be surprised if all three of them are keeping tabs on this lab. But we're going to find out who's behind this!"

"There you are!" Kip stuck his head into the lab. "I thought I heard your voice."

Charlie was confused by his presence.

"It's eleven, remember?" Kip asked. Kip had brought Tommy over.

"Christ, Kip, I don't have time now!"

"Come on, Charlie," Beth soothed. "I think we should find out what Tommy has to say." She didn't have to say the rest. Ralph Masco's death might hold the key to the puzzle.

"Okay," he agreed unhappily. "Let's go to my office."

Tommy was sitting there when they arrived. It all seemed unreal to Charlie. His office looked the way it always did—comfortable, academic, carefully insulated from the outside world. He felt lost, confused as to what he was doing.

But Tommy looked the worst of all. He sat facing the door, glancing out every few seconds, looking like a scared rabbit ready to run. "Where's the doctor guy?" he demanded.

"Oh, shit," Charlie said. "I never even managed to call him. I've been so . . ." He stopped, remembering again what had happened so far that morning. It kept slipping from his mind, every chance it got. "Busy," he finished.

"I wanted him to be here, too," Tommy said. "Call him now."

"Goddamnit!" Charlie roared. "If you want to say something, say it, or else get the hell out of here! I'm tired of this stupid-ass game!"

Tommy looked at Charlie with terror. "Okay, okay! Jesus, I just wanted him here, too, that's all. I can tell the three of you. Don't get all keyed up, okay?" Charlie just waited for him to say his piece.

Tommy turned to Kip. "Kip, I'm sorry I treated you so bad when you came down yesterday, but I had to! This thing with Masco is a lot bigger than I want anything to do with!"

"Go on," Kip said, trying to calm him, "just tell us what happened."

Tommy looked at the three of them. "Well, I went over to Masco's apartment last week—when I got back in town. I thought I'd find out what they knew. Well, as soon as I started asking, they jumped all over me. They demanded identification, said they'd take me in if I didn't show some."

"Who were they?" Charlie interrupted.

"Two guys. A guy named Patterson and a short guy —I don't remember his name." Charlie nodded. "So I showed my driver's license, and they wrote down my name and all. Then the short one said to me, 'I guess you haven't gotten the message.' I didn't know what the hell they were talking about. And then Patterson said that Masco had been wasted for sticking his nose where it didn't belong and talking to strangers when he shouldn't. 'Now, why do you want to poke your nose into something like that?' he asked. I didn't know what to say. I sort of made some lame excuse, and then Patterson said that I'd do best to forget that I ever knew Masco and not to talk to anyone about it." His gaze kept jumping to the door. "They said they'd be watching me."

"Then why'd you come here?" Beth demanded.

"Because I figured if I'd told other people, then they couldn't get to me so easily, because others would know that they'd threatened me!"

"Could you have been followed?" Charlie asked. He

didn't want Patterson, whoever he was, knowing how many pieces they had.

"No," Tommy replied. "I drove, and there was no way . . ." The others didn't see the man walk past the door. All they saw was Tommy's face turn ashen and his lips start to tremble. "Oh, Jesus," he whimpered, cringing into the back of the chair. "They did—they followed me."

Charlie turned and looked at the empty door. "What are you talking about?"

"Patterson's buddy, he just walked past the door." He looked frantically around the office. "You've got to hide me—please, you've got to!"

Charlie pointed to the couch, and he and Kip started pulling it out from the wall, while Beth headed into the hall. She saw the figure turn into her lab. Terrified, she followed, unable to avoid the confrontation. She stepped carefully into the lab.

"Oh, hi, Beth." She jumped at the voice. Turning, she saw Jim Karls coming over to greet her. "Remember me? Squaw Valley?"

She nodded dumbly. "Of course!" she said. "I mean, of course I remember you." She tried to smile, but it wouldn't work.

Karls didn't seem to notice. "I'm looking for Tom. Is he around?"

She shook her head, not trusting her voice. Behind her, she could hear Charlie and Kip coming down the hall. She heard them walk into the lab, but didn't turn around. "Charlie, Kip," she said, her voice trembling, "this is Jim Karls, from the Squaw Valley meetings?"

Charlie muttered something under his breath that Beth didn't hear. But she heard Kip's "You're right!" Kip stepped past her, looking more closely at Karls.

Karls looked at him nervously, then past him at Charlie. Charlie had moved to block the door. Karls smiled and stuck his hand out to Kip. "Pleased to meet you."

Kip just looked at it. Smiling tightly, he spoke to Beth without taking his eyes off Karls. "Beth, I'd like you to meet an old friend of Charlie's and mine. Peter Alder."

Karls paled. The recognition was mutual. His mind raced. How much did they know about the project? If they knew what it was all about, it was over for sure. Frantically, instinctively, he tried to cover. "Sorry," he replied, "you must have me confused with someone else. My name's Jim. Jim Karls." He tried to smile, but failed.

"You remember, Beth," Charlie called from behind her, his voice amazingly menacing. "The agent provocateur that Kip found out was working for the CIA? Remember, Doc said they were too smart to leave him in Boston, where people could recognize him? Looks as if they're not so smart after all!"

Karls froze for an instant, then stalked toward the door. "This is absurd!" he shouted, and tried to push past Charlie. But Charlie grabbed him by the arm and wouldn't let go. "The goddamn CIA!" he shouted, right in Karls' face. "Does that put it all together, Beth?"

Beth stared at Karls. "Your question at Squaw Valley! You asked if it would be possible to produce geniuses by causing general cranial enlargement. Everyone laughed at the question, but you were already doing it."

"I doubt it," Kip snarled. "More likely just testing it. I'm sure that if they got it to work it would be the CIA producing geniuses for their own use, not for anyone else."

Karls moved to break loose, but Kip grabbed him, too. "You're not going anywhere until we say you are!" Kip shouted. The two of them dragged him over to Darnell's desk and forced him down in the chair.

Suddenly Karls realized that the game was over. "You stupid fool!" he snapped. "You'd just let this country run downhill until anyone could walk all over us! But we could produce humans that would rule the world, an American world!"

He started to say more, but the phone rang. Charlie glanced at Beth. "It might be Tom. Get it!" He turned to Karls. "If you make a sound, you're going to lose all your goddamn teeth!" He picked up a hammer off the benchtop and held it threateningly. Beth answered the phone.

"Yeah, he is, but can he call you back later?" She listened, and her face turned pale. "Just a second," she whispered. She looked at Charlie, knowing that it was too soon, way too soon. "It's for you," she said, holding the phone out to him.

Not understanding, Charlie left Karls to Kip and took the phone.

"Hello, Charlie?"

"Yeah?"

"Charlie, it's me, Ann. Come and get me, Charlie. I'm in labor. We're going to have a baby. It's two weeks early." She had never been so happy in all her life.

Afterword: Science Fiction or Science Fact?

When this novel was first conceived, genetic engineering, the science of recombinant DNA, was a new field, almost unheard of outside professional scientific circles. But since that time it has grown both in its technological capabilities and in its public interest. Thus, as we finish the novel, we find ourselves faced with the question of how unreasonable the story line presented here actually is. In partial answer to this question, we have put together this afterword, dealing with some of the ideas presented in the novel. The final answer, unfortunately, must await the decisions of future writers.

The CIA

In June 1975, the Rockefeller Commission on the CIA reported that during the forties, fifties, and sixties the CIA carried out studies on certain behavior-influencing drugs, such as LSD. As early as 1953, these drugs were given to unsuspecting subjects, tests which resulted in at least one death.[1] Yet such tests were continued until 1963. Just how much testing of this sort was done will never be known, since most records connected with this program (over 150 files in all) were ordered destroyed in 1973.

The extent to which the military or even the President himself is aware of such testing is unclear. In 1975, CIA stockpiles of nerve poisons, enough to kill tens of thousands of people, were discovered. In clear violation of international treaties signed by the United States, the stockpiles were maintained even after orders were given by then-President Ford to destroy all biological warfare weapons.[2]

Whether the CIA would consider embarking on a project to create a "master race" cannot be answered. The concept, however, is not one that is universally rejected, even by notable scientists. As long ago as 1962, such concepts were discussed at a CIBA Foundation conference in London.[3] One idea discussed there was to increase the number of brain cells in an individual by injecting the developing fetus with a growth hormone before the final number of nerve cells in the brain had been established. Another was to use viruses to carry novel DNA into human fetuses, thereby producing hereditary changes in their genes. Together, these two ideas constitute the CIA project presented in this novel.

The Military

If the military has not constructed and tested the likes of Stanley Johnson's botulinum influenza, it certainly isn't for lack of trying. During the sixties, scientific publications emerging from Fort Detrick, the army's "biological defense research laboratory," suggested that they were actively investigating plague, anthrax, yellow fever, Q fever, tularemia, and encephalomyelitis, among other diseases.[4] There are also strong indications that the army actually went so far as to stockpile biological warfare agents in Southeast Asia during the Vietnam War.[5] In 1972, a report from Detrick discussed attempts at genetic engineering.[6] This paper reported attempts to transfer genes from bubonic plague to other, less harmful bacteria, ostensibly to study the genetics of virulence. These experiments, which reportedly failed, could presumably be done relatively easily with the new techniques of recombinant DNA enzymology.

As for military tests of such agents, information has recently become available concerning germ-warfare tests carried out by the army within the United States.

Between 1949 and 1969, the army conducted 239 germ-warfare tests in the open air of San Francisco, New York, and Key West, Florida. A test in San Francisco, using what was considered to be a harmless type of bacteria, *Serratia marcescens,* was followed by eleven cases of *Serratia*-related pneumonia, and one death. Despite this, the same bacteria were used again in 1966 during tests conducted in the subway system of New York City.[7] Whether field tests of more dangerous substances have been made is currently unknown to us, but it is perhaps worth keeping in mind that a weapon that has never been tested cannot be relied on, and hence is almost valueless in the preparation of strategic plans.

Technically, the development and stockpiling of biological warfare agents is now prohibited by international treaty. The effectiveness of this ban, unfortunately, is not clear. Negotiations over a similar treaty that would ban chemical warfare agents have been very neatly deadlocked by the invention of "binary agents."[8] These are containers which contain two harmless chemicals, separated by a thin wall. Puncturing the wall results in the mixing of the two compounds and production of a highly lethal nerve gas. The army's claim is that until this thin wall is pierced, something that does not occur until the weapon is employed, there is no "lethal nerve gas" and, hence, stockpiling of this weapon is not in violation of the treaty. One can only assume that similar "clever" tricks will permit the stockpiling of biological warfare weapons.

Industrial Concerns

An interesting group that has stayed out of the public spotlight during the recent spate of attention given to genetic engineering has been industrial concerns interested in the application of this technology. In addition to agribusiness, the major industrial concerns involved are the pharmaceutical houses. As the military and intelligence arms of the government are perhaps the greatest threats in terms of the malicious use of genetic engineering, these industries probably pose the greatest threat of accidental injuries to both humans and the environment in general.

It will not be long before pharmaceutical houses will be utilizing specially designed microorganisms in the production of medically useful compounds such as insulin and human growth hormones. The profits involved in the successful production of such bacteria are astronomical. But for these companies, profits depend on being first, and speed, rather than safety, might tend to be the rule. Example after example of industrial accidents leading to severe, if not fatal, injuries to plant employees and local residents can be found. In one of the worst, ICMESA, a subsidiary of Hoffman-LaRoche, accidentally released 4½ pounds of the chemical dioxin into the air, contaminating some 10,000 acres of land near Milan, Italy.[9] The compound is so dangerous that one-trillionth of a pound will kill a guinea pig. It has been reported that notification of nearby residents was withheld at the company's insistence, and was only given after several residents were hospitalized. In another case, a multimillion-dollar fine was levied against Allied Chemical Corporation in connection with the injury of several plant employees working with the pesticide kepone. In announcing the decision, the judge stated that corporate executives knowingly withheld from employees already showing signs of neurological damage, information that the pesticide they were working with was in all probability the cause of their injuries.[10]

It seems likely that industrial use of genetic engineering will soon raise the same questions currently being raised by nuclear power plants, where the fear of disaster has been an extremely potent cautionary force.[11]

Attack, Accident, or Coincidence?

In dismissing the risks of genetic-engineering research, a noted scientist was recently quoted as saying that in four years of work on recombinant DNA throughout the country, not a single illness had resulted. This statement points up one of the biggest dangers involved in this type of research. How does one identify an illness that has been caused by a newly synthesized, experimental bacterium or virus?

With nuclear power plants, it's easy to monitor radioactivity in various areas that might have been contaminated. But with biological organisms, how would one know what to look for? How would one distinguish a genetically engineered virus or bacterium from a normal one, one that perhaps had never been noticed before? And with industrial concerns willing to cover up accidents or, reportedly, even present faked data on the danger of their products,[12] how could an accidental spill of a dangerous new organism be distinguished from an attack?

Two bizarre events involving dangerous biological organisms occurred in the early part of 1976. In February, several hundred soldiers at Fort Dix, New Jersey, were stricken with the flu. At least a dozen of these, including an eighteen-year old who died, apparently were infected by a "new and more worrisome" form of the virus.[13] The result was a Presidential directive to immunize all Americans against this new strain of swine flu, so called because of its resemblance to a flu which normally infects pigs. But while millions of Americans were being vaccinated, the disease strangely disappeared, without a single new case appearing anywhere in the country. It was as if the disease had mutated away.

Then, in July, a scant five months later, the Legionnaire's Disease hit in Philadelphia. One hundred and seventy-nine cases, including twenty-eight deaths, were identified. Although preliminary evidence now suggests that a bacterial infection, unlike anything previously reported, was the cause, it is unclear whether the true cause will ever be known.[14]

The possibility that the disease was the result of biological warfare research was not overlooked at the time, and both the CIA and the army went on record denying any connection with the outbreak.[15] By September, other reports were suggesting that the disease was the result of a covert Russian biological warfare test.[16] Meanwhile, the deadly disease had disappeared without a trace, with absolutely no secondary infections. As if it had mutated away.

So, concerning research into the production of new and unpredictable forms of bacterial and viral life, the question remains, how does one tell an accident from an attack from a normal mini-epidemic? Until solid answers are found to this question, the risk of undetected accidents and attacks remains a serious problem.

The Universities

Most of the attention concerning the control and possible banning of recombinant DNA research has been focused on the academic world. The reason for this is that members of this community were the first to raise serious questions concerning these possible dangers.[17] The result was the Asilomar Conference on Recombinant DNA Molecules sponsored by the National Academy of Sciences. The conference, which included mostly academic researchers but also government and industry representatives, set up voluntary guidelines suggesting the restriction of much of this research to special "safe" facilities and recommending the banning of certain types of recombinant DNA research.[18] Subsequently, the National Institutes of Health (NIH), a subdivision of the Department of Health, Education, and Welfare, produced similar guidelines that became legally binding on researchers supported by NIH grants.

The Future

As of this writing, there are no legal restrictions to any genetic-engineering research, development, and production, except that sponsored by the NIH. Industrial concerns are under no control, and academic research not funded by the NIH is similarly uncontrolled. The only legislation submitted to Congress to date which would place restrictions on this research on a national level was withdrawn by its sponsors in November 1977, following intense lobbying by researchers.

Although there is still discussion of federal regulations, they are yet to materialize, and whether they will control industrial production, as well as research, remains to be seen. It would seem inappropriate for standards and restrictions to be placed on academic research that did not apply equally, if not more stringently, to industrial research, development, and production.

In both academia and industry, fame and fortune await those researchers who first make various "major breakthroughs" in the field. The result of these incentives is keen competition, where speed is essential. And it is in just such an environment that the danger of accidental or intentional violations of safety precautions is the greatest. In June of 1977, a team of researchers at the University of California, San Francisco, reported that they had isolated the gene controlling the production of insulin, and transferred it into bacteria. The team, which had been racing a similar group at Harvard, received world-wide acclaim for their feat. Subsequently, it became clear that the UCSF team had used methods prohibited by NIH guidelines in their work on the project. Despite denial of intentional wrongdoing, it was reported that "It was clear that everyone knew that [the method was] not certified." [19] In addition, one researcher at UCSF complained that "People would stop talking when you came into the room, or change the subject if you tried to make conversation about how the insulin project was going." [19] It seems reasonable that for the most dangerous types of research, where strict measures must be taken to prevent the escape of potentially dangerous bacteria and viruses (P3 and P4 levels), only a handful of facilities should be constructed. It seems outrageously reckless to allow every university and every pharmaceutical house to build its own facility in order to join in the race for profit and glory. Perhaps here, where the dangers are the greatest, industrial and academic concerns should be required to cooperate, to minimize repetition of potentially dangerous experiments.

We have said nothing about control of military and

intelligence uses of genetic engineering. Besides being banned by international treaty, it seems clear that the work should not be permitted. But we have no faith in the promises and claims of these interests, and feel that control of them is impossible as things stand now. This leads into a morass of ambiguities. We have been talking as if military, industrial, and academic research are three distinct entities. In fact, nothing could be further from the truth, as military and industrial money supports academic research, and academic and industrial researchers hire themselves out to the military as consultants. In fact, when one supports any of the three, one supports all three, and for the present there is no way around this quandary.

In the end, we are left with a hope and a fear. There is no question but that there are valuable gains possible from research and development of recombinant DNA technology, and that this research and development carries a grave risk. In approaching this dilemma, two points should be kept in mind. First, there are no panaceas about to appear through research into recombinant DNA. There are no cures for cancer, heart disease, and birth defects just a few months or years away. Second, an accident could occur at any time, and the results could be far worse than all the possible advantages combined. Unlikely though it is, it remains possible that humanity itself could be destroyed by an error.

References

1. Report to the President by the Commission on CIA Activities within the United States. U.S. Government Printing Office, Washington, 1975. p. 226ff.
2. New York Times. Sept. 17, 1975. p. 1.
3. See G. Wolstenholme, ed., Man and his Future. Churchill, London, 1963.
4. S. Hersh, Chemical and Biological Warfare: America's Hidden Arsenal. Bobbs-Merrill, New York, 1968. p. xiii.
5. J. Cookson & J. Nottingham, A Survey of Chemical and Biological Warfare. Sheed and Ward, London, 1969, p. 310.
6. W. Lawton & H. Stull. Journal of Bacteriology, Vol. 110, pp. 926-929; 1972.
7. New York Times. March 9, 1977. p. 1.
8. Nature. Vol. 253, pp. 82-83, 1975.
9. New York Times. July 29, 1976, p. 3, and July 31, 1976, p. 3.
10. New York Times. October 6, 1976, p. 1, and December 31, 1976, p. 20.
11. See for example, "Too Hot to Handle", by R. Severo. New York Times Magazine. April 10, 1977.
12. Nature. Vol. 264, pp. 308-309, 1976.
13. Time Magazine. April 5, 1976. p. 50.
14. Morbidity and Mortality Weekly Report. September 3, 1976. p. 271ff.
15. New York Times. August 8, 1976, p. 1, and August 31, 1976, p. 11.
16. National Examiner. September 27, 1976. p. 5.
17. Science. Vol. 181, p. 1114, 1973.
18. Proceedings of the National Academy of Sciences. Vol. 72, pp. 1981-1984, 1975.
19. Science. Vol. 197, p. 1342, 1977.

About the Authors

Bob Stickgold (Ph.D., biochemistry, University of Wisconsin) is a research scientist in neurobiology at Harvard Medical School. In 1974-75 he was a Postdoctoral Fellow in Stanford University's departments of Genetics and Biochemistry. The author or co-author of eleven published papers in genetics and neurobiology, Bob is married and has a daughter. He enjoys squash and bicycling.

Mark Noble (Ph.D., genetics, Stanford University) is a Postdoctoral Fellow working in neurobiology in the Department of Zoology, University College, London. Mark is an avid back-country hiker and guitar player. He is married to Barbara Hyams, a well-known medical illustrator and accomplished horseback rider.

Catch a Rising Star!

Jack L. Chalker

A JUNGLE OF STARS	25457	1.50
THE WEB OF THE CHOZEN	27376	1.75
MIDNIGHT AT THE WELL OF SOULS	25768	1.95
DANCERS IN THE AFTERGLOW	27564	1.75

James P. Hogan

INHERIT THE STARS	25704	1.50
THE GENESIS MACHINE	27231	1.75
THE GENTLE GIANTS OF GANYMEDE	27375	1.75

Tony Rothman

THE WORLD IS ROUND	27213	1.95